FISH out of WATER

ALSO BY NATALIE WHIPPLE

Transparent
Blindsided

FISH out of WATER

NATALIE WHIPPLE

HOT
KEY
BOOKS

First published in Great Britain in 2015 by Hot Key Books
Northburgh House, 10 Northburgh Street, London EC1V 0AT

Text copyright © Natalie Whipple 2015
The moral rights of the author and illustrator have been asserted.

A CIP catalogue record for this book is available from the British Library.

ISBN: 978-1-4714-0430-6

2

This book is typeset in 10.5 Berling LT Std using Atomik ePublisher

Printed and bound by Clays Ltd, St Ives Plc

www.hotkeybooks.com

Hot Key Books is part of the Bonnier Publishing Group
www.bonnierpublishing.com

For my grandma Carole, who, though I never quite understood her, I loved just the same

Chapter 1

The goldfish are uneasy, but who wouldn't be when their potential killer stares them down so gleefully? The little boy bounces in front of the tank while his mother looks at bowls. I stand at my little island in AnimalZone's Aquatics department, hoping they'll leave without buying one of my precious fish.

"How many goldfish can live in these?" The woman holds up a one-gallon bowl, seeming slightly irritated by her squealing son.

"Actually . . ." I glance at the boy, who is now banging on the guppy tank and giggling as the fish scatter, "those bowls are intended for betta fish. That's not big enough for one goldfish. They need at least ten gallons to do well—twenty, for some varieties."

She gives me the "Are you crazy?" look. "Really?"

I nod, wishing I could point to where my nametag says *Aquatics Expert*. "They produce a lot of waste, so it would be most humane for the fish to live in a filtered, large aquarium. The ten-gallon starter is only fifty."

"Well, aren't you the little saleswoman . . ." She glances at my nametag. "Mika. I'll take the bowl, some fish, and some food."

"Okay." Apparently *Aquatics Expert* means nothing to this woman. I do as I'm told, not bothering to recommend some rocks and plants in the bowl. That way the fish could hide when her son comes to enthusiastically torture them each day of their short, horrible lives.

"That one! No, that one!" the boy screams as I try to capture the fleeing fish. He's pointing to the one with the black spot on its forehead, but I really like that one and can't send him to his death. His mother tells me to grab three of whatever and hands him a candy.

I bag each fish and say a prayer that they'll go peacefully. People like to think fish don't have feelings, but as I watch the last guppy squirm in his bag his eyes plead with me to put him out of his misery. I get the sense he knows just as well as I do that bad things are on the horizon.

"It would be good to buy water conditioner," I say as I hand over the fish. "The chlorine in tap water can kill them."

"Right. Thanks." She takes the fish and heads to the front, not even a glance at the conditioner.

There will definitely be a fish funeral in less than a week, which is why I don't mention they can return dead fish within two weeks for a replacement. At least not to people like that, who are clearly here for a "cheap, easy pet."

I check on the remaining goldfish guppies. They're huddled in a tight mass, traumatized by the little boy. I don't blame them—it's like a crazed maniac coming into your house, flailing and screaming, and then leaving just as quickly as he came. How can you not huddle there in shock?

"Mika?"

I whirl around, finding the storeowner, Clark Wainwright, at my station. He's a nice guy, despite his looking a little shady—I blame the creepy mustache and gold watch. But I couldn't ask for a better boss.

There's a new face next to him, one that doesn't seem particularly excited to be here. He doesn't look at me while I take in his dark eyes and messy hair that walks the line between brown and blond. He wears the signature ugly AnimalZone uniform—lumpy black polo and pleated khakis.

"New employee?" I ask.

Clark nods. "This is my nephew, Dylan. He just graduated and will be working here for at least the summer, maybe longer."

"*Not* longer," Dylan says. He makes no effort to be friendly, as if he's pretending with every fiber of his being not to be here. I can't tell what he's like past the serious slouching problem and sullen expression.

"Better get your act together if you think that. Probably couldn't get a job at all without nepotism."

"Whatever."

Clark looks back at me. "He doesn't have much work experience, but he'll pick up on things quick."

"Cool." I try to put on a nice face, though I doubt he's right. "If he's anything like you I'm sure he will."

"Suck up," Dylan coughs under his breath.

Hard as it is, I ignore the comment and smile, which earns me a disturbing glare. "I'm Mika, by the way."

"Figured, since it's on your nametag," Dylan says.

So he's gonna be a jerk like that. Great. If Clark weren't here,

I'd ask Dylan if he were PMSing, but instead I force my smile wider. "Oh good, you're observant. That'll help."

Clark pats him on the back. "I'll give Dylan the run-down today, but I thought we'd start him on Aquatics for training, since you'll be volunteering at the Aquarium this summer, right?"

"Yup." I beam, not at all embarrassed to show my excitement. My parents are marine biologists at the Monterey Bay Aquarium, and I finally convinced them to let me "intern" with them. It'll look amazing on my college applications. "Sounds great. I'd be happy to train him."

"Don't underestimate her, Dylan." Clark points to me. "She might be younger than you, but she knows her fish and you better listen."

Dylan doesn't answer. I have a feeling listening isn't one of his strong suits. As I watch the two head back down the aisle, I regret agreeing to train him already. He's clearly going to be a pain in my side.

After a quick lunch and wardrobe change, I hop on my bike and head for the Aquarium. The weather is beautiful now that the morning fog has worn off, and even over traffic the ocean can be heard. AnimalZone is pretty close to the Aquarium, so it doesn't take me more than ten minutes to hit Cannery Row in all its touristy glory. It sits right on the water, a collage of old industrial buildings that don't quite match with the beachy bungalows in this area of Monterey. What were once canning factories for seafood products are now rows of outlet shops and restaurants. It's one of the "must see" places for visitors, so it's always bustling with people and choked with traffic. The Monterey Bay Aquarium stands at the very end, a monument to all the environmental repairs made to the bay after the canning industry nearly destroyed it.

Even if it's kind of fake, I don't mind so much. My parents told me a long time ago not to be one of those jaded locals who complains about the tourists. Mom and Dad would be out of jobs without them, since the Aquarium is non-profit and depends on people visiting.

I lock my bike outside the entrance, where Mom told me to meet her today. She and Dad usually work at the research facility nearby, but she often comes to check on the Aquarium animals in the public buildings.

After I get through the line, I use my season pass to get in. Since I'm the daughter of prominent and long-time employees Stan and Yumi Arlington, I've had a free pass for as long as I can remember. This place is almost like a second home, the Living Kelp Forest and Outer Bay exhibits as familiar as my own bedroom. I've always dreamed of volunteering here, but you have to be at least eighteen. Except all that's about to change. Finally, *finally*, Mom and Dad have given into my constant begging, though I'm still seventeen.

Mom stands by the information desk, chatting with an obviously star struck receptionist. She has that effect on people. With her long black hair and youthful face, she oozes intelligence and beauty all at once.

"I hope it will be a busy summer!" she says, her Japanese accent barely there. She tries hard to mask it at work, but I love that it still slips out, a reminder of where she came from. She spots me and smiles wider, leaving the desk to meet me. "Mika! There you are."

"Hey," I say as she gives me a hug. "So what are we doing today? Checking on the otters? Taking water samples? What?"

Her face lights up. "Actually, I have good news to tell you first!"

I tilt my head, unable to imagine what could make this day better. "What?"

"Do you remember that grant from Stanford we applied for?"

I nod. Of course I do. I was drooling over the proposed studies they'd be doing in the bay. There was supposedly a lot of stiff competition for the money, but Mom and Dad are rock stars in their field. "Did you get it?"

"We did!" She bounces a little, she's so excited.

I join in. "That's awesome! Please tell me I get to help."

"We have to take on a few interns, but as far as I know, yes."

"Sweet!" I selfishly hope they are attractive male interns. "I didn't think this summer could get any better!"

Mom puts her arm around me. "You've earned it. You've worked hard at the pet store, and you take such good care of our aquariums at home. We know how serious you are about pursuing this, and we're so proud."

"Thanks, Mom." I lean on her shoulder, soaking in the moment. "What are we doing today then?"

She laughs. "Well, I hope you aren't too disappointed, but your father and I actually have a meeting with the grant administrators in about thirty minutes. So you'll have to wait a little bit longer until we get all the details worked out."

"No worries." While I'm a bit disappointed not to be starting right now, it'll be worth the wait. "I guess I'll just have to go home and be lazy or something."

"It *is* summer break."

"See you later." I float out of the Aquarium. I'm so high on the awesomeness of my impending summer that I treat myself to some ice cream and decide I deserve a present. I end up back at AnimalZone. My eyes dart back and forth as I check to see who's on the floor. I hope Clark doesn't spot me. He always teases when I come in after my shift, especially when I come back for the reason I have today.

Dylan stands at my Aquatics island, looking as bored as humanly possible. It takes him a second to recognize me in my sundress and leggings, but when he does his eyes go wide. His sour expression comes back as he says, "Aren't you off for the day? Or do you live here?"

I clench my jaw, determined to hang on to my good mood. "Thought I'd come back and give you a test."

"A test. Sure." He says it like it's a joke. It was, until he mocked the idea.

"Yes, I'd like to buy a fish."

He rolls his eyes. "Which one?"

"Something easy to keep."

"A goldfish then."

"No." I put my hands on my hips. "So fail. Big time fail. No fish is easy to take care of. They all have specific needs, and if you don't respect those needs then you'll kill the fish."

He sighs. "Great, I have to work with a crazy fish girl. Is this hell? I think I'm in hell."

All my happy feelings vanish. I get the strongest urge to push him out of my spot and tell Clark I'll never train him. He obviously doesn't care, and there's nothing I hate more than people who don't care about what they do. It shouldn't matter if you work at a pet store or in the White House—you should do your best.

"Yes, I'm a crazy fish girl. Get used to it." I tip my head up with pride. "Don't ever tell a customer fish are easy to care for—they already come in with enough misconceptions. It's your obligation to make sure those fish get the best possible care."

"I thought I was obligated to sell pets."

My eyes narrow. "And if those fish keep dying, we not only lose money through replacements but people stop coming here to buy them. Healthy fish and educated customers make this place money."

His upper lip curls, but he says nothing.

I smile victoriously and head for the goldfish guppies. "I'd like the one with the black spot on his forehead. Clark taught you how to bag a fish, right?"

Dylan grabs the net and stands, stalking over like I challenged him to a duel. He looks over the fish. "I don't see one with a black spot."

"Right there." I point to my fish. "So much for observant."

His look is all daggers, but he sticks the net in and attempts to catch my fish. It takes a ridiculously long time, and I almost feel guilty for enjoying his struggle. After several failed attempts, he throws the net on the ground. "Get your own damn fish!"

I stare at him as he heads back to the island. He has his back to me, and his shoulders rise and fall with angry breaths. I pick up the net, wondering what the hell his problem is. "Can't put a contaminated net in there."

He flips me off.

"I'll have to talk to Clark about your customer service skills." I lean over the island to rinse the net. "Because, wow, that was a serious mantrum."

Double flip off.

I seriously wish I hadn't come back here, because it's ruining my good day. Dylan acts like I'm the one at fault here, and it makes me mad. He should at least be grateful his uncle is giving him a job, but he's not even trying. I almost point this out, but it doesn't feel worth it. So I prepare a bag of water and net my spotted friend in seconds. Then I give it a puff of air and tie it off. The guppy swims around happily—at least there's one thing in this situation that's nice. Smiling at my new fish, I head for the front counter to pay my twenty cents.

"You really wanted that fish?" Dylan says when I'm half way down the aisle.

I stop and turn around. "Yes."

His face softens only slightly, as if he's curious. "So you weren't just messing with me?"

I shake my head, patting my water-filled bag. "I almost had to send this guy to an early grave this morning and decided he needs a real home. Everyone deserves one of those, right?"

One of his eyebrows quirks. I don't know what to make of the expression, so I wait for an explanation. Dylan just stares at me. A tiny part of me hopes for some kind of apology, though he doesn't seem like the kind of guy who says sorry. When it's clear an answer isn't coming, I continue on my way.

Chapter 2

Our place is a quaint beach house that's, ironically, not very close to the beach. Juniper bushes guard our small front yard, which is zenned-out with rocks and sand, raked to look like water ripples. A single cypress tree shades the path to our door, and I park my bike on the porch.

The house is quiet, or at least as quiet as it can get with so many aquarium filters humming. Dad jokes that if an earthquake hits, our house will flood from all the tanks breaking. I never found it funny as a kid, picturing all my fish friends meeting such a traumatic end, but now that I'm older I get his joking. We have at least one tank in every room, if not several. Five of them are mine, and that's not including my koi pond in the backyard.

I head for my room, where my tanks are lined up against the wall. Each one contains goldfish—from comets to bubble eyes to blackmoors. It probably looks like overkill to most people, but there's just something about goldfish that makes me happy.

My new guppy is tiny. When I hold up his bag to my "Baby Fish" tank, I worry he might be too tiny even for that. I don't want him getting pecked at, so I decide it's time to move the biggest fish over to my "Teen Fish" tank. Opal, a pretty white fish with an orange forehead, doesn't protest much when I scoop her up and place her bag in the adjacent tank. I do the same for my new fish, watching him as I decide on a name.

I smile wide as the image of Dylan's mantrum flits into my head. He was totally out of line, and though he ruined my mood it was nice to put him in his place. I laugh to myself like a dork. This poor fish will forever be tied to that memory. "I'll have to call you Dill, sorry. Hopefully you won't be as sour as your namesake."

The doorbell rings, and I shoot up from my bed in surprise. Not that we don't have visitors, but my best friends—Shreya and Olivia—are either working or on vacation. Everyone knows my parents wouldn't be home. I creep to the door and peek through the peephole, expecting a salesperson.

All I see is a fluff of gray hair and the beginning of an old woman's forehead. Our only elderly neighbor is Mr. Choi across the street, so I'm not sure what to expect when I unlock the door and turn the knob.

"Hello, is this the Arlington residence?" she asks, looking me up and down in a way that makes me uncomfortable.

"Yes?" For a second I wonder if she could be a reporter interested in my parents' grant, but she seems a little too old and her clothes are more like pajamas than business attire. She can't be here for an interview.

"Are you the daughter?" I don't have a clue who she is, but it feels as if she's picking apart every inch of my face, clothing, and frame. "There are so many Orientals around here it's hard to tell. You all look the same."

My eyebrows shoot up, and my tongue goes dry. Not that I've never heard a racial slur before, but most people at least *try* to be respectful.

"Well?" she says when I stay mute. "Do you speak English? Or did your mother only teach you Japanese?"

"Um . . ." I force myself to swallow the shock. "Who are you again?"

She sighs. "You don't recognize me at all?"

I try to look past her words, try to focus on not letting my anger boil over. I don't know how old she is, but she looks at least as old as my *Obaachan* in Japan, who we video chat with every couple weeks. Her lips are completely gone, she's heavy, and she sports a fairly visible mustache. Her eyes are a pretty hazel, even though she scowls at me. I can't recall ever meeting her in my life. "I'm sorry, I don't. Maybe you got the wrong Arlington?"

Her frown deepens as she scratches her head, then her face goes oddly blank. Finally, she nods. "I could have. Sorry for taking up your time."

As awful as her comments were before, her apology is so sincere it takes me off guard. "Don't worry about it. Hope you find who you're looking for."

"Me, too." She heads back down the path, makes a left onto the sidewalk, and I watch her as she reads house addresses. For a moment, I wonder if I should take her in. She didn't seem dangerous. Maybe she's really lost—majorly lost—and needs to call the police for help. Not that I have much to go on, but something felt off about her.

13

Then I'm closing the door, and I'm back on the couch in front of my laptop, looking at Instagram and getting super jealous over Olivia's pictures of some beach in Tahiti. Her mom has been saving up for years, but still. I want to be in Tahiti, not alone in my bedroom on a perfectly nice day. I remind myself I'll soon be out on the bay, studying with my parents—that makes me feel much better.

The home phone rings, and I pick it up even though no one important ever calls on it. "Hello?"

"Uh, hi. Is this Mika, I'm guessing?"

"Yes?" I swear I know the voice but can't quite place it, so I decide not to hang up.

"Great—I figured, since it's summer and all. This is your Uncle Greg. Do you remember me?"

"Yeah, of course!" That's why he sounded familiar. Uncle Greg is Dad's younger brother who lives in Seattle. We used to visit him every fall break when I was a kid, but it's been years now. Dad's not very close to his family, for some reasons I know and some I don't. "How are you?"

His laugh is a lot like Dad's. "Okay. I was just wondering if your dad's cell number changed, because the one I have isn't working."

"Well, he got a new phone a couple years ago . . ."

"What's the number?"

I rattle it off, trying not to think about Uncle Greg having a cell number that's over two years outdated. I may not have siblings, but I hope I'd talk to them more often than that if I did.

"Great, thanks, Mika." He hangs up without a goodbye, which makes me wonder what would be so urgent that he needs to talk to Dad right now.

14

As I set the phone on its charger, the doorbell rings yet again, and the peephole reveals the same fluffy hair. When I answer, the woman examines me just like before and says, "Is this the Arlington residence?"

I sigh. This woman is obviously lost and a little off her rocker. If I don't help her, who will? "Come in, ma'am. I think it's time to call the police."

Her eyes bug out. "Oh no, I'm just looking for the Arlingtons. Please don't call the police."

I look at the clock in the living room. It's ten to five. An hour at least before my parents get home, but I hate to think of this poor woman wandering the streets more than she already has. She seems harmless enough. "My parents aren't home just yet, so how about dinner? Are you hungry?"

Her eyes glisten with tears. "That would be lovely."

"I'm Mika." I hold out my hand, and she takes it. "What's your name?"

"Betty Arlington."

Without thinking, I pull my hand from hers, too shocked to speak. It can't be a coincidence, and now that she's said her name I can see traces of Dad in her features even though I've never seen so much as a picture of my grandmother. Dad hasn't spoken to her in decades, and I can't imagine he'll be excited to see her now.

Chapter 3

I only know a few things about my dad's mom, and none of them are good. When I was old enough to realize I was missing a grandma, I asked about her. All my dad said was, "Mi-chan, Grandma Arlington wasn't happy that I married Mommy, so we can't talk to her until she gets over that."

I didn't quite get it back then, but I took his word for it. As time passed I've learned to read through his carefully constructed statement. Because there are only a couple reasons why someone would disapprove of my intelligent, beautiful, kind mother, and those would fall into the racist category.

From the few words I've exchanged with my grandmother today, it's clear I haven't been wrong about her prejudices all these years. But now that she's in front of me I'm not sure what I'm supposed to do about it.

"So . . ." I manage to get out. "Betty, I take it you're my dad's mother?"

"Is your dad named Stanley?"

I nod.

She sighs, like this is more disappointing than exciting, the first face-to-face with her granddaughter. "Told him his kids would look nothing like him."

I want to tell her she's wrong, that I got things from my dad that are super obvious, like my stubby fingers instead of Mom's skinny, long ones. I have a bigger bridge in my nose like him, too. And my hair is wavy, not my mom's never-gonna-curl-ever hair. But I don't tell her. I just stare, trying to figure out if I should make good on my dinner offer or not.

"Aren't you gonna let me in?" she asks.

I jump out of the way before I can find the courage to say no. It won't be long. At least I hope it won't, because I already don't want to be around her. She inspects our entryway with the same hard glare, and I head for the kitchen to find something decent to cook. It's not as if my parents are champs in that field. They usually grab take-out on the way home.

"You can sit here," I say, pointing to the kitchen table. "Is there anything you don't like or are allergic to?"

"Nothing ethnic or spicy, please." She sits, looking exhausted. "There are a lot of fish in this house."

"Marine biologists and fish go together, right?" I open the fridge and inspect the boxes of restaurant leftovers, wondering what exactly she means by "nothing ethnic or spicy." Does that include pizza? Because that's Italian and pepperoni is spicy to some people. What about the enchiladas? And would Dad's beloved Polska kielbasa also be ethnic? Or is it just the non-European stuff?

I shouldn't have offered to feed her.

"I thought the fish would be a phase," she says, smiling at the nearest tank with a dreamy, far off look. "If I'd known that book on marine life would have sparked all this . . ."

17

"You don't like Dad's job?" I settle on a can of chicken soup. Surely she can't complain about chicken soup being anything but standard.

She purses her lips. "His job is fine, except that he had to go away to college, and then on that internship to Japan, and work all the way across the country. Why he couldn't just stay in Vermont . . ."

I didn't know she lived that far away. "Isn't Vermont landlocked?"

"So?"

I turn to the soup, deciding it's better not to point out that a person who studies marine life might want to *live* by the ocean. If she understood these sorts of things, there wouldn't have been problems to begin with. As I stir with one hand, I pull out my phone with the other. Even from the first ten minutes with this woman, I can tell Mom and Dad need a warning text.

Did Uncle Greg get hold of you? I figure that's why he called— he somehow found out that Betty was on her way here.

Yes. Is everything all right? Dad sends back.

We have an interesting visitor.

We're on our way.

I breathe a sigh of relief. There is no way I'm capable of handling this situation, and honestly, I don't want to. Betty doesn't hide her displeasure with pretty much everything around her. Why did she even come? She's obviously not here to make nice.

"So your name's Mika?" she says, but it sounds like *my-kuh*.

"*Mee-ka*," I say as I set the soup in front of her. No complaints, which I feel bad for expecting, but they do seem to spill out of her.

"Have a middle name?"

"Grace."

She nods. "Do you know why you got that name?"

"Dad said he liked it."

She slurps down a spoonful of soup. "Of course he does. Grace was my stuck-up, free-thinking sister who thought everything he did deserved a trophy."

"Was?" I can't bring myself to eat my soup, so I keep stirring it around and around. "Did she die?"

"Twenty-five years ago." Her spoon splashes soup onto the table when she sets it down. "And good riddance."

It's kind of funny that my grandmother's name is Betty, because all I can think when I look at her is *bitter*. She reeks of bitterness. I have no connection to this woman, even if I share her genes. It seems like I should have some positive emotions about meeting my grandmother, but I can't feel anything but annoyance. An image of Dylan pops in my head, and I try not to laugh at how similar they are. He should be related to her, not me.

We eat in silence for a while, and then I hear Mom and Dad's car pull up in the driveway. Their footsteps are hurried, and when they reach the kitchen it looks as if they're expecting to walk in on a scene from a horror movie. Dad in particular, his curls wild and mad-professorish. He even has his lab coat on still.

"My, Stanley, you've gotten old," Betty says.

Mom looks to him, as if everything hangs on what he will say. I suppose it does.

"What are you doing here?" he asks.

19

"Is that any way to greet your mother?"

Dad clenches his jaw and it looks like he has a lot pent up, though nothing comes out. Finally, he takes a deep breath and attempts to tame his hair. "Yumi, Mika, if you wouldn't mind I'd like to talk to my mother in private."

"Of course, honey, take your time," Mom says.

I open my mouth to protest, but Mom already has me by the wrist and half way out of the kitchen. I manage to get free by the time we reach the hall. "I want to know why she's here! I'm the one who got to spend all this time dealing with her."

Mom puts her finger to her mouth. "He's just trying to protect us. We'll find out more listening to them from here, anyway."

Trying not to smile, I lean next to her on the wall. Sure enough, Betty makes no attempt to be quiet, her voice carrying through the house. "Looks like you're pretty comfortable here, Stan. Gotta admit I hoped to find you divorced and eating humble pie."

I imagine Dad pinching the bridge of his nose, which is what he does when I talk back. "What do you want?"

"Who said I wanted anything?"

"You wouldn't be here otherwise!" Dad's voice is almost a yell. I have never heard him yell. "What do you need money for this time? Did you lose the trailer? Because I was shocked when Greg said you flew here."

"Jenny's got the trailer. She kicked me out." Betty says this as if it's no big deal, but Jenny is Dad's older sister. My aunt. Never met her, either.

Dad scoffs. "And you thought I'd be more sympathetic?"

20

"No." The spoon and bowl clatter in the sink. "Just figured you'd have more money than your tree-hugger brother. What is it with you two and nature?"

"I told you ten years ago I wasn't giving you any more money." Dad's voice is so cold it's hard to believe he's speaking to his mother. He doesn't talk like that to anyone.

"I don't need money. I need a place to stay."

"Even worse."

"Well, you ain't got much choice, son, because I have Alzheimer's and nowhere to go and no money to get there anyway. Spent the last of it flying here."

Dad doesn't answer, and suddenly his footsteps are approaching. Mom and I scramble for my bedroom, shutting the door just in time to hear Dad stomp past and lock himself in his room.

Chapter 4

I sneak out of the house early next morning, deciding not to attempt breaking the angry silence that has fallen over my place. Last night my mom coaxed Betty into the guest room. I'm not sure how Mom ignored all the comments about ruining the family and the importance of staying loyal to one's country and race, but she did. And then we all took to our rooms like the cast of some soap opera.

"We clean the more populated tanks every day," I say, though Dylan makes no attempt to listen to me. Instead, he tosses a pen, higher and higher each time. I try to take it from him, but he dodges. "Do I need to call your uncle?"

"You're the kid who used to tattle on people at recess, aren't you?" He holds the pen up, way out of my reach.

"No." I give up, going back to the tank I'm cleaning. I so don't have the patience for this today. "But this is work. We're being paid to do a job, not to mess around."

He snorts. "Yeah, babysitting fish is majorly important."

"It *is* important. Every job is important." I have a strong urge to grab the mop so I can scrub out my aggravation. Between Dylan and Betty showing up, my summer has turned into

22

a disaster overnight. *Think of the grant and the bay and the potentially hot college interns . . . it's not all bad.*

There's a long pause, but finally he says, "Why take such good care of an animal that can't remember you for more than a few seconds?"

I stop scrubbing, and for some reason Betty flashes through my mind. I don't know much about Alzheimer's, but I do know it makes you forget until your brain shuts down entirely. Maybe I don't like her, but I do feel sorry for her. Even so, I hope Dad won't let her stay with us. "Even if that were true—which it isn't—shouldn't we make every moment they remember a good one?"

Dylan's face does that same thing it did yesterday when I took my new fish home. If I knew him better, I might understand what it meant. It's a mystery, and it remains one, since he walks away after that. I go back to work, happy not to have to deal with him more than absolutely necessary.

Right before lunch, Clark shows up at the Aquatics island. He's still brushing hair off himself, probably having just fed the cats or dogs. "Hey, Mika, how goes the training?"

I wince.

"Say no more. Dylan is a pain, but try not to judge him too badly."

"Yeah, he's making it hard."

Clark gives a tired sigh. "Let's just say this summer isn't turning out how he expected. I think we can win him over, though."

"With what? The catnip?"

He laughs. "Maybe. Hey, so I know you're about to clock out, but Tanya called in sick. You mentioned your parents'

23

study in the bay has been delayed—would you mind covering a couple more hours for a few days?"

As much as I don't want to be around Dylan more this afternoon, I figure it's just as bad as going home to Betty. The idea that she's still in my house at all makes me uncomfortable. "I guess I can do that."

"Thanks, Mika.

"I'll be back after lunch then." I hate going out in public in my AnimalZone uniform, but I need some *saag paneer* just as much as I need Shreya. So I bike over to her family's Indian restaurant, Shades of Bombay, where the noon rush is just slowing down as people head back to work. The tiny eatery is crammed between a nail salon and a tanning place, almost invisible in the non-descript strip mall, but all the locals know it's the place to get curry.

The front door dings as I walk in, and Shreya smiles when she sees me. "Mika! We're still a bit packed but I'll sneak you in back."

"Thanks." As I head towards her, I try to ignore the angry glares of a few people waiting. My mouth waters at the smell of this place—the richness of the spices comforts me. Shades of Bombay is practically in my blood, what with my best friend owning it and my parents' insatiable appetite for anything not cooked at home.

Shreya gives me a warm hug when I get to her, and I sigh. "You have no idea how bad I need *saag* right now."

"Uh oh." Her warm brown eyes fill with concern. It's funny how the color is about the same as mine, and yet I always see hers as warm and mine as cold. Maybe it's the difference in skin tone—I'm paler, like my dad. "I have a break in ten. I'll meet you then, 'kay?"

I nod.

"Mom! Mika's coming back!" she yells.

"Okay!" I hear from behind the kitchen door, and then Shreya is off to tend tables.

The kitchen air is hot and thick with curry. Her father and three older brothers work the line, and her mother stands at the pass making sure all the food goes out perfectly. She analyzes me when I sit at the table in the corner. Her long hair fights to escape the scarf she uses to cover it. "Let me guess . . . *saag paneer.*"

I smile. "How did you know?"

She holds up her hands. "It's a gift. Or I've taken your curry order for years."

I laugh. She probably has my family's favorites memorized.

Shreya comes in just as her mom sets down my food. I grab the *naan*, warm and soft and the best of breads, and stuff my face. I've learned if I go for the curry first, I'll burn my tongue and ruin the meal. As I spoon *saag* and rice onto my plate, everything feels better. It may look like green mush with white bits in it, but it's magic. I take a bite, and the spice with the silky *paneer* cheese makes all the bad feelings go away.

"Do I need to get you a room?" Shreya asks, one of her thick eyebrows arched.

"Yes." The food garbles the word, but I don't care. "And *The Princess Bride.*"

She laughs. "Did you break up with a secret boyfriend? It's been a while since you had one."

"You speak as if I'm never single."

"I just thought you'd have found someone else by now. You broke up with Cyrus, what, two months ago?"

I nod. It was right before Prom, since I didn't want to complicate things with him going off to college anyway. "It wasn't *that* long ago, though I gotta admit I really miss the kissing and—"

Shreya plugs her ears. "I'm not listening!"

"Fine, fine." This is why I need Olivia to not be in Tahiti. We respect that Shrey isn't ready to date, but I need someone to talk to and Olivia is wilder than I'll ever be. A month without her is too long.

"So if not a break up, why are you in *saag* mode?" Shreya asks.

"Where do I even start?" By the end of my tale, her jaw is slack and she's stopped twirling her long black hair.

She stands. "Let me get you more curry."

"Butter chicken!" I call, suddenly craving it after all that *saag*. I almost feel guilty for horking it down so fast, but it couldn't be helped.

Shreya shoves her way into the little kitchen, and her brothers yell at her in Hindi. This means they don't want me to know what they're saying, because they speak English perfectly well. I get them back by insulting them in Japanese. They shoot me glares, but they treat their friends in the kitchen just as much as Shreya treats me.

"Idiots." Shreya puts the fresh curry in front of me, and I dab my *naan* there while I wait for it to cool. "I wish they'd get married and move out."

"Seriously."

Shreya's brothers are all much older than she is—by at least ten years—and they were born in India before her parents saved up enough to come here. Despite the sibling squabbles, they really care about her, making sure they're always around for school events and whatnot.

"So, I need to know one thing," Shreya says as I dig in. "Is this Dylan guy cute?"

I nearly choke on a piece of chicken. "Shrey, c'mon! Are you kidding me?"

She holds up her hands. "I'm just saying. You *have* been single for a whole two months, and it's not like you have much to look at during work, between Supervisor Clark, Old Lady Miriam, and Tanya the Gumsmacker."

"Do not mock my co-workers." I shake my head, trying not to laugh at the ragtag AnimalZone team. "They are lovely people."

She wears a smug smile. "I didn't say they weren't, but attractive they are not. So what about Dylan?"

"I don't know." I lean back, the curry sloshing inside me. "I was too distracted by his overall hatred of the world to notice."

"Perhaps I'll have to make my own assessment." She leans in to whisper. "If I can ever get off work, that is."

"Tell me we're still on for Saturday at least."

"Of course. That's, like, our thing."

I laugh. "Pretty much. I better get back to work—Clark needs me to fill in for Tanya a couple hours."

"I gotta get back out there, too." She stands with me. "Don't you just hate Olivia right now? If she posts one more picture of Tahiti . . ."

"Seriously." But at least Shreya and I can share in our no-vacation summer misery. This is my only comfort as I bike back to work. When I get there, Dylan is still lounging at my Aquatics island, messing with the pens. Old Lady Miriam mans the register, where she cheerily chats with a lady about her ragdoll cat. She may be the slowest checker on the face of the Earth, but she is also the sweetest. Tanya the Gumsmacker works the shift after me, so I don't see her often, but I do get stuck with her hours or Miriam's when they can't come in.

I don't want to deal with Dylan, but I force myself back to my station. He might be slightly more tolerable than Betty. Maybe I should be grateful I don't have to go home. "Did you have lunch already?"

He doesn't look away from the pens. "None of your business."

"I was just asking because now that I'm back you can get out. Sorry for trying to be considerate."

"I heard you talking to my uncle earlier," he says. "I know he's trying to get you on the fix-Dylan train. Don't bother. I don't need fixing."

"I have no clue what you're talk—" My phone rings, but when I pull it from my pocket I don't recognize the number, so I let it go. "Look, I'm just trying to do my job, and I really hope 'fixing you' isn't part of it, because that has a very different meaning in a pet store, you know."

That earns me a disdainful glance.

"Though I hear fixing dogs really calms . . ." Whoever it was leaves a message, and I decide it's better to listen to that than deal with Dylan. The voice I hear is definitely not one I expected.

28

It's my neighbor, Mr. Choi. "Hi, Mika. I couldn't get a hold of your parents, so I thought I'd try you. Um, there is a strange woman in front of your house ruining your zen garden. I tried to ask her about it, and she called me a rather distasteful name and said it was her house. I thought I should call you before I called the police. Call me back if you can."

My lungs can't seem to get air. My parents left Betty alone at the house? Are they insane? I assumed at least one of them would stay with her. And my mother's zen garden! She is obsessive about getting those lines just right. I redial the missed call number, and he picks up immediately. "Hi, Mr. Choi? Don't call the police—she's my grandmother. Yeah, my dad's. Yeah, that's the one."

Dylan's ears perk up at this, and I'd rather not have him hear about my new family drama. I take a few paces away from him and speak quieter. "My parents are probably in meetings. Let me talk to my supervisor and see if I can get there before she destroys the whole thing."

"Police, huh?" Dylan says when I hang up. "And here I thought you were a tight ass."

I give him my best glare instead of flipping him off like I want to. "Don't. I have more than enough to deal with right now. Try not to kill any fish while I'm gone."

Clark is kind enough to let me go early, even though he needed me to cover Tanya's hours. Then I speed off to whatever disaster my grandma is causing.

I have a feeling it won't be the last time.

29

Chapter 5

When I pull up to my house, I can barely believe what I'm seeing. How can an old woman do so much damage in so little time? Betty has managed to shovel all the gravel into piles, like tiny mountains scattered about our yard. And now she's digging at the packed dirt below for no reason I can guess.

Across the street, poor Mr. Choi stands nervously in his driveway. He's been such a good neighbor, and sometimes I babysit his grandchildren when his kids come home for holidays. I better get his account before I attempt to break Betty out of her furious digging.

"How long has this been going on?" I ask as I wheel my bike across the street.

"Since this morning. I was returning from my early walk when I spotted her. At first I thought perhaps your parents hired someone to tend the yard, but then I realized it would probably be a younger person." His eyes might be wrinkled with age, but they still show a hint of anger. "She called me a dirty Jap when I asked her what she was doing. I'm not even Japanese, but still."

I cover my mouth in surprise and embarrassment. He's Korean-American, but it seems Betty is one of the many people who are happy to lump all of Asia together. And use racist words while they're at it. "I'm so sorry. She showed up yesterday. I don't think my parents realized her condition was this bad."

"Condition?"

"She said she has Alzheimer's."

"Ahhh." He nods, some compassion returning at the news. I'm not sure I should be happy about that or not. Does her disease exempt her from being kind to my neighbors? That doesn't seem fair. "I swear we'll make it up to you. Treat you to dinner or something."

He shakes his head. "Don't worry about it. I just knew Yumi would be upset."

"Yeah . . ." Mom loves the zen garden. It's her only real hobby. She says it gives her peace, sitting out on the front porch with her tea most every evening. "Maybe I can get it almost back to normal before they get home."

"Good luck." He straightens his glasses, looking over my shoulder at Betty. "Perhaps your parents should take her to a doctor."

"Yeah. Thanks for calling."

He nods, and I head back to my house. Betty doesn't look up from her work as I lock my bike to the porch. I watch her for a second, still unsure of why she's digging a hole in our yard.

"What are you doing?" My voice is angrier than expected.

She looks up at me, seeming confused by my presence, until it clicks. "Grace, you're back."

"Actually, it's Mika."

31

"Oh . . . I'd rather call you Grace." She goes back to digging. "Did you know that's my sister's name? I love my sister. We make dollhouses together."

"You told me about her yesterday. Except you said you're glad she's dead."

"What?" She laughs. "No I didn't."

I roll my eyes. "So is there a reason you piled all the gravel into little hills? Because my mom will be pissed about that."

"Who has rocks in their front yard? You need grass. And more trees."

I raise an eyebrow. "Are you seriously crazy enough to think you can re-landscape our yard?"

"If I want it done right I have to do everything myself—that's what my mom always says." Her arms strain as she works, and a gust of wind blows her unpleasant scent right in my face. She's drenched in sweat.

"You can't do this. It's not your yard. You don't have a right to change it just because you don't like it." I grab her arm, though there's no way I could pull her up.

She freezes, then slowly turns her head to me. All the pleasantness in her expression drains. "Don't touch me!"

"I was just—"

"I don't want your dirty hands on me!" She stands up, looking surprised by her surroundings and the trowel in her hand. "I need a bath."

Words fail me. Maybe because I've never been so insulted in my life, and by my own grandmother. Mom prepared me for prejudice from strangers, not from my own blood. How am I supposed to handle this?

Betty disappears inside before I can figure out what to say, but I know one thing for certain—my parents were right to cut her out of their life. She's awful.

I get to work on the gravel, which is surprisingly heavy. How Betty got all this piled up is beyond me. At least I'm used to the lifting, what with how much I haul at work. I only get five mounds smoothed out when I hear, "Grace! Grace! Help!"

Shooting up, I run for the house with no clue what I might find except that it must be bad. I don't know enough about Alzheimer's to deal with her. And I don't want to. I rush through the door, where I'm met with *way* more old lady flesh than I ever wanted to see in my life. "You're naked!"

"I don't have any clothes!" She's crying like a child, soaking wet from what I can only assume was her bath to clean off my dirty touch. "I think someone stole my clothes."

"Ugh." I shield my eyes, wishing I could go back to work. Stupid Dylan is better than this. Barely.

After all that digging, she really doesn't have any clothes that aren't dirty. She didn't even have a purse when she showed up yesterday, which makes me wonder how she managed to get on a plane and all the way to Monterey. I head into the living room and grab a blanket. "Here. Let me see if I can find you anything."

She nods slowly, wrapping the blanket around her chest.

I head to my parents' room in attempts to find something for her to wear. The search doesn't go well. Betty is not a small woman, and my mom has never been bigger than a size two. Even my dad is thin and lanky, and none of his stuff looks remotely big enough. But I have to get her something because I can't handle her naked, on top of everything else.

It comes down to the kimono my mom wore for her big twentieth birthday celebration or my dad's favorite bathrobe. Seeing as one of my mom's prized things has already been destroyed today, I grab the bathrobe. At least now it's even.

"How's this?" I ask her, holding out the robe.

She smiles meekly. "Yes, thank you."

I look away as she dresses right in front of me. "Can you not ruin anything else now? Just watch TV or something."

She frowns as she grabs the remote. "I don't know how to make it work."

I sit her down and show her how to use the remote. It seems to take her more than normal time to understand, and my patience is long gone. This isn't fair. I shouldn't have to be doing this while my parents are working. They're the adults—they should be here.

After I start the washer to clean her sweaty clothes, I sit in my dad's recliner and let out a long sigh. Betty watches the TV, but she glances at me, seeming confused. "Where's Martin?"

"Who?" I ask.

"My husband. Do you know where he is?"

I shake my head, exhausted with her. "I don't know anything about you. Watch your show."

Betty shrinks into Dad's robe, looking sad. "I don't know either. He just left. No note. No calls. Jenny and Stan and Greg keep asking where he is, and I don't know what to say. Business trips don't last forever, you know?"

"Whatever." I have no idea if what she's saying is real or not. Dad doesn't talk about his family. As far as I know, his life began in college. That's as early as he'll go.

"Everyone leaves me." Her voice is soft. "You will, too, Micah."

"Mika."

She cringes. "Does your name have to sound so foreign? Couldn't they have at least given you an American name?"

"I've always liked my name just fine."

Long pause. "I think I'm hungry."

Rolling my eyes, I stay put. "Can't you get your own food?"

"Your refrigerator smells weird."

What the hell is that supposed to mean? I decide it's better to feed her than listen to her talk. "I'll make you a sandwich or something."

As I rummage through our meager food stock, I wonder if I should call my parents again. But then I hear their car drive up and the garage door rumble open. Maybe Mr. Choi left them messages as well. I run out the back door, into the garage, and spot my parents out front surveying the damage, but I stop short of them.

Mom's face slacks in shock at the sight of our ruined front yard, and then she turns on Dad, livid. "Look at this!"

"I'm not blind, Yumi." Dad heads for the piles of gravel. "You're the one who said she'd be fine on her own."

"Don't you dare put this on me. She's your mother, and she hates me. Of course I didn't want to stay home with her!"

Then my dad explodes, and they're arguing in front of our house where everyone can see. Taking a few steps back, I decide to go back inside. I stand in the kitchen, reeling. I've never seen them fight before.

I don't like it.

Chapter 6

"What do you mean you don't know?" Dad's on the phone with his sister, Jenny. "She didn't show up with anything but the clothes on her back. How could you put her on a plane without . . . that is no excuse . . . ugh, you're just like her, you know that? I can't believe you've been living off her, using her trailer, and you can't even tell me who her doctor was or if she has any insurance. What about Medicaid?"

Mom and I eat breakfast in silence. Betty hasn't gotten up yet. From what I've gathered so far, Jenny is not the beacon of responsibility my dad is. It sounds like instead of physically escaping, like Dad and Greg did, she chose a more . . . chemical route.

"You know what? Forget it. I'll deal with it, like always." Dad sets his phone on the counter, looking like he's about to burst. "Jenny said there was a carry-on bag—Mom probably didn't take it off the plane, so I get to call the San Jose airport next. There's no telling where her purse ended up."

Mom frowns. "What are we going to do? Two days, and she's already ripped a hole in our lives. How much does Alzheimer's care even cost?"

"Probably more than we can afford, but what choice do we have?" Dad sits at the table, seeming exhausted, though the day has only just begun. "Greg will chip in, but forest rangers don't make much. Jenny has nothing—she'll probably use Mom's social security money if we don't hurry and transfer it here."

I sip my tea, trying not to look freaked out. Jenny sounds messed up if she'd actually do that. "But Betty needs to get out of here. Like now."

My dad's eyes soften when he looks at me. I told them about the naked situation yesterday, and they both felt bad for putting me through that. "I know, sweetie, but I can't do that until I find out what it'll cost or who diagnosed her." He leans back in his seat, resigned. "I'll have to take time off work. She obviously can't be left alone."

Mom sighs. "I'll find a way to tell the director. I can handle finalizing the grant preparations on my own. Your mother? Not so much."

Dad doesn't seem happy about what Mom said, but he doesn't reply. It feels like there's residual anger left from their fight yesterday, and I won't be the one to bring that up again. I grab my messenger bag. "I gotta get to work. Good luck, Dad."

He nods. "Thanks."

The morning is warmer than usual as I pedal my way to AnimalZone. It is technically summer, so I hope it's a sign of some sunnier days to come. If my life is so complicated, at least the weather should be agreeable. It makes me wish it were Saturday, then I could hang out with Shreya at the beach instead of facing Dylan again.

By a stroke of luck, he's nowhere to be seen when I get there. I don't dare ask Clark where he is, favoring to do my job instead. The fish make me happy. As I feed them and clean their tanks, I feel like everything is normal for a second. There's one goldfish in particular—one with giant telescope eyes—that I keep going back to. The moment I bring one home, I always find another at work to get attached to.

When I take my morning break, I discover Dylan has been shoved into the inventory room, where he's stacking a new shipment of dog food. It makes me happy to see him doing grunt work. Clark must be punishing him for something.

"Excuse me," an older man says. It's about noon, and he's the first customer all day to make eye contact with me. I don't bother asking the browsers if they need help—they usually get tense and uncomfortable, like I'm hoping to sell them something.

"How can I help you?" I ask.

"I'm having problems with my goldfish. I thought he was dead this morning because he was upside down, but when I went to scoop him out he flicked back around and scared the living daylights out of me." He puts his hand over his heart. "Does that mean he'll die soon?"

I shake my head, smiling. "He probably has swim bladder. Feed him a couple shelled peas every week, and he'll be fine."

He looks surprised. "It's okay to feed them people food?"

"Not *all* food, but goldfish are omnivores. They like a variety of things—peas, carrots, oats, worms, shrimp, even raspberries. It's good to give them treats, helps them digest better."

"I didn't know that. Thank you, you've been very helpful."

"You're welcome. Do you need anything else?" This customer is just what I needed. He asks me to point him to a better food for his fish and even buys a bigger tank at my recommendation. His fish is a lucky one. Most people hardly care or notice when theirs start acting out of character.

I wonder if anyone noticed when Betty first started acting strange. Jenny doesn't sound like the kind of person who would worry about her mom's health. Something drastic, like yesterday, must have happened before Betty even went to the doctor.

After I help the man to the register, I turn to find Dylan back at my Aquatics island. *Urgh*.

"Sure had that guy eating out of your hands," he says.

I roll my eyes. "It's called being polite. Maybe you should try it sometime."

He smirks. "Maybe. But seriously, what's with you and fish? I've never heard someone go on about them like that, let alone a person my age."

His voice is the least venomous I've heard it, and it takes me off guard. For a second I consider not answering, but if this means he's trying to be nice I'll encourage it. My life would be much easier if he wasn't such a jerk. "My parents are marine biologists—I've been around fish my whole life. I can't remember a time when I didn't like fish."

"So . . . you like them because your parents like them? I don't buy that."

"It's not just that," I say, sounding way more defensive than I like. "Have you ever heard the legend of koi?"

He shakes his head.

"It was my favorite story growing up. My mom would tell it to me before bed, how the koi would swim up the Yellow River but were met with a great waterfall at its source. Most of the koi would give up at that point, but some kept on trying to scale the waterfall. They tried and tried for one hundred years, and finally one koi reached the top of the falls—when it did, the gods turned it into a dragon."

I smile at the wall of goldfish beside me. "I still picture all these little fish as potential dragons, I guess. And it's a good reminder not to give up, even when things get hard. Maybe someday I'll reach the top of the falls, too, you know?"

Dylan is quiet for a moment, his brow knit tightly over his eyes. "Question."

"Okay?"

"If a koi was born at the top of the waterfall, in whatever spring was up there, would it turn into a dragon?"

I tilt my head. "Huh?"

"I'm just wondering—is it the trying to get to the top that makes a koi a dragon? Or is it being at the top?"

I'm not sure why he wants to know, but it is an interesting question. Who knew he had it in him to get all deep and ponderous? "I think it's the journey and effort the gods found favorable enough to merit dragonhood."

"But if that were so, what about all the others still banging their heads against the rocks? Don't they deserve it, too?"

"I . . ." I search for something, but can't put my thoughts into words.

"Ahem." I whirl around, finding Clark watching us. "How do you feel about me treating you guys to lunch? Mika

40

deserves it, and I am currently obligated to feed Dylan."

"As long as it's not cheap food, fine," Dylan says, looking at the floor.

"Fair enough." Clark turns to me. "How 'bout it, Mika?"

There's something weird about the way he looks at us. "You've never treated any of us to lunch before. Why now?" I ask.

Clark clears his throat. "Well, I just thought maybe you two would get along better if you learned more about each other. It's to improve our work environment. Employee bonding and junk."

He's totally lying. I get this sinking feeling in my stomach. Is he seriously trying to set us up? Oh, hell no. "Uhh, I actually need to run home and check on . . . stuff. Sorry, maybe next time."

Clark raises an eyebrow. "You can just say you don't wanna go."

"No! Really." I search for something to tell him, and then the image of my dad alone with Betty hits. "It's family stuff. My dad's home for the day, and I wanted to bring him lunch."

"Does it have to do with the cop thing?" Dylan asks.

My eyes go wide. "No. There were no cops. Shut up."

Clark gives me a skeptical look. "Well, have a nice time with your dad. Hope everything is okay."

"Thanks."

Though I didn't originally plan this, I go to my dad's favorite Mexican place, Su Casa, and order enough enchiladas for the two of us. I'm not sure what to get Betty and end up picking a cheese quesadilla. As I park in front of our house, I'm afraid of what I'll walk into. I just hope it's not more yelling.

41

Chapter 7

When I open the door, I'm not on edge because of any fighting, but because it's so *quiet*. The only sound is the TV, and when I round the corner there's Betty watching as if she's completely normal and nothing at all strange happened yesterday. Dad sits at the kitchen table, poring over his laptop. He looks up first. "Mi-chan, I didn't know you were coming home for lunch. Didn't you say you were covering for Tanya?"

I hold up the bags. "Yeah, but I thought you might want to share?"

He smiles—truly smiles, for the first time since his mom showed up—and that makes the trip worth it. "Did you really bring me enchiladas?"

I nod.

"C'mere." He hugs me, and we pull open the boxes. The enchiladas kind of look like someone threw up in a tin platter, but they taste amazing—the sweet pork, the hot sauce and cilantro. I'm drooling already.

There's no reaction from Betty, and I can't help but glance over at her. "Has she been like that all morning?"

"It was a fight to feed her breakfast, but yeah, pretty much. I think she's tired from all that digging she did yesterday, which she doesn't remember, by the way." He takes a huge bite of the cheesy mess, then shoves a spoonful of beans in along with it. "Mm, so good. I needed this."

"Thought you might." I dig into my own, taking only slightly smaller bites. Mom hates how we eat, says we act like the food will vaporize if we don't shovel it in. I lean in to whisper. "She makes me crave *saag* like nothing ever has."

He laughs. "I know the feeling all too well."

"I bought her a cheese quesadilla, just in case. The first day she said she didn't like anything spicy or 'ethnic,' though."

He rolls his eyes. "Whatever that means."

"I know, right?" I love my dad. He's not the stereotypical strict kind. Of course he expects me to do my best, but he also seems to encourage me to question things and follow my own path to the answers. Maybe he does it because he didn't get that, growing up.

"I'll give it to her after you leave," he says through his food. "You've already had your share of her for the week."

"Okay." I look at her, a strange pity-anger mix hitting. I can't help but wish we didn't have to deal with this, especially since my mom and I hardly know her. "Dad, can I ask you something?"

"Of course."

"Did you have an aunt named Grace?"

He pauses mid-bite, staring at me. "How . . .?"

"She asked me my middle name, and when I told her it was Grace she said you must have named me after her sister. I wasn't sure if it was true or not."

43

He lets out a long sigh. "It's true. Aunt Grace was . . . amazing. I don't know much about my mom's childhood, but they were very poor, as poor or poorer than I was growing up. Aunt Grace didn't want to be that way forever, and she fought, Mika, just like me and your mom fought. She was a lawyer in Boston, and she encouraged me to do well in school and go to college. I owe everything to her."

I nod. "And she died?"

"Right after I got into college. She was only forty-five." He stares at his food, I think maybe to hide his expression. "Cancer. She left what she had to me, Greg, and Jenny for school, but it wasn't much after all those medical bills and the funeral."

I know I'm already pushing it, but these stories from my dad's past fascinate me. He seems like an entirely different person, and yet the same. "Did your father really just up and leave you guys?"

"S-she told you that?"

"She said it yesterday. She was telling me she didn't know what to say to you guys."

"He did, but I don't want to talk about it." Dad won't look at me after that, and it feels like he's put up ten-foot walls. "I better get back to researching care facilities."

The idea makes me excited. "So she's not staying here?"

He shakes his head. "Not if I can help it. Thanks for lunch."

"No problem." I get up, needing to get back to work anyway, and head for the door. But I take one glance at Betty and stop. She's still staring at the TV, and I swear there are tears running down her face. Weird. It can't be from the show—they are doing some cooking segment—and then I realize she heard everything my dad said.

44

Did it hurt her?

Everyone leaves me, she said.

I look at my dad. I've always been proud of him, how hard he's worked to get where he is. But I never really thought about who or what he left behind. Though if Betty felt so bad about it, why didn't she ever try to fix it?

"Mi-chan?" he says.

I whirl around. "Hmm?"

"Something wrong?"

I shake my head. "See you in a few hours."

Chapter 8

I always show up to the beach early, though I know Shreya is always late. But Lovers Point isn't a very big place, and I have to stake out a good spot where the sand is perfect and close to the tide line. I roll out a few towels I brought to claim our place and sit to watch the sunrise. Yes, rise. Lovers Point curves into the bay, making it one of the few places on the West Coast where you can watch the sun come up over the ocean.

This, of course, makes it a busy tourist spot, but that's pretty much why Shreya and I pick this beach so often. We're show-offs. When your art is as fleeting as sand sculpture, the goal is to have as many people as possible see it before it crumbles.

The beach is still cold this early in the morning, so I pull my hoodie up and nestle deep into my favorite fleece blanket. Opening my current sketchbook, I draw out ideas for today's piece in the slowly increasing sunlight. An opulent castle. An old man making sand angels. A dragon crawling up from a spring.

Shreya will probably hate them all—she's a much better artist, honestly—but I always sketch anyway. It's nice to let my mind wander, to draw whatever shows up there.

When I'm not sketching, I shamelessly people-watch. As the sun rises, they make their way down the cliff to the beach, walk along the park paths with their dogs, take pictures of the Victorian-style bed and breakfast places lined up across the street. I check my phone, wondering just how late Shreya will be. It tends to vary based on how busy the restaurant was Friday night.

Finally, I see her on the cliff stairs. She has her usual equipment strapped to her back, and she waves when she spots me. I wave back, ready to do something normal after this crazy week.

"Good spot," she says when she gets close enough. "I have all day, so let's try going bigger, okay?"

"Hell yeah," I say. "I brought lunch, no reason to leave."

"What did you draw this morning?" She snatches my book from me, looking at the latest stuff. "I like the dragon. I'm so in the mood for a dragon, but—"

"You have a better idea?" I ask.

She laughs. "Just some modifications! We'll totally keep it an Asian dragon. Way cooler."

"Fair enough."

We get to work planning the dragon. Of course her ideas take my sketch to the next level. She wants to make it look like it's just about to take flight, its front feet pushing up from the ground, its head lifted to the sky. "It'll look awesome from the cliff, like it's about to shoot up and take someone out."

"Totally."

We get to work mapping out the size and proportions in the sand—its giant head, the arch of its back in the center, the tail resting on the other side of the pond. I even run up to the cliff top to make sure it looks like a good size. Then it's time for sand packing, which is the least fun part. But firmly packed sand is key to a sturdy sculpture, so we take our jackets off and begin.

"This part never stops sucking," Shreya says, huffing as we shovel sand into our five-gallon buckets. "Can't sand weigh less? Stupid sand."

I laugh. "But hey, our arms are ripped."

She flexes her triceps, which are seriously cut, then her biceps. "I do look hot, don't I?"

"Totally hot." I move on to my next bucket. "What we need is Olivia."

"Psh, she always whines."

"She has good stories, though, and it feels weird without her to entertain us." When Olivia is not in Tahiti, she works at the Pebble Beach Spa with her mom, who's a masseuse. Olivia's basically a gofer for the rich ladies who hang out while their husbands play golf, and she constantly has some dramatic tale to tell us about them.

"True. Olivia is our creamy Oreo center."

"I miss her." Olivia's the one who doesn't take life too seriously—Shreya and I have a tendency to be too "goal oriented," as Olivia says.

"Me too, but I will channel her. I want to hear more about Dylan," Shreya says.

I roll my eyes, though Olivia *would* ask me about him. "There's nothing to tell. Still doesn't do anything I tell him to do. Still acts like he'd rather have his nails ripped out than work there. You really need to get out if you're desperate enough to talk about him."

She snorts. "I know I do! But that's what my parents are worried about, even when I've told them I don't want to date until college. Seems like the older I get the more they want to keep me at the restaurant. They have another thing coming if they think I'll let them pick my husband, though."

Her face goes dark, and I frown. Shreya's parents had an arranged marriage, but I didn't think they'd do that to her. "Shrey, is that really what they're planning?"

She shrugs. "Not completely. Yet. I don't know. My dad doesn't want me to marry a non-Indian, though. We kinda had a huge fight about it last night. Not that I *don't* want to marry an Indian guy—I'd just like to have a choice, you know?"

I'm not sure what to say, because it seems weird that this still happens. I can't help thinking about my parents, how being in love made so many problems with my dad's family. I sigh. "We're only seventeen. You have time to win them over."

She smiles, but it's sad. "I'm not sure it works that way, Mika."

"Why not?"

"I don't know. It should be that simple, shouldn't it?" She grabs a smaller bucket to fetch water.

"Yes, it should be."

"But it isn't." She walks towards the waves, tugging at her ponytail. That means she's upset. It makes my heart ache. Shreya is my best friend. She shouldn't have to choose between love and her family. They should go hand in hand.

Within a few hours, we've packed all the sand into giant mounds that will form the foundation of our dragon. It's a simple enough design, though bigger than we usually go, so I figure it'll take us well into the afternoon to finish. We stand next to each other, surveying our work.

"I'll do the head," Shreya says.

"I was just gonna say you should. I'll do the rest—it's mostly scales." I grab the sketchbook, and we spend a few minutes collaborating on the look of it to make sure our pieces will match. Then it's time for the fun to begin.

I start from the top. We learned pretty quickly that starting anywhere else was bad. I begin by smoothing out the upper arch, so that the shape is just right, and then I hand pack ridges for the spine scales. Now that morning is in full swing, the beach is bustling with people. Many of them watch us work, which made me nervous when we first started getting serious about sand sculpture. But now I'm used to the camera clicks and the kids who stare on as if we're the goddesses of sand. I'm also used to the annoying people who ask if it's really sand.

"Yes, it's definitely sand," I say to a man watching on. He doesn't look convinced.

"You can pack it all next time, sir, if you'd like proof," Shreya says. "Just show up before dawn with a shovel. We'd be happy for the extra manual labor."

He snorts and walks off.

Once I have the large spinal scales as crisp as possible, I start on the tedious process of adding small ones to the whole body. I'm just starting to remember why it's been a while since we did a dragon when I hear, "Mika?"

I look up, blinking a few times because the scale pattern is burned into my retinas. Creepy mustache and running shorts just a touch *too* short. His sulky companion glares at me.

"Supervisor Clark?" I choke out.

"Hey! What a coincidence!" He pats his nephew on the back. "Dylan, look, it's Mika."

"I have eyes." Dylan wears running gear, too, except his fits much better than his uncle's. The red shirt clings to his form, revealing way more muscle than I expected. His black shorts hit at the knee. His shoes look flashy and expensive. I hate to think it, but he looks like he stepped out of an ad for running wear.

"*That's* Dylan?" Shreya says, clearly taken in by this version of him.

I want to say he looks a lot worse in the AnimalZone uniform, but I have a feeling I'd insult my boss. "Yeah. This is my best friend, Shreya."

Clark holds out his hand, and they shake. "Nice to meet you."

Dylan turns to the ocean, clearly trying to pretend he's not here. I give Shreya an I-told-you-so look.

She smiles. "Looks like you guys went running."

"Yup." Clark nods in Dylan's direction. "It might not look like it, but he does like to run. And I've always liked Lovers Point, touristy or not."

"Us too," I say.

"I had no idea you made sand sculptures." Clark looks over our work, which is maybe one third done. Something in me starts to squirm. I'm positive I mentioned it to him before, because I told him I had to have Saturdays off. "How long have you been doing this?"

"Pretty much every good-weathered Saturday since we were ten," I reply. That's when Shreya started at my elementary

51

school. We became instant friends, and we'd go to the beach and build sandcastles. "The sculptures just got bigger."

"Right." He glances at Dylan like he wants to kick him for being a jerk. "So, let me guess . . . a dragon?"

I nod. "Maybe you'll have to come back in a few hours when it's done. It doesn't look like much right now."

"Or we could stay! I didn't get to treat you to lunch the other day like I wanted—you deserve it for putting up with Dylan. I could run and get something, be back in like thirty minutes."

Dylan looks over his shoulder, glaring at his uncle. "I'd rather shower."

"Being dirty builds character," Clark says to him, and it feels like I'm missing something. "Hang out with the girls. Maybe you could even help."

His jaw slacks. "But, Unc—"

"No buts! I won't feed you if you leave." Clark sprints off. "I'll be right back with sandwiches!"

I watch in shock as he gets farther and farther away. "Did he seriously plan this?"

"Yup." Dylan sits in the sand. "And I fell for it."

Chapter 9

"You *can* just leave," I say to Dylan as I work. "Clearly you don't want to be here, and I don't want you here, either."

"Mika!" Shreya says, seeming surprised. "When did you get so mean?"

"I've been trying to be nice all week. I'm tired."

Dylan sighs. "I can't leave. He really won't feed me if I do. All the food at the house is locked up."

Shreya and I exchange a puzzled glance. Clark has always seemed like a nice guy to me, but that sounds a little weird. "Can't you go buy something?" I ask.

"I don't have any money. Not even my wallet."

I stick my carver in the sand and tromp over to the cooler I brought. Setting a sandwich down in front of him, I say, "Eat this and leave, then."

"So I'm supposed to tell him I stole your lunch and left? Do you know how much trouble I'd get in? He'd probably starve me all day, and I'm already dying from running." He lays back, looking pretty tired. "Jerk didn't even leave water."

I raise an eyebrow. "Why is he doing that?"

"Not your business." He covers his eyes with one arm.

"Can you leave me alone? I really am exhausted."

"She's only asking because it sounds batshit crazy," Shreya points out. "Like you're a prisoner. And I thought my parents were strict."

"Seriously, shut up, your voice hurts my head," he says.

That does it. Nobody talks to my friend that way. Grabbing my cooler, I pluck out the first cold water bottle I see, unscrew the top, and pour it right on his crotch. He flies up, and I fling the rest of the water in his face. He gasps for breath, his eyes full of fire. "What the hell?!"

"Either apologize to Shreya or leave. Because I'm so done with your crap."

"You can't make me leave."

I fold my arms. "But I can scream about the weird guy who peed himself and is bothering us. Or maybe . . . is that . . . You were doing *what* in public?"

His face goes slack with shock. "You wouldn't."

"You wanna bet?"

"You're bluffing."

I take in a deep breath, but only get out a partial scream before he lunges at me and covers my mouth. His weight takes me off guard, and I hit the sand. I stare at him, his face just inches from my own, his wet hair dripping onto my forehead. He glares at me, seething. "Are you crazy?"

He doesn't move his hand, so I don't know how he expects me to answer. He just stares and stares, and I don't know why but I keep looking at him, too. There are gold and green flecks in his brown eyes that you'd never see from a distance. And his lips glisten from the water. Maybe it *has* been too

54

long since I had a boyfriend, because his weight on me . . .

"Get off her!" Shreya yells.

That snaps him out of it, and he springs back. People gawk at us. One woman even has her phone out, as if she's just about to call 911. I pull myself up, brushing off the sand and whatever it was I felt. When she sees I'm okay, she lowers her phone, but I can feel her eyes on me.

"Well," I say. "You did a good job humiliating yourself all on your own, didn't you?"

Dylan sits in the sand, his head to his knees. His ears are vibrant red, and I'm pretty sure it's not a sunburn. I purse my lips in an attempt not to laugh. Grabbing another water bottle, I hold it out in front of him. He doesn't take it.

"C'mon, I know you're thirsty. And it's not like you can stand up to get your own drink."

He looks up at me. I expect something mean to come out of his mouth, but he takes the water and cracks the top. In about five seconds, the bottle is empty. He doesn't say thank you.

"Don't think I've let you off on the apology. But you can save it for later if you need to rehearse." I go back to sculpting. I have to go slow because my hands are shaking. I'm not sure why, since I'm not mad anymore. Better just focus on the scales.

"Sorry, Shreya," Dylan says after about five minutes.

She gives him a puzzled look. "Thanks, I guess."

"Here's the deal," he continues. "When my uncle gets back, I'm betting he'll have some excuse to leave again. If we don't play nice, he'll probably keep trying to orchestrate these run-ins. So can you pretend we get along while we eat, and then I'll leave you alone?"

"Why is he doing this, anyway?" I ask.

He shrugs. "Thinks I need new friends. You're the only person my age he knows."

"Great."

"Yeah . . ." Dylan stares out at the waves, where a few people are surfing. He does seem genuinely exhausted. I almost feel bad for him, and a small part of me wishes he wouldn't be so determined in his rudeness. He might not be so bad if he'd talk nicely like he did about the koi legend.

"So why are you here if Clark is so harsh on you?" I ask, going back to my endless scales.

"It was the lesser of two evils."

"What happened to your parents?"

"They got sick of me."

I pause. What his uncle said comes back, how this summer isn't turning out how Dylan wanted. "So . . . they threw you out?"

"Yup." He slouches more, and I feel like I've been kicking a puppy that lost its two front legs.

"I'm back!" Clark calls. He holds a few Subway bags, and Dylan runs to him like he can't stand another second of not eating. His uncle holds the bags back. "Let me check something first. Mika, how was he?"

My eyebrows raise. "What?"

"Was he nice?"

Dylan gives me the saddest look in the world, and somehow I know his eating relies completely on what I say next. I don't like this pressure. He might be mean, but he doesn't deserve this weird punishment. And I shouldn't be the one to decide. "He was fine," I say. "Quiet, mostly."

"Good. We're making progress." Clark hands Dylan his sandwich. He grabs it and steps back like his uncle still might take it away. "If you keep being civil, maybe I'll give you food privileges soon."

Shreya and I look at each other, and I wonder if her "What the hell is going on?" expression matches my own.

Clark hands us sandwiches, too, and then sighs. "Well, I got a call from Miriam at the store. Sounds like Tanya didn't show, so I need to go in. Dylan, would you prefer to haul more pet food or enjoy the beach with Mika?"

Dylan looks at me, feigning surprise. How did he call that? "You mean you'd give me a day off?"

"I told you that's how it works. If you make good choices, you get good things. Plain and simple."

Dylan nods. "I guess I'll stay here then."

"Great! I'll come back for you at six." Clark turns to me. "Don't let him leave, Mika."

I nod, feeling like a traitor.

When Clark goes, Shreya and I head to our towels to eat. Dylan doesn't join us. He's maybe twenty feet away, devouring his lunch like he hasn't had food in weeks. Shreya watches him, and I flick her leg. "Ow! Can't I enjoy the view?"

"What view?"

She glares at me. "C'mon, Mika. You can't tell me he's not gorgeous. How did you not notice? Even I can see that and I'm not boy crazy like you and Olivia."

"Uh, hello? Did you hear anything that came out of his mouth?"

She shakes her head, still staring at him. "I'm starting to forget."

I roll my eyes, even though I might agree with her more than I want to admit. With the afternoon heat upon us, the sand will start drying faster. We need to get the dragon finished before then. When we get back to work, I'm keenly aware of the fact that Dylan hasn't left the beach yet. He occasionally looks at me, but mostly stares at the ocean. I can't imagine what's going through his head.

Hours pass. Our dragon looks awesome. Shreya did an amazing job with his facial expression, and as we put on the finishing touches the crowd around us becomes a solid ring of people and camera phones.

I spot Dylan on the cliff, looking down at our work from the same place I surveyed it this morning. I can't quite tell, but I think he's smiling.

Chapter 10

The koi gather at the edge of my pond in the backyard, right near my feet. They swim over each other, excited, and I smile. Who says fish are dumb? They know just as well as any pet that it's feeding time, and they have an incredible sense of smell. They don't react this way to anyone but me.

My parents' voices float out the kitchen window. I can't quite make out what they're saying, but the tones are not nice. Again. This has been the case for over a week now. My dad doesn't want to stay home anymore. We all want Betty in a care facility, but it would cost like a third of their income even with Uncle Greg's help. I don't know what they'll do with her if we don't have the money. Hopefully not anything crazy. Like keep her around.

I sprinkle the food over my koi, and they gobble it up like the endlessly hungry fish they are. At least it's mostly peaceful out here. Our backyard is one of my favorite places. Though it's small, there's a giant tree that takes up most of the space. The limbs are so thick even an adult can sit on them. My koi pond is right under that, surrounded by bushes, with a small waterfall at the far end. The rest of the space is devoted to a deck with lounge chairs.

Stooping down, I reach out to pet my fish. Shreya once told me that was creepy, but I don't care. They aren't slimy like people usually assume. It's more like silky.

"They sure like you," Betty says, and I jump up in surprise. What is she, a ninja? She stands right next to me, her eyebrows raised high. "Sorry, I scared you."

"No, it's fine. Just didn't hear you." I eye her warily, never sure of what I'll get when she opens her mouth. The doctor my parents took her to said she was likely in the beginning of moderate Alzheimer's, which I guess means she'll need more and more help.

She points her thumb back at the house. "Do they always fight like that?"

I look away. "Actually, no."

"Ah, so it's my fault."

"Yup." I figure she should know how much she's invaded our lives, even if she might not remember tomorrow.

She stoops down by the pond, puts her fingers in the water. My fish scatter. "At least you have parents who care."

Though I don't really want to talk to her, my curiosity betrays me because maybe I'll get more stories about my dad. If he won't tell me what happened, Betty is all I have. "You didn't?"

"I used to, until the war." Her hand stops, one finger still in the water. "Gracie, why'd you have to go first? Everything would have been better if it was me."

"What are you talking about?"

She shoots up, her face way too close to mine. In her eyes, I'm sure I see fear. "Do you know what happens in those homes?

60

That's where they send you when you're too far gone. That's where I'm going to *die*. Alone. I bet Martin won't even visit me!"

Whoa, talk about swift topic change. "You mean my dad, Stan?"

"See? It won't be long until I can't say anything." She bursts into tears, and I don't know what to do. It seems cold just to stand there and watch her, but last time I tried to touch her she said she didn't want my "dirty hands" on her. "I don't want to die, but there's nothing else left to do."

"Those care centers aren't *that* bad. Have you talked to my parents about it?" Because this is way too heavy for me. Why does she always pick me when she wants to say crazy stuff?

She wipes at her tears like an angry child. "They don't like me. Honestly, I don't like them very much either."

I don't like you, either. "But you'd still rather stay here?"

She nods.

My stomach turns with guilt, thinking about how she'd rather be with people trying to get rid of her. Her life must suck if she thinks that's a good option. "Why?"

Her face goes blank again, and I have a feeling she can't remember. But then she sighs. "I miss my Stan, even if he never missed me, just like I miss my sister and my Greg and my Martin and my dad. Why do I still miss my dad? Why can't I forget that instead?"

"What happened to your dad?" I ask.

That gets me one of the worst glares yet. "Go to hell, dirty Jap."

My eyes widen as I watch her storm back to the house. I stand there, stunned. No one has ever called me that to my face. It hurts. Even knowing she's losing her mind, it doesn't stop it from repeating over and over in my head. I've been as

61

patient as I can with my grandmother, with this person who deserves no kindness from me, and this is what I get. I blink back tears as her screaming comes from the house.

"You're all going to hell! I hate you! You ruined my life! You ruined the world!"

Screw it.

My parents better put her in a facility tomorrow. I'll even pack her stuff and drive her there as long as I never have to deal with this crap again. Instead of going inside, I head around the house to the front. Mom's zen garden is finally back in place, and I hop along the stepping stones until I reach the porch.

My bag is still inside. I haven't eaten breakfast. I don't even have my uniform on yet, just yoga pants and a t-shirt. But I unlock my bike and go.

I have to get away from here, because if I tell my parents they'll just freak out more and I'm so sick of drama. Give me my old life back, please.

It would be nice if I could ride to a beach or the Aquarium to watch the fish all day. Better yet, I wish I had a boat so I could go out on the bay and be surrounded by the ocean. But I have work. Stupid work. I take the long way, trying to calm myself down so I won't risk bursting into tears.

Dylan would revel in that.

We may have reached a silent truce in the last week, but the image of him sneering at me steels my face. I won't be weak in front of him. Not ever.

"I think you forgot something," Dylan says when I get to work.

I grab the blue apron from one of the shelves in the Aquatics island. It'll have to do for today. I just hope Clark doesn't ask any questions. "I forgot a lot of things, actually. Did you clean the tanks yet?"

"Of course not."

I pinch the bridge of my nose. We've gotten to the point that he'll do stuff when I ask him to, but if I don't mention it he pretends it magically doesn't need to be done. "Good. I need to scrub."

His eyebrows go up. "Did something happen to you?"

"Why would you care?" I grab the cleaning supplies. "Go check the shelves to see if there's anything we need to restock."

"Okay . . ."

His expression might be concern, but I'm already too upset to be impressed by his small show of compassion. I grab the big magnetic scrubber, attach it to the glass, and get to work. Try to forget the words she said. Think of anything else. Everything else. She's just a crazy old lady who doesn't know what she's saying.

Which is actually *more* frustrating, because I can't cuss her out for being such an awful person. She probably wouldn't even remember if I did.

"Ugh!" I struggle to get the magnetic scrubber off the glass. They are super strong and get slippery in the water. "Stupid thing!"

"Mika?"

I look up to see Clark staring at me like I've sprouted horns. I stand straight and wipe the water off my hands. "Yes?"

He looks over my outfit disapprovingly. "Did that tank do something to hurt your feelings?"

"Sorry." I stare at my feet, realizing how crazy I must look.

"Dylan said there was something wrong with you, but I didn't expect him to be right."

63

I snap my head up, eyes wide. He tattled on me? After all the times these last two weeks I restrained myself? I'll kill him for this, freaking hypocrite. "I just . . . it's . . . family stuff."

"What happened?" His voice is so kind when he says it, but I can't bring myself to explain.

"It's personal," I choke out. He would never understand, and I can't bring myself to say the insult.

He nods. "Well, I'm sorry for whatever it is, but I hope this doesn't happen again. You have to wear the uniform, Mika. It's not like you to ignore rules, so I'll assume this is a one-time thing."

"Definitely."

"I need to feed the kittens, but if you feel like talking at some point feel free to holler at me. I know family stuff can be hard—we've had our fair share lately, with you know who."

"Like what?" I ask before I can stop myself. Despite my best efforts, I'm still curious as to how Dylan ended up here. He is kind of ruining my life, so I feel like I deserve to know.

He purses his lips. "My brother and I don't exactly get along—very different world views, you could say. He's always been overly ambitious, nearly cutthroat in how he approaches life—he thinks I'm a lazy slob."

Clark is a bit odd, but "lazy slob" is definitely the wrong descriptor. "But you own a business, and you work really hard to keep it running."

"Why thank you, Mika." He smiles wide, like he's relieved to have validation. "I feel the same way, but my brother doesn't think much of one pet store when he owns . . . well, it's a lot more than one store. He's never even come to visit this 'dirty flea hole', so."

I raise an eyebrow, curious. If Dylan grew up with such a stuck-up sounding father, no wonder he's so condescending. "What does he do?"

Clark waves it off. "It doesn't matter, but suffice it to say I never liked how much they neglected Dylan, and yet also expected him to do everything they told him to. They sent him off to boarding school so they didn't have to deal with him. Now they're not happy with how he turned out, and I find it rather . . . frustrating."

"Is that why you took him in?"

"Partly," he says, looking at the school of fish nearest him. "Also because I believe family is family, even when they're not behaving how you'd like. Of course you can't be an enabler, but you don't just throw people away. Especially in their darkest hours, when they need you the most."

His words hit me right in the gut. Scary how much they apply to me. "You really think that?"

He nods. "Now get back to scrubbing, and I expect you to change at lunch."

"Yes, sir."

As I continue cleaning the tanks, Clark's words repeat in my head. Mom has always told me that taking the high road is better, even though it's harder, and I agree with Clark that you shouldn't throw people out. But I'm not sure that applies when said "family member" has never been part of your life because your parents knew they'd only hurt you. Besides, wasn't Betty the one who threw my parents out?

I don't know what happened with Dylan, but he's not Betty. She's already had enough second chances. She needs to leave, and I'll do what I have to in order to make that happen.

Dylan manages to avoid me until after lunch, but now he approaches the Aquatics island slowly, as if he's trying not to anger a tiger. He better be careful, because I'm still pissed about him ratting me out. "You better scrub these tanks all week, otherwise I'll tell Clark you're still a jerk to me, and he'll make you clean up all the poop in the store."

"Probably. You are teacher's pet," he says.

My eyes narrow. "I'm not the tattler. And after I covered for you at the beach and everything!"

He holds up his hands. "Fine, maybe I shouldn't have, but you looked really messed up, okay?"

"Gee, thanks."

He leans on the island, seeming to have decided that I will not, in fact, decapitate him. "C'mon, that's not what I meant. I figured you wouldn't want to talk to me, and my uncle has this annoying habit of being ridiculously level-headed when other people are freaking out."

I purse my lips, appraising him. If I'm not mistaken, I think he might have been worried about me. Weird. I thought he hated me, but maybe I'm wrong. "That is an annoying habit, but you still get tank duty. My standards."

Instead of the glare I expect, he smiles. "Fine."

I look away, surprised at my blushing.

Customers come in and out for the next couple hours. Tanya the Gumsmacker is actually here today, but now Old Lady Miriam has a doctor's appointment. Between those two missing work I'll be here full time all summer. But I actually wish the time would go slower, dreading what might happen at home tonight. The afternoon is always slow, so

66

when the door dings I automatically look up.

"Shit!" Dylan says before I can process who's there, and then he drags me around the corner. "You can't tell them I'm here."

"Who?" I ask, pulling my arm away from him.

"That girl and guy who just walked in." He clasps his hands together. "Please. I'm actually begging you."

"Why?"

He clenches his teeth. "Just because, okay? The guy's not so bad, but meet that girl once, and I'm sure you won't want her hanging around. I'm gonna hide in the back."

He dashes off before I can argue, and I go to my island plotting all the ways I'll make him pay for this. The two people talk with Tanya, who smacks her gum and takes them in with her classic "I don't give a crap" expression. She points over to me, and I straighten my shoulders in preparation.

As they walk down the aisle, I can't help but notice how expensive they look. The girl is over-tanned, manicured, glossy haired, and wearing preppy clothes. The guy is clean cut and attractive, with dark skin and a swagger only the financially secure possess. They look like the kind of people who vacation in Carmel, the kind of people Olivia and her mom take care of at Pebble Beach Spa.

And that's when it hits. Dylan is not just rich, he's loaded. Or was? Clark's words suddenly make a lot more sense.

"The lady up front told us Dylan Wainwright works over here," says the girl, who has warm brown hair and bright blue eyes. "Do you know where he is?"

"He went home already," I blurt out. "Sorry."

The guy frowns. "Damn."

"Well, do you know where he lives?" the girl asks.

"Nope. I don't know much about him." Except that he's the laziest person I've ever met.

"Clearly." The girl looks me up and down. It feels like she deems me lacking in every possible way. I hate admitting Dylan was right—I don't want her around at all. "Can you at least tell him that London and Brock stopped by?"

"Sure."

The guy, who must be Brock, leans on the island and smiles at me. "Maybe we'll see you again . . ." Nametag glance, and also a boob glance. Lovely. "Mika. What a pretty name."

London rolls her eyes. "You really will hit on anything with boobs, won't you?"

Brock doesn't look at her. "Ignore her. She gets jealous of girls who are prettier than her."

"Oh please." London shoves him, then gives me a glare that seems to prove Brock right. "If Dylan wants to see us, we're staying at the usual place. He'll know what that means."

"Okay." I try not to glare at them as they leave the store. My time is up for the day, so I head to the back to get my stuff and clock out. Dylan is there, lounging in the break room with his feet on the table.

"Are they gone?" he asks.

"They said you can meet them at 'the usual place' if you want. Oh, and the guy tried to hit on me." I grab my bag, punch my card. "He seems like a keeper."

He frowns. "You're joking, right?"

"Nope, not at all," I say in my best sarcastic voice. "You owe me."

"I do." He puts his hands behind his head, smiling like he just got away with murder. It makes me wish I'd turned him in to those people. "Thanks, Mika."

I leave, refusing to react to his first real show of gratitude and decency. He won't win me over that easily. He obviously has plenty of other girls hunting him down. I refuse to add myself to that list.

Chapter 11

A few days pass, and Mom and Dad still haven't gotten rid of Betty. Every time I come home and see her still there, anger flares inside me over our last conversation. I've refused to talk to her since then. If my parents don't decide where to put her soon, I might lose *my* mind, too.

"I don't *want* to go to bed!" Betty's voice is so loud I can hear it through my bedroom door. "I'm not a child!"

"I didn't say you were . . ." Dad's tone has grown increasingly aggravated over the last few weeks. This "family crisis" has put back their grant work, since they can't start without Dad. It's made us all even crankier, knowing we're missing out on valuable research time. Their bedroom door shuts next, so I figure that's Mom signing out.

I turn up my music.

As I look over Olivia's newest string of beautiful pictures on Facebook, I can't help being distracted by the search bar at the top of the page. All I'd have to do is type in Dylan's whole name and . . .

I close the tab before I go there. I won't be a Facebook stalker, because that would mean I actually care and I don't.

Sighing, I watch my fish and try not to feel like I'm trapped in my own aquarium. Ever since Betty got here, I've been hiding out in my room more and more, like avoiding the problem will make it go away. Truth is, so much about her scares me. Not just her disease, but who she was before and what she can do to us now.

My computer starts ringing, and I check to see who it is. I smile at the icon and click "accept." Olivia's very tan face and bright white smile appear on the screen, and she laughs when she sees me. "Hey, Mika, you're up! You miss me?"

"Yes! Stupid time difference—you're never on when I am." I'm so happy to see her I barely restrain a squeal. "Shreya and I are lost without you."

"Of course you are." Her smile gets bigger. "But you'll have to endure it, because Tahiti is freaking amazing. The guys, Mika, you have no idea."

I laugh. Olivia has always been boy crazy and proud of it. I guess that's what happens when your mother is a professed "old bachelorette" who will never settle down. Olivia was the first in our group to kiss, to have a boyfriend, to go all the way. I've gone to her for advice on guys since I started liking them. "How many have you kissed?"

"Four," she says like it's no big deal. "But we just got to our hotel on the other side of the island, and I have my sights set on a *very* attractive bus boy at the restaurant across the street. I'm thinking he'll be my vacation fling."

"Good luck with that."

"Thanks! What's up with you?"

I cringe when I think about the past few weeks, but as I tell her everything that's happened I feel better. Olivia gasps

71

and swears and frowns in all the right places, and it reassures me that I'm not blowing these events out of proportion. My summer really has sucked.

"You know what you need to do, right?" Olivia says when I finish my tale. "You need to kiss Dylan."

"What? No!" I put my hand on my cheek, the idea making my face burn. "Why is that your answer for everything?"

She laughs. "C'mon! You're all tense anyway, and you clearly have chemistry whether you admit it or not. Making out with him will make him very nice at work, and it'll chill you out so you can deal with Betty."

I roll my eyes, though her logic is disturbingly sound. "You know I don't do the casual thing. I have to at least like the guy, and there are few people I despise more than Dylan."

"Psh, you and your fake relationships." She puts her face right in the camera. "You never date anyone seriously anyway! You like to stay emotionally detached while they fall madly in love with you."

"That's not true!" Okay, it's kind of true. All three of the guys I've dated were leaving in one way or another—moving, going to college, only in town for the summer. It made it easy not to get too attached, to practice liking someone without falling in love. But I don't see what's wrong with that. When I do fall in love, I want it to be permanent like my parents. May as well try a few guys before that, figure out what I really want.

Olivia leans back into her pillows, her expression skeptical. "Whatever. I still say you should make out with him."

I sigh, not wanting to talk about this anymore. Yet all I can think of is Dylan tackling me in the sand last week. And he was worried about me the day I went to work in pajamas, so maybe he's not all bad . . . I shake my head. "Enough about me—I want to hear more about your exploits."

She gets this big grin on her face. "You're so avoiding, but the bus boy's name is Waka. While my mom was out with some businessman, I went . . ."

There's a knock at my door, and then my parents pop their heads in. "You have a second, Mika?" Dad asks.

My heart skips. This must be it—they've found a place for Betty and they've come to tell me. We can finally get back to our lives and the grant and this nightmare is over. "Yeah. Olivia, I gotta run. My parents need me."

She frowns. "Fine. See you in two weeks!"

"Bye!" I close the video chat as they settle on the edge of my double bed. They look hesitant, and this washes away all my excited feelings. "What's wrong?"

My dad purses his lips as he looks at Mom, but finally says, "I know you won't be happy about this, but Betty needs to stay with us."

There's a long moment of silence as I stare at my parents. I couldn't have heard them right. The only option they ever entertained was a care facility—they never mentioned *once* that they were considering keeping her here. They look at each other when I don't reply, and Dad soldiers on. "I know you don't like her. Believe me, I'm well aware she's not a pleasant person. Not by a long run. But looking at all the options, this one makes the most sense."

"Have you two gone nuts?" I say before I can think better of it. "We can't take care of her! We know nothing about

Alzheimer's, and besides, we all work."

My parents aren't looking at me, and I get the sinking feeling I'm involved in this plan much more than I want to be. Dad gulps. "The truth is, Mika, we don't have the money to put her in a home. We'll all have to help out. Even you. If you stayed here in the afternoon with her while we—"

"What?!" I cut in. "Are you saying I'd have to give up working with you this summer?"

They look at each other, wincing.

"No, you can't do that. You promised me!" This can't be happening. All I've wanted for years was to help them with their research, to be part of their marine biologist world. Now they're going to rip it away because of Betty? It's hard enough having her around—I can't believe they're asking me not only to give up the internship, but to take care of her on top of it. This can't be the only choice. "What about Uncle Greg? I thought you said he'd help."

My dad deflates. "He said he could maybe give us five thousand, but Marietta is finally expecting and their funds are limited as it is. Forest rangers aren't exactly rolling in cash."

"And Medicaid?"

"Not every facility takes it, and it won't cover it all anyway." He puts his hand over Mom's. "We just can't afford it, even with the help we'll get."

"No, you have to find a way!" My voice is desperate, but I don't care. "She's awful, Dad. She's already called me horrible names, and she doesn't treat you guys any better."

Mom's brow pinches, and I hope this is a good sign. "What did she call you?"

I tell them what happened in the backyard though I hadn't planned to. These are dire times, and I need to play every card I have. "I was so mad I couldn't even be here, and I went to work in my pajamas and got in trouble. How could you keep her around when she does that to me?"

This story has a big effect on my parents. I can see them wavering in their conviction. Dad sighs. "This is exactly why we've kept you away from her all these years. My worst nightmare is coming true."

"There has to be a way to pay for it," I say. "What if you use the money I make at AnimalZone? Would that help at all?"

"It would have to be a lot more than what you make, sweetheart," Mom says in a cloying tone. It makes me feel like a kid. I already know I make pennies in comparison to them—way to rub it in.

Dad chews on his lip. "There's only one other option we've thought of. But I don't think—"

"What is it?" I lean forward, excited by another possibility. Maybe they don't want to do it, but I could talk them into it.

"We've been talking about taking from your college fund . . ."

My eyes go wide. "Excuse me?"

"We were only discussing it," Mom says. "It was a last resort. And you'll probably get scholarships—we'd know that early next year. It would be the only way to pay for it, but even that would only last a few years."

It feels like someone knocked the wind out of me. They've been hard on me all these years, but I take it because I believe it's made me a better person. I'm responsible, hard-working, well-rounded, and everything they wanted me to be. They never let me walk the easy route, but they were at least planning to help me with college. Now Betty has even put that in jeopardy?

"So let me get this straight . . ." I put my hand over my mouth, trying not to scream. "Either I agree to pitching in with my racist, crazy grandmother I don't even know, willingly walk away from the summer of interning you promised me, or I give up my college fund and screw over my future?"

Both of them cringe.

"That's bullshit!" I shoot up from my bed, unable to contain my anger while sitting. I want to scream and punch things. I want to tell them to go to hell because how could they do this to me? It's so beyond unfair that there's only one choice to make—I'm not giving up my future. Leaving in a year, after I graduate, is all I have to cling to right now. "So what? Do I have to quit my job and stay at home with her all day while you have all the fun at work?"

"No!" Mom comes over and puts her hands on my shoulders. I'm so mad I push them off. She doesn't even tell me I'm being disrespectful. That's how I know they're aware of what jerks they're being. "We've looked into respite care. It's much more affordable and would give us all a break from her when we need it."

"Respite care?" I repeat. "What's that?"

Dad stands now, too. "There are caretakers who specialize in Alzheimer's, and they come to your home part time to help with the hardest parts. If we paid for someone to handle the mornings, you could do the afternoons, and Mom and I would take the evenings."

"So it would be just me and her all afternoon?" I ask.

They nod.

This summer keeps getting worse and worse. I wish I could swear to move out. But I can't. *College is right around the corner. Just tough it out.* "This sucks."

Dad raises an eyebrow. "Does that mean you'll help?"

"What else can I do when all you've given me are shitty options?"

Even though I'm clearly pissed off, Mom still gives me her proudest smile. "We'll make it work, okay? I'm not happy about it, either, but maybe it won't be as bad as we think."

Try as I might, I can't restrain the eye roll.

She hugs me in return. "I'll ignore the attitude, because I know you probably want to do a lot more than that."

"You think?" I mumble into her shoulder.

"Goodnight, Mika." They head for my door, victorious in ruining my life completely.

"Night," I grumble as I flop onto my bed. My head spins when I think about what I begrudgingly agreed to do. It's one thing to tolerate Betty's presence, but to have to *interact* with her every day? Take care of her? That takes compassion, and she dried up mine weeks ago. I don't know how I'll do this.

Just as I'm about to turn out my light, my phone chirps. Grabbing it, I find a text from Shreya. *Are u available for a sleepover?*

I purse my lips, confused. Shreya and I have never had a sleepover—her parents don't want her at other people's houses overnight. *Did something happen?*

Her reply is immediate. *Oh, u know, stormed out of house w/o thinking it thru.*

I have a feeling this has something to do with what she mentioned about her parents and marriage.

I fought with my parents tonight, too. It's like we're soul mates.

Seriously? You guys never fight.

Come over. I'll prep movie and popcorn.

Ur the best :)

Don't forget it ;P I squeeze my eyes shut, a sudden wave of tears threatening to break through. If it wasn't for Shreya, I might have spent the whole night letting them fall to my pillow, but at least now I have something else to focus on.

Chapter 12

Shreya has nothing but her bike with her when she arrives. Her eyes are swollen from what I assume was a lot of crying. She bends down to lock the frame to my porch. "I can't tell you how much this means to me."

"Shrey, of course." I put my arm around her as we go inside. "Even if you'd shown up out of nowhere, I would have let you in."

"Do your parents . . .?" She looks down, embarrassed.

"They're fine with it." Not that I actually told them, but they better be fine with it after the bomb they just dropped on me.

She gives me a hug. "I didn't know what else to do."

"C'mon." I lead her to the living room, and we get comfortable in front of the TV. I hand her a bowl of popcorn and a soda. "Do you want to talk about it?"

She curls in on herself and clicks her nail on the can. "I probably made too big a deal out of it. It wasn't even about me, but it felt like it could be next time."

"What happened?"

"Pavan brought a girl home . . . a blond girl who can't look any more white." She shakes her head, now glaring at the soda.

"He is such an idiot. He could have at least mentioned he was dating her—well, now they're engaged. My parents blew up and threw them out."

I can hardly believe it. I don't know Pavan well, only that he's the middle brother and somewhere around twenty-nine years old. "Then what happened?"

"They started screaming at us." Shreya's tears come anew. "They told us they'd throw us all out if we ever did the same thing, that they are ashamed to have raised Pavan. I never thought . . . they told us we can't even *speak* to Pavan."

Rubbing her shoulder, I try to imagine such chaos. "It came as such a surprise, maybe they'll calm down after awhile."

She snorts. "Ever the optimist. Even when your own parents went through pretty much the same thing."

"It's not the same. Your parents don't hate people—they had to know coming to America meant this could happen, right?"

"You'd think. Maybe I'll just never get married, and then I'll never have to hurt anyone." She pulls her knees in, cradling the popcorn like it's the only good thing in the world. "If Pavan's feelings don't matter to them, mine won't."

Refusing to admit she might be right, I decide to change the subject. "Let's watch a movie. And eat stuff we shouldn't."

She smiles the tiniest bit. "*The* movie?"

"As you wish." I waggle an eyebrow, and that gets a laugh out of her. *The Princess Bride* is kind of ancient, but when we first watched it at Olivia's house we were hooked. From eleven years old and on, it's been our go-to movie whenever one of us is down. It's impossible to feel bad while watching it, with all the ridiculous lines and Westley being so hot.

My phone rings just as they reach the Cliffs of Insanity. I cringe when I see the number. "Shrey, it's your mom. What should I do?"

She looks terrified. "I don't know . . ."

Neither of us are the rebelling type. I'm still reeling over the fact that Shreya left her house in the first place. Olivia's the wild one who pushes us out of our comfort zones. She'd know what to do. Too bad her phone doesn't work overseas.

The call is about to go to voicemail when I hit "accept." "Hello?"

"Mika!" Shreya's mom sounds like she's sobbing. "Is Shreya there?"

I look at my best friend, hoping she'll tell me what to do. Shreya hangs her head, and I sigh. "Yeah, she's here."

Her mom says something in Hindi. It sounds relieved. "I'm so sorry to impose. I will come and get her."

"She can stay," I say quickly. "You guys have had a rough night, and I'll take care of her. She just got scared is all—she's not mad. We're in the middle of a movie."

There's a pause, which I use to say a little prayer. *Please, please let her have this one thing.*

"Her father won't be happy," her mom says. "But it would be good for her to be somewhere else while he calms down."

"Thank you! I promise I'll have her to work on time."

When I hang up, Shreya looks like she could squeal in excitement, but since there are sleeping people she flails around and giggles. I try not to laugh, because I'm just as happy that we finally get to do this.

81

"I can't believe you convinced her!" Shreya says. "Let's take a picture and post it so Olivia can be jealous she's missing our first sleepover."

"Yes! We have to!" I run and get my laptop, and we spend the next few minutes trying to get a decent picture on my webcam. When I do, I post it to Instagram and tag Olivia just because it'll bug her. Then Shreya logs me out and gets on her profile to comment and be even dorkier. Soon it's like nothing bad ever happened.

Westley and Princess Buttercup escape the Fire Swamp as Shreya says, "Do you know Dylan's last name? Is it the same as Clark's?"

My stomach flips. "No, Shrey, don't."

She starts typing.

"Shrey!" I lunge for the computer, but she hops up and over to the kitchen table. She's pulled up Facebook just like I guessed, and she's already done the search I promised I'd never do.

"Inconceivable!" she says. "You gotta see this, Mika."

"I don't want to." I stare at the TV, determined to stay in place and watch the movie like I should.

"His wall is a running spam of scantily clad girls asking why he's not around and when he's coming back. I guess he's cut off from technology along with food and who knows what else." A few clicks. "His profile info is a bunch of crap. *Location: In Your Pants.*"

"Ugh, gross."

"And yet kind of funny. Dang, his photos are private."

I whimper, my conversation with Olivia still too fresh. "Can we not talk about Dylan? I have enough of him in my life."

"You're no fun. I'm trying to distract myself here." She shuts the laptop. "Is he really that bad?"

"Pretty much." Except then I picture him smiling at me, saying thanks. Why, out of all the stupid things he's done, does that stick out? I prefer him being a jerk.

Chapter 13

There is a decidedly nervous energy as we wait for the person my dad hired to care for Betty. It took him another week to decide on the right service—which was nothing short of torture—but he finally went through a place called Monterey Meadows Home Care, which sounds non-threatening enough.

"I don't like this," Betty says to her oatmeal as she lets a clump plop back into the bowl.

Dad sighs. "But you asked for oatmeal."

"I did?" She frowns. "Why would I ask for this crap?"

I swallow my last bite of toast, beyond exhausted over her food complaints. Every morning she insists on oatmeal, and she always hates it. She doesn't seem to like much of anything. I just want her to be quiet, so I say, "We told you it wouldn't taste good plain. Do you want some brown sugar in it now?"

She nods.

"I can't wait to go back to work," Dad grumbles under his breath.

Yeah, go have all the fun while I'm stuck with Dylan and Betty, thanks. I still have a hard time talking to my parents after they betrayed me. Mostly I curse them in my head and glare. I grab the brown sugar from the counter where I left it because I was sure Betty would want it. As I sprinkle it over her oatmeal, there's a loud knock at the door.

Mom and Dad jump up, and even I can't help but follow behind them. Maybe I hate the plan my parents came up with, but after another week of dealing with her on our own I'm ready to have expert help. Monterey Meadows said they would send a caregiver that fit Betty's needs, based on a questionnaire my dad filled out. But it seems impossible that they would know the right kind of person from that, and now that person will probably be a big part of our lives for who knows how long.

Mom opens the door, and there stands a perfectly manicured man in scrubs. Rhinestone-studded scrubs. He's not very tall, but he's fit and looks like he's never been happier in his life. He gives us a big wave, and says, "Hello, Arlingtons! I'm Joel, and your life is about to get *so* much easier because of me."

I wish I could scowl to show my displeasure with the plan, but I can't help smiling. He could not be more perfect. At least for my entertainment; maybe not for Betty. Oh well.

Dad grins like a fool. "Nice to meet you. Come right in."

"Thank you." Joel steps inside and points to my mom. "Now, let me guess—Yumi." Then to me. "Mika." And to my dad. "Stanley. So that leaves my lovely new best friend, Betty. Where is the lucky lady?"

"This way." Mom leads Joel to the kitchen, where Betty is still scowling at her oatmeal like it gravely offended her.

Joel smiles wide. "Betty! How are you today?"

She looks up from her bowl, surprised at the sight of this new person in her life. "You have rhinestones on your shirt."

He laughs. "If you had to wear ugly scrubs all day, wouldn't you want to pretty them up?"

She thinks about this for a moment. "I suppose so."

"Right?" Joel sits next her, his hands placed under his chin. "I think we'll get along perfectly. I'm Joel, by the way."

She nods.

He turns to us. "Now, can I give you the run-down? How much time before you need to go?"

"Oh, sure. We have a minute," my dad says.

Joel claps his hands together. "Perfect! First and foremost, I believe in positivity. Patients tend to become negative, so we all need to laugh and have fun as much as possible, all right? All right."

Okay, maybe I *won't* like him, because I won't be chipper about this.

He goes into the kitchen and starts looking through drawers like he owns the place. I guess this will be his home five mornings a week. "I'm happy to help Betty with all the basics—dressing, washing, eating—so you won't need to worry about her hygiene. I also like to help keep the house clean if I can." He gives us a stern look. "But I am *not* a maid. I'm Betty's best friend, and we'll all get along if you don't forget that."

"Of course," my mom says. "We're so grateful for you already and happy to take any advice."

Joel smiles. "Now that's what I like to hear. Can you show me her room and the bathroom?"

I grab my work things while my parents acquaint Joel with the rest of the house. Betty stares at the hallway, a quizzical look on her face. "Is that man really my best friend?"

"Yes?" I say.

"He does seem very nice, though I'm not sure I've ever seen a man wear rhinestones . . ."

I gulp, realizing Joel could easily end up on her hate list if she realizes he's gay. Time to break out a lie. "Really? Guys wear rhinestones all the time—it's totally in fashion. He's really cute."

She laughs. "I always was a sucker for the blond ones."

Joel and my parents emerge just as she says this, and he narrows his eyes. "Were you two gossiping about me?"

"Only good things," I say, shouldering my bag. "I should probably get going. It was nice to meet you, Joel."

"I'll walk you out!" He hooks arms with me when I'm in range. "Your parents told me I'll be handing Betty over to you in the afternoons. Is that right?"

"Yup." My voice is cold, and I can tell he picked up on it.

He looks me over. "I get the sense you're not happy about this."

"Why would I be?" I look at the ground, the anger as fresh as it was the day they told me I was stuck doing this.

He nods, and I hate to admit it seems like he understands. "Alzheimer's isn't easy to deal with, no matter the circumstances. I can't promise it'll get better, but if you choose to really take care of her, Mika, you will come to love her. That will make it easier in some ways, but harder in others."

This advice makes me uncomfortable. I don't want to take care of Betty, let alone love her. But saying this out loud will only make me sound like a jerk, especially when Joel does this for a living. "Well, I guess I'll see you this afternoon."

He squeezes my shoulder. "Yup. And you'll do great. Just remember that transitioning to a different caretaker can be hard for her; any change will be. It's not your fault if she has a hard time adjusting when you get home. So many family members feel guilty for things they shouldn't."

Whatever. I nod. "See you later."

"We'll be great friends, Mika. I just know it!"

Can he be more over-the-top happy? It makes me want to punch something. I'm glad Joel's here to help, but he can't wash away the negative aura that has permeated our house since Betty showed up almost four weeks ago. As I ride to work, I keep thinking about how nice it would be if I didn't have to go back home in four hours.

When I get to Aquatics, Dylan is lounging at the island doing nothing, like usual. I grit my teeth. The one week he promised to clean tanks without a fight is over, so of course he doesn't bother. I'm about to run over there and cuss him out when a high-pitched squeal hits the air.

"Dylan!" says a vaguely familiar voice. If I'm not mistaken, it's that London girl who was looking for him before. I duck down the nearest aisle—he's totally on his own this time—but I linger to listen.

"I can't believe you're actually here, man!" a guy's voice says. Brock.

"London . . . Brock . . ." Dylan doesn't sound particularly excited to see them. "What's up?"

"Just hanging out in Carmel, playing some golf, you know," says Brock. "Are you seriously working at this place? Rumor has it your parents cut you off from everything."

"It's not as bad as I thought it'd be," Dylan says.

"You poor thing." London sounds like she's talking to a little kid, and it makes me want to gag. "Let me take you to lunch. You need expensive sushi. I can tell."

"I don't think that's a good idea . . ." Dylan's voice sounds nervous, and I wonder if he's worried his uncle will overhear. I doubt expensive sushi would fly with Clark's weird training program.

"Why not?" London whines.

"Because . . . I'm kind of seeing someone, and I don't think she'd like me having lunch with you."

I'm pretty sure that's a lie, even though it doesn't sound like it.

"For reals, dude?" Brock laughs. "You're dating a local, huh? Is she hot? Of course she's hot."

"Yup."

"Well, who is she?" London has dropped the baby talk and now sounds pissed. "I seriously doubt anyone around here is good enough for you."

"That's pretty shallow," he says.

"You're avoiding the question! Which means you're full of it, so there's no reason I can't take you out to—"

"Her name's Mika, okay?" Dylan says.

My stomach drops to the ground. Part of me wants to run out there and beat him senseless for using my name, but then my cheeks are on fire and I'd rather not have those rich people see me in my ugly AnimalZone uniform again.

"Wait . . ." London says. "The girl who works here?"

"Got a problem with that?"

"Duuuude. Beat me to it." Brock laughs. "Work hook up!"

"I still don't believe you," she says. "That girl is so not your type."

"You have no clue what my type is, London." Dylan's voice has lost all warmth. "If you did, you wouldn't be hunting me down just to take me to lunch."

"Fine then. Prove it. If she's really your girlfriend, then she'll come with you to Cypress Point for a round of eighteen. Otherwise, I'll assume you're still fair game."

"We'd be happy to come," he says.

"Saturday. Nine o'clock tee time." London's heels clack down the aisle.

I lean on the nearest shelf, trying to get enough air. Who the hell makes up crazy lies like that? And *Cypress Point*? That place makes Pebble Beach look like the ghetto. It's one of the most elite private golf courses in the world, and the fact that these kids can get in means they must cry diamonds.

"Mika, there you are," Dylan says. I look up, and he's smiling at me like I didn't just hear what he said. "I have a favor to ask you."

Chapter 14

"No." I head down the aisle in search of Clark and safety.

Dylan's hand comes around my wrist, and he pulls me back. "I haven't even told you what the favor is yet!"

I wrench my arm from his. "I can already guess, and the answer is hell-freaking-no. You can go out with London and eat sushi and leave me out of this."

He curses. "You heard us."

"Duh."

He runs his hands through his hair, leaving them at the back of his neck. This seems to be his post-London stress pose. "Please. I know I shouldn't have done that, but your name was the first one that popped into my head. Just this one time, and she'll be appeased and leave me alone. I swear."

"Why do you *want* her to leave you alone? You seem perfect together! I can't think of two people who deserve each other more."

His eyes narrow, and his arms come down. "That's cold."

"Whatever." I stand strong. "I won't even begin to consider this without knowing why you'd rather pretend we're in a relationship than go out with her."

"Fine," he says through his teeth. "London doesn't like people—she likes money and prestige. She doesn't like *me*, she likes my family name and status and thinks she can fix the rest. I'm sick of people thinking they can make me into whatever they want me to be, so I'd rather not be her trophy."

I raise an eyebrow, the answer deeper than I expected. Almost commendable, even. "And why is she so persistent when you shut her down so hard?"

He cringes. "We . . . may have hooked up a couple times. She got the wrong idea."

"Ugh, I'm out." There's no way I'm getting involved with him and his obsessive stalker hookup. I turn back around, head for the kitten aisle where Clark probably is. "You can sleep in that bed for all I—"

His hands come down on my shoulders. "C'mon. I was smashed. That's all."

"So not helping your case." I shrug him off.

"It's not a big deal! You're acting like such a prude."

I glare back at him. "I am not. Stop assuming I'm some innocent, straight-laced girl."

His eyes light up, and it makes me want to kick him. "You're not?"

"I'm just a girl who thinks hookups are stupid. Maybe I'm old-fashioned, but I prefer being intimate with someone I care about and enjoy being with. You're neither, so you can wipe that pervy grin off your face." I start walking. Fast.

"So that's a no?" he calls.

I force myself not to smile. That was *not* funny. This time I'm the one flipping the bird.

92

Clark is in the kitten room cleaning out litter when I find him. The kittens jump all over him, and he laughs. The guy might be weird, but he loves his job and I respect that. I tap on the glass, and he gives me a nod that means, "I'll be right out."

I force myself not to pace, to calm down, to think of something happy. It's sad that nothing comes to mind except bedazzled Joel trying to tame Betty. That has to be sitcom material. Horrible situations are always funnier on screen than in real life.

"What's up?" Clark asks when he comes out. There's a fresh scratch on his arm, which he dabs with a paper towel.

"Oh, I just wanted to let you know that our aide came today." I didn't want to tell him about Betty's arrival and all that's happened since, but I had to so he'd know I couldn't keep taking on extra hours.

He nods. "And how's the aide?"

Sparkly. Annoyingly happy. Painfully thoughtful. "I think he'll be a huge help."

"That's good to hear." His smile is so genuine. I don't know how he can be related to his liar of a nephew. "Do you need anything else?"

I'm tempted to tell him about Dylan's friends showing up, but I can't get myself to do it. Maybe because I don't know which would be worse for Dylan—dealing with London or facing his uncle's punishment. For now, my bet is on London. "Nope. I'll go check on the fish now."

When I get back to my station, Dylan has this smirk on his face that makes me uneasy. He usually scowls all day. As I inspect the tanks, he even starts laughing to himself. I glare at him. "What?"

"Nothing," he says, but I can't shake the feeling that I have something on my face. Or my fly is down. Or my hair is messed up.

I take a deep breath and force myself to ignore it. He won't get to me. About an hour later, one of my favorite customers shows up—Mr. Castillo. He's a goldfish enthusiast like me, and I wave as he approaches.

"Mika! How are you?" he says with his smooth accent.

"Good. It's been awhile since you've been in. What can I help you with?"

"I'm looking for a new fancy." He eyes the tanks. "I recently bought a bigger tank for my full grown oranda and blackmoor, and I'm thinking they need a more . . . colorful companion."

I smile. "Definitely. How big are they now?"

"About this big." He holds out his palm. "So I need one that's pretty large."

"Yeah, you do." Goldfish are known for eating just about anything, and sometimes that means smaller goldfish. I look over the tanks, but even the two biggest might not be large enough. "You know, I have one at home named Simba that's bigger than these. He's a pretty orange one with white fins."

Mr. Castillo lights up. "Really? You'd give me one of yours?"

I nod. "I buy my fish here—I've sold them on occasion when I know they'll go to a good home. He's about two years old. Should I take a picture of him for you so you can see if he fits the bill?"

"That would be wonderful. I'll stop by tomorrow."

"Great!" I wave to him as he goes. That's when I realize Dylan is staring at me like I'm a difficult math problem. "Seriously, what?"

94

"You have a two-year-old goldfish?" he asks.

I brace for the impending criticism. "I have a ten-year-old goldfish and pretty much every age under that."

His eyebrow raises. "Just how many do you have?"

"Including the koi? Thirty-seven."

"Really?"

I sigh, not particularly interested in whatever insult will come out of his mouth next. "You already know I'm the crazy fish girl. No need to act so surprised."

"Do they all have names?"

"Of course they do."

He snorts. "Sand sculpture. Goldfish. You are so weird."

"At least I'm interesting." I tip my chin up. "You're boring. You just sulk all day, and when you do talk it's rude or critical or a lie. Maybe you should get a weird hobby so you actually have something valuable to say."

"Maybe." To my surprise, he looks away. "Except I'm never allowed to *do* the things I want. You have no idea how lucky you are."

His face is so sad that I feel bad for what I said. "Why don't you get to?"

"Because it's not who I'm 'supposed' to be."

"What does that mean?"

His chest heaves up and down, and it feels like he has words building up inside him. "Never mind."

He walks away, and I'm left to work alone. Though this time I almost wish Dylan had stayed and told me what was on his mind.

Noon comes quickly. I have an hour before I need to be home. As I head for the back, I run through places I might go for lunch, but the closer I get the more I catch the distinct scent of curry. I take in a big whiff to make sure I'm not hallucinating. No, I'd know that smell anywhere.

I run for the break room, and when I catch sight of Shreya my jaw drops. Dylan smiles wide at my reaction, and I get the feeling this is why he was smirking all morning.

"Surprise!" Shreya holds out her hands to the curry, which is set up and ready to eat.

"How . . .?" I manage to get out.

"Dylan called me to ask what your favorite food was—he wanted to buy you lunch! Isn't that sweet?" Shreya looks over at him like he's a shining example of romance.

"Where did he get your number?" I glare at him, knowing very well that this is a bribe to get me to come to Cypress Point. He hasn't given up on the fake date yet, and I'm starting to worry his insistence will only get worse.

She looks sheepish. "He called me on your phone."

I grit my teeth. "So he went through my purse and stalked you down? That's not sweet—that's creepy."

Dylan frowns. "I just wanted to surprise you."

"The answer is still no." I sit down, because good curry should not be wasted. And Shreya brought all my favorites—*saag paneer*, shrimp *korma*, butter chicken. I will eat it all and refuse his pleas. Win-win.

"We'll see." Dylan tries to grab the *korma*, but I move it away from him. "So that's how you're gonna be?"

"Yup." I take a big bite. "You bought it for me, right? Who says I have to share?"

Shreya laughs. "You guys are so cute together!"

I give her my worst glare, but Dylan laughs. "See? Shreya's on my team."

"Traitor," I grumble between bites.

"Tell her she has to go to Cypress Point with me on Saturday." He tries to get the *saag* but I snap that up too. "She totally turned me down. It hurt."

Shreya gives me a disapproving look, but I smack her. "Don't feel sorry for him! He's trying to make me go on a fake date so his hookup stalker will think he's taken!" I point at him. "Don't lie to my friend."

"Do you always have to be so tech—?" Dylan's eyes go wide, and I spin around to see Clark emerging from his office. He folds his arms over his chest, and it's obvious he heard what we were talking about. "Uncle Clark, look, it's not . . ."

He stops when Clark holds up a hand.

A huge smile breaks out on my face. Dylan is so dead.

Finally. There is justice in this world.

His uncle stares at him, seeming to contemplate which punishment would be best. "I think you should go, Mika. Dylan needs help getting away from that girl. I'll let him borrow my car."

Dylan bursts into laughter, and I hang my head in defeat.

Chapter 15

After the great AnimalZone betrayal, I'm actually excited to go home to Betty and Joel. Surely even they wouldn't agree with this mock date ridiculousness. And I'm still not going. I don't care what anyone says. I can't think of a worse way to spend my Saturday.

When I get there Joel and Betty are sitting on the porch sipping tea. Joel gives me a big smile. "Welcome home! Would you like some?"

"Please." I pull my bike up the step and lock it in place. "How did things go?"

Betty glares at her tea. "He tried to *undress* me. It was very rude."

Joel laughs as he hands me a cup. "I wanted to help with her buttons. It might be good if you invested in some clothing that's easier for her to take on and off unassisted."

I take a sip, and it calms me. "I'll let my parents know."

"Excellent." He hops up. "You stay here while I grab my things, and then I'll get you up to speed."

He dashes into the house, and I take his seat next to Betty though I'd rather take a nap after all that curry. She looks out to the street, and I study her face. It's so different from mine, and yet the more I see her the more Dad appears in her features, and therefore mine as well. I'm not sure I like that.

I make no effort to start up a conversation, but as usual, when she's in the right mood, Betty talks to me like I'm an old friend. "We had a porch like this when I was a little girl, and we'd sit and drink iced tea in the hot summer evenings. Grace and I would play in the front yard, while Mom and Dad looked on with big smiles on their faces. Those were the good times. I wish I could live in those moments forever."

I want to ask her why, but last time we got on the topic of her father she got hardcore racist and crazy. There's no way I'm going there again, even if I am curious.

"Did *you* have a good childhood?" she asks.

"I think so." I take another sip of my tea, unsure of what else to say. My parents have been amazing as far as parents go . . . at least until recently, but the circumstances have messed us all up. Still, I know more than anything they want me to be happy.

She sighs. "I think what hurts most is that I can't blame Stan for leaving. He turned out a lot better because he did . . . you have everything I wished for growing up."

I hate it when she says stuff like this, because in these moments my heart traitorously warms. If she were always this way, I think I could like her. Then she starts crying. I try not to panic, but it seems like I have a way of doing this to her.

"Why did he have to leave?" she sobs.

"I don't know . . ." I'm not sure who she's talking about, my dad or her father or her husband. All the options make me feel bad for her, and I squirm at the thought that I could pity her when she's been so rude to me. I should straight up hate her, but . . . I don't know what to feel.

"Mom said he died, but I knew—*knew*—she was lying." Must be her father then. "The men in uniform came to your house when soldiers died. That's what happened to my friend Mabel. They never came."

"Betty!" Joel says when he comes out. "Why all the tears, sweetie?"

I wince. "Sorry. She started talking about her childhood. I didn't know what to do, so I just listened."

He gives a sad smile. "She's been nostalgic today. Sometimes that happens. You may want to write it down because she'll lose those things eventually."

"Okay." I never thought about writing anything down, but since Dad won't talk about it the stories might be lost forever otherwise.

"Let me give you the run-down," Joel says. "She had her lunch, but she gets distracted while eating. We need to keep her on task there. Despite her protests, we got her cleaned up and she had a blast while I did her hair. As for your part, try to get her moving. Maybe a walk around the backyard or down the street. She needs a snack around two or three—your parents should take care of dinner and bedtime."

"Okay. Thanks," I say.

"You are very welcome. We'll have a lot of fun, Mika." He waves as he gets in his little blue car.

I manage to convince Betty to take a stroll around the block. There's no more talk about her childhood, but she has plenty

100

to say about all the rock yards. She hates rock yards. She finds them unfriendly and ugly and pretty much the worst idea ever. I try to distract her with the beautiful trees or flowers *also* in these yards, which works for about a minute before she tells me no one in their right mind would put rocks in their yard. By the time we get home, I am on the verge of screaming at her for being ridiculous.

She stops when we get back to the house. "Is this the right place?"

"Yup. I know it has rocks, but can you look past that and come inside?"

She scrunches her face. "I guess."

I get her settled in front of the TV. She picks a talk show while I grab my laptop. We still have three hours until my parents get home, and that feels like an eternity. She makes comments on the show, and I do what Joel suggests—I type down what I've learned about her so far.

Hardly any of it is pleasant, but as I read over what I've written something overcomes me. I'm not quite sure what it is, except that reading what I wrote makes me smile more than it should. I think about how Joel said taking care of someone leads to love. Could this be the beginning of affection? I shut the laptop, refusing to think about it more.

After a couple hours, I get a call on my cell. I don't know the number, so I don't pick up. It rings again. After the sixth consecutive attempt I pick up. "Hello?"

"So you *do* know how to answer your phone. I was starting to wonder."

My eyes go wide at the voice. "Dylan?"

"Yup. I haven't been allowed to use a phone for a month and Clark only allowed it so I could call you. Don't you feel special?"

"No."

"Well, you should. We need to shop for the clothes you're wearing on Saturday. When's a good time?" he says matter-of-factly. "Are you still there? Hello?"

"How'd you get my number?" AnimalZone only has our landline number, not my cell, so I know he didn't get it from Clark.

"Shreya."

"I'm gonna kill her." I pinch the bridge of my nose, trying not to explode. "I don't care if Shrey and your uncle think I should go with you. I'm not."

"I guess I could pick out your clothes myself, but don't complain if you don't like them. What size? I'm guessing two."

"No!" I yell, and Betty glares like I'm interrupting her at a movie. I head to the kitchen. "I'm not going to Cypress Point. I'm not shopping with you. This fake relationship is not happening. Tell London to leave you alone, like a normal person!"

"I have. Several times. It doesn't work." He lets out a long sigh. "Fine, I get that this isn't fair to you at all—I'm not stupid—but do you really want her showing up every week at the store?"

I cringe, but hold firm. "That's not enough incentive. What if she comes after me for this? What if your stupid plan doesn't even work?"

There's a pause. "You need to be less smart."

"I'm choosing to take that as a compliment." I lean on the counter. "You already owe me. I want some kind of payment before I agree to any more of your crap."

"Since I've only been paid once, I don't have much money . . ." There's a feeling of panic in his voice, as if the idea is the scariest thing in the world. "Between the Indian food and your outfit, I won't have anything until my uncle pays me again."

My heart traitorously skips. "You don't have to buy me clothes."

"No offense, but you don't want to go to Cypress Point wearing the wrong thing. It'll be hard enough as it is, and it's not fair to make you pay for them."

"I still haven't said I'm going . . ." I hate to admit how close I am to being convinced. Cypress Point is legendary—it would be incredible to see in person, a once in a lifetime chance. I just wish the company was more agreeable.

"Please, Mika. I'm actually begging you. I'll do anything."

"Anything?" If I'm going to say yes anyway, I may as well get something out of it. "Even if it's cleaning every fish tank in my house for the rest of the summer?"

"Yes."

"You don't even know how many there are."

"Don't care. If that's what it takes, I'll do it."

I purse my lips. This is an incredibly bad idea, I can feel it. But at the same time it'll tell me everything I need to know about Dylan. And I'm curious. It's stupid, but I have to know what he's really like. Because as annoying as he can be, there have been hints of something underneath that I might actually like. Time to roll the dice. "Fine."

Chapter 16

Betty is actually eating nicely at dinner, and my parents seem happy. I want to be more bitter about everything, but they've been awesome about taking over the second they get home. They even encourage me to go out and have fun so I don't have to be around Betty all the time. It's starting to make me feel guilty for the silent treatment I've been trying to employ. I swallow my bite of pizza, deciding that this might be the time to tell them about Cypress Point.

"So, um . . ." I start, but then the words get caught in my mouth.

"What is it, sweetie?" Mom looks tired, her long hair pulled back into a messy bun. They must have worked extra hard in the bay today.

"I just thought I should warn you that I'm going to Cypress Point on Saturday."

My dad's jaw drops. "What?! With who?"

"He's—"

"A guy?" Dad says with too much interest. "How did you meet a guy who has access to Cypress Point? Are you dating him? Can I get in on this?"

"Dad!" I knew he'd be more excited than concerned, since Dad loves golf but rarely gets the chance to play. I don't need any more Dylan fans. "No, you can't. And his name is Dylan. He's my boss's nephew. His friends invited us, so it's not really a date. I just couldn't say no . . ."

Dad snorts. "You think? You better take pictures."

I put my hand to my face. "I'm not acting like a tourist in front of them."

"You can't ask her to do that," Mom says.

"I can't believe you get to go to Cypress Point and you don't even know how to play golf." Dad takes a huge bite of his pizza.

"I can't believe you're jealous of your teenage daughter," Betty says out of nowhere. I'd almost forgotten she was listening. "Shouldn't you be more worried about the fact that she's going with a boy?" She's says "boy" as if being male is a criminal offense.

Dad slouches in his seat. "I try not to think about it."

Mom tips her chin up. "She dates. She's responsible. We trust her."

"I trusted Jenny, too, and she still got knocked up at sixteen." Betty glares at me like I could be pregnant this very second.

I look to Dad instead. "I have cousins?"

"Three good-for-nothings," Betty answers.

Dad straightens his glasses. "I wish I could refute that, but last I heard Slade was in jail. So."

Slade? I have a cousin named Slade. Who has been in jail for who-knows-what. Shaking that information off, I say, "I swear it's not like that with Dylan. He's barely a friend. I just have to find time to buy clothes is the problem. Should I tell him I have to do it at night?"

Mom and Dad look at each other. Then Mom says, "We're finally getting started on the grant work now that Betty is taken care of. We won't be able to get home any earlier."

I nod. "I just needed to know what time to give him."

There's a long silence before Dad clears his throat. "So tell me about Dylan. Mainly, how he'd know people with Cypress Point memberships when his uncle runs AnimalZone."

"Daaaaad." I give up on my pizza and get up from the table. "I actually don't know. It's not really something you ask a person."

"Sure it is! You say, 'Hey, so how did your parents get filthy rich and important?'"

Throwing my plate in the sink, I glare at him. "He doesn't like to talk about his parents. I'm going to my room now."

"You're no fun!" he calls, and I hear Mom swat his arm.

I try not to slam my door, but I still shut it loudly. Pacing my room, I can't quite figure out why I'm so angry. But there's something I don't like about my parents' reaction. My dad usually goes pale the second I mention a guy, but he didn't even bat an eye this time. Have I just had too many boyfriends? Are they immune now?

Or is it the money?

It feels like the money. Dylan is more of an ass than my three exes combined, and yet he gets a pass because his name is tied with Cypress Point. That is supremely unfair.

Though their reaction makes me want to back out, I call Dylan. "Hello?" he says.

"I can only go after six. For the shopping thing."

There's a pause. "But you get off at noon."

I sigh. "I have something else after that, and I can't get out of it."

"What?"

"Not your business. It's six or nothing."

"Hmm . . ." I can picture his smug face, and it makes me even angrier that I gave in like everyone seems to. "I guess that should be enough time, if we're efficient. Are you a slow shopper?"

I raise an eyebrow. "No. Why do I get the feeling you *like* shopping?"

"Because I do. Tomorrow okay?"

Maybe shopping is fun when you can buy whatever you want. "Yeah, bye."

I flop onto my bed, mad at everything. Myself included. How did this happen? Why did Dylan have to say my name to London? He could have made up anyone, but no. A wave of nerves crashes over me—I've never felt insecure about my family's social or economic standing, but these people . . .

I'm so out of my element.

My phone chirps. I glare at Shreya's name. *Did Dylan call u yet?*

I'm so sick of his name I could scream. And I can't stand how everyone in my life seems happy to shove me right into his arms.

When I don't reply, Shreya sends another message. *Are u mad @ me?*

Pressing the power button, I turn off my phone.

* * *

107

The next day, Betty sits on my bed while I rifle through my closet. I don't know why I feel the need to dress up, but I do. Maybe I want to prove that the AnimalZone uniform is not my best look. I swear it adds ten pounds.

"You have a lot of fish," Betty says. For the third time.

"Yup." I pull out a blue top and some black skinny jeans. Normally I'd be running my outfit by Shreya and Olivia, but I'm still mad at Shrey and Olivia needs to stop being in Tahiti. At least I can count on Betty for brutal honesty. "What do you think of this?"

She scrunches her face. "What are you trying to say? Because that says, 'I want to impress you.'"

"Ugh." I throw the clothes on the floor. "Not that then. I want to look . . . pretty, but not in a seductive way. This isn't a date."

She nods thoughtfully. "You look pretty in everything, though."

I raise an eyebrow, surprised she'd say something like that. "You really think so?"

"Yeah. Thin, nice legs, exotic."

I hold in my laugh. Yes, I'm so exotic. Next I grab a black tank and red jeans. "What about this?"

She frowns. "You'd look tough in that."

"Tough. I'll take it." I shoo her out for a moment while I dress, hoping she doesn't do anything while alone. We had a scare earlier today when I took a bathroom break—came out to find her hand in one of our aquariums. She had a fit when I told her she couldn't pet the fish.

Luckily, she's standing right in the hall where I left her. She comes back in, appraising my look. "What shoes?"

I smirk. Maybe she's more useful than I thought she'd be. "How did you know I was about to ask that?"

"It's not the first time I've gotten ready for a date, Mia."

"It's Mika, and this isn't a date." It's preparation for a fake relationship. "Sneakers or flats?"

She points to the flats. "In case you have to buy shoes, too."

"You have done this before." I slip them on, spin around once. "So I look okay?"

For a second I think I'm seeing things, but Betty is tearing up. I get the sense that she's . . . proud of me. Weird. "You are beautiful, and a very good person. Even if you are Oriental."

I deflate. She has a gift for balancing out those nice words with horrible ones. I hear a door slam and then footsteps. "Sounds like Mom and Dad are home. How about you go see them while I finish my makeup?"

"Sure."

I stand at my closet mirror, applying blush and eye shadow and wondering if I'm overdoing it. Part of me wants to rebel and wear grungy clothes, but my bet is we'll be going to a nice store and I don't want to stand out. Why is my insecurity suddenly winning?

The doorbell rings, and my heart doubles speed as I run to get there before my parents. I pull it open, and there, standing next to Dylan, is Shreya.

Chapter 17

Shreya shrinks under my glare, looking genuinely remorseful, though I'd rather not admit it. "I'm sorry, okay? I was just excited to surprise you with food and thought it would be fun. I didn't think you'd freak out—I had no idea what it was for."

"It's true," Dylan says. "I totally lied to her."

I'm not sure how to react, because I'm fairly certain he brought her to help make up for having to do this. Which is really considerate of him. I'd much rather have her help with clothes than his. "Why am I not surprised?"

He shrugs. "Old habits die hard."

"Is this Dylan?" my dad says. I spin around, finding my parents looking on curiously.

"Yup. I'll be back in a few hours." I grab my bag and hurry out before my dad can ask any embarrassing questions about Cypress Point.

"Are you ashamed of me?" Dylan says as we head towards Clark's non-descript silver car, which I usually see parked behind AnimalZone.

"Yes, that, plus my dad fantasizes about Cypress Point. I'd rather not have him latching on to you."

"I see." He opens the door for me, and I stare at him as the reality of this arrangement sinks in. He really is trying to make it look like we're together . . . and it doesn't seem like he minds as much as I do. Why are his eyes so soft as they take me in? Cue freak out.

"What?" he asks when I don't get in.

"Nothing." I move to the backseat door and open it myself, determined to make this look nothing like a date. "Shrey, go ahead and take shotgun."

"Can you be more stubborn?" She rolls her eyes but gets in.

Dylan looks like he wants to say something to me, but he shuts Shreya's door and heads for the driver's side. I get in back, happy to have space. He starts the car, and we're off. No one talks as he heads for whatever shopping place he's decided to go to, but from his direction I'm guessing we're headed to Carmel. Of course we are. Carmel is where rich tourists like to hang out and take themselves too seriously.

My phone chirps, and I grab it, relieved that I have something to busy myself with. I try not to laugh when I read Shreya's name. *Please don't be mad anymore.*

I'm fine. This is just weird, I type back.

It is. I'll give u that. He really asked u to be his pretend gf?

More like told a lie and now has to cover his tracks.

I need details.

Later. It's involved.

"Are you guys seriously texting each other so I can't hear what you're talking about?" Dylan asks.

"Maybe." I look up. He's eyeing me in the rearview mirror.

"You're talking about me, aren't you?"

111

"Yes."

Shreya laughs, and I can't restrain my smile. I expect Dylan to glare at me, but when his eyes meet mine again they look sad. For some reason this makes it impossible for me to send another text, but I'm not planning on starting a conversation, either. Was he expecting me to give in and embrace this? He has another thing coming if he did. I plan on dragging my feet every step of the way.

In complete predictability, Dylan parks at the Carmel Plaza, a ritzy shopping center full of designer stores. I'm glad I at least tried to look nice. He takes in a deep breath, looking practically giddy. "I've missed this. Even if I'm not shopping for myself, this'll be fun."

I stare at him. "You're weird."

"You're one to talk, Fish Girl." He grabs my hand, and I reflexively pull back. He doesn't let me go. "Just in case. London or other people who know her could be here."

"You seriously expect me to buy that?" I growl, trying to get free of his grip. "What, does she live at the mall or something?"

"No." He points past me. "But her parents' second home is about five minutes that way. And they stay in Carmel every summer and hold all sorts of parties. London's favorite place to eat is the Patisserie Boissere, which is here. So chances are good."

I cringe because he has a point, but I'm not ready for this. The way his hand feels in mine . . . no, I can't go there. "The deal was one day."

"Which is twenty-four hours—Saturday will only be seven,

112

tops." He gives me a wicked grin. "That, plus three tonight, means I'll still have fourteen hours left to use."

Shreya puts her hand over her mouth, probably knowing I'll kill her if she laughs. I relax my arm, but I refuse to hold his hand back. "Exploiting me, huh? You can't make up extra loopholes."

He pulls me along, seeming to have no problem with my resistance. "You should have specified terms if you didn't want loopholes."

"What are you? Some kind of lawyer?"

"My father hoped I'd get a law degree. After business school, of course." His voice is colder than usual, but then he stops and clears his throat. "Never mind that. I'm guessing you can't play golf, right?"

"She's even bad at the miniature variety," Shreya says.

"Thanks for pointing that out." I put my free hand on my hip. She gives me a mock innocent look. "No, I am not interested in golf and thus I suck. My dad took me to Poppy Hills once and refused to let me try after the tenth dent."

"Divot. Not dent," he says with a surprising lack of condescension. He purses his lips, thinking. "Then the goal should be to avoid playing—I can't have you ruining the green. London is really good, and she'll tear your form to pieces."

"I would prefer to avoid tearing."

"So that means not golf attire?" Shreya asks.

"Precisely, but it still has to have the right look." He starts walking again, and, kill me now, we end up at J. Crew. I was secretly hoping for Anthropologie.

Dylan and Shreya practically skip through the racks, picking out clothing that gags me with its stuffiness. Then I get thrown in a dressing room and am ordered to come out and show them every single outfit whether or not I think it's ugly.

"Can you at least not frown?" Dylan asks. "It's distracting me from the clothes."

I glare at him as he analyzes the sweater and pants like this decision is life and death.

"Angry is better than pouting," he says.

"I like the sweater. The teal looks nice on her." Shreya touches my arm. "Ooo, soft."

"It's cashmere. Better be soft." He puts his finger to his mouth. "I like the sweater, too, but not with those pants. Maybe with—"

"Dylan Wainwright, is that really you?" a woman says. She's older, but the kind of older that also looks like she's had a lot of work done. Her face lights up as she comes closer, while Dylan's fills with dread. "It is!"

"Hi, Mrs. St. James," he says as she does that European kiss greeting. "How are you?"

"Just wonderful. Carmel is always a nice break from the hectic school year. You know how the boys keep me busy." She eyes me and Shreya suspiciously, but tries to concentrate on Dylan. "And how are you dealing with everything? Your parents have been very worried about you."

His smile is tight. "Sure they have. You can tell them I'm fine if you want."

She puts her hand on his arm, and now I'm really curious. She has to know him super well if he'd let her do that. "They'll be happy to hear that. Truly."

Dylan nods.

Finally, she turns her attention to us. "And who are your . . . friends?"

"This is Mika Arlington, my girlfriend, and her friend Shreya." Hearing "girlfriend" out loud makes my stomach twist. He shouldn't be telling this woman such a lie—she doesn't seem like the kind of person who refrains from gossip.

"Oh? Well, isn't she darling?" Mrs. St. James pastes on a huge smile as she comes to do the kiss thing to me, too. "Nice to meet you, Mika."

"You too," I say.

"I hate to cut this short, but I really have to get going. Need to pick out wine and cheese for our next soiree before the shops close." She looks back at Dylan, and I can't make out her expression. "Can I tell London you said hi?"

I force myself not to react, but I'm pretty sure I just met London's mom.

"Sure," Dylan says.

We all hold our breath until she leaves the store. Dylan plops down in a chair, practically hyperventilating.

"Was that as close as I think it was?" I ask.

"Yes. Told you we could see them." He rubs his temples, and for some reason it makes me want to comfort him. "I hate that woman almost as much as her daughter."

"I'm lost," Shreya says. "Who was that?"

"Later." I can't seem to take my eyes off Dylan. He doesn't look like the arrogant guy I first met, but instead like a guy who's been through a lot. For some reason, I don't like seeing him like this. "So if you like the sweater, Dylan, what pants should I try with it?"

115

He looks up at me, and in his eyes I think I see gratitude for the distraction. "The brown plaid, I think. Your butt looked amazing in those."

I narrow my eyes. "Don't look at my butt."

"What should I look at then?" He leans back in the chair, his eyes locked on mine like he's daring me to flirt with him. I rush back into the dressing room, and I don't come out until my face stops burning.

With the sweater, pants, and a pair of admittedly beautiful red snakeskin flats, the total comes to almost nine hundred dollars. Which has to be Dylan's entire paycheck from AnimalZone. I gulp as he hands over the cash like it's nothing. He grabs the bag and my hand, and we head back outside. It's dark now—I didn't realize we were in there so long.

"I feel like I need to take out an insurance policy for these clothes," I say.

Shreya snorts. "No kidding."

He sighs. "Just take care of them, okay? I did work a whole month for them. First money I ever earned on my own, too."

Now I feel like a jerk for giving him a hard time when today was all about me. He didn't have to do this. He could have let me look stupid and poor on Saturday. I squeeze his hand, and he looks at me curiously but says nothing. He opens the car door for me again, and this time I comply. He takes Shreya home first and then heads for my place.

"What was with you back there?" he asks.

I know he's talking about the hand squeeze. "Nothing."

"You really suck at lying."

I sigh. "Fine, I wanted to say thank you, okay? Even if I feel

116

like a huge fake in these clothes, it's better than London having another chance to laugh at me."

There's a long pause, and it feels like he's looking at me though I don't dare check. "Are you okay?"

"I'm scared." My fingers run back and forth over the bag's handle, as if I have to make sure the clothes don't disappear. "This isn't me. And you're right, I'm a horrible liar."

"Just follow my lead, and it'll be fine." He turns onto my road. "And really, there won't be much lying involved anyway. It's not like we have to spend the day making out to prove we're in a relationship—unless you want to."

I smack his arm. "You wish."

"What if I do?" He stops in front of my house, stares at me in a way that makes me want to run and stay all at once.

"Doesn't mean much, seeing as you'll hook up with girls you apparently hate."

He smiles. "Touché. But I'm not drunk right now."

I unbuckle my seatbelt and get out, determined not to look back at him. Because if I do and he's still giving me that disgustingly cute grin, then I'm in big trouble.

Chapter 18

I lay out the fancy clothes on my bed, staring at them in the faint morning light. There's no denying they're pretty, but they still feel like someone else's. Taking a deep breath, I push down the nerves. It'll be over soon enough, and then I'll have someone to clean tanks for the rest of the summer. And goldfish tanks are nasty.

I smile, picturing Dylan grumbling about how many he has to clean. He'll regret giving London my name if it's the last thing I do.

Heading for the bathroom, I decide getting ready for today should count towards my twenty-four hours as fake girlfriend. Usually my Saturdays are spent in grungy beach clothes, but today I have to do the full run-down.

I scrub my hair, shave, moisturize, pluck, and blow dry like I'm going to Prom. Not that I've ever been, but I imagine it's at least this involved. As I stare at my reflection, trying to decide what to do with my hair, my phone rings. The name in the window is not what I expected, but I'm happy to see it.

"I'm baaaaaack!" Olivia says when I pick up. "And you should see my tan. You'll be jealous."

I smile, her voice putting me at ease. "I already saw enough pictures to make me green with envy."

"I noticed—flaunting your slumber party in my face, jerk."

"It was impromptu. But you still missed out." I pull out my makeup to put on while we talk. "So what's with the early call?"

Olivia laughs. "I miss you guys! I wanted to know what beach you were sculpting at today so I could see you and Shrey."

"Actually . . ." My stomach drops. How do I begin to explain I'm about to go out with Dylan when last time we talked I was so against it? "I'm going to Cypress Point today, so no sculpting."

There's a pause. "Like, the golf course?"

"Yup."

"Uhhh, did you win the lottery since we last spoke?"

"The lottery from hell." I apply mascara liberally, dang short lashes. "I'm sure you remember Dylan."

"No. Way."

"It's not what you think—he lied and told some people I was his girlfriend. I got roped into pretending it's true for a day." I pull open the bathroom door and head to my room to dress.

She laughs hysterically.

I'd strangle her if she were here. "It's not funny, Olivia!"

"Oh, it is. You don't have to be so stubborn. It's okay to change your mind about a guy. He obviously likes you, and if you actually agreed to this I bet you like him, too. Whether you admit it or not."

"No. I don't. Trust . . ." I stop, staring at my bed in shock. My clothes are gone—just the shoes remain at the foot of the bed. "Olivia, I gotta go. Call Shrey. She'll fill you in on the rest."

I hang up before she replies, my heart pounding as I spin around my room. They can't be gone. No one is even awake yet. I hold my breath, trying not to panic, and that's when I hear it:

The washer is running.

Sprinting down the hall in my towel, I make it to the laundry room just in time to see Betty put my cashmere sweater in the water. The pants are about to go in, but I dive for them. "No!"

She gives me a look that implies I'm the crazy one. "I was just washing your outfit—you have to wash clothes once before you wear them."

"How could you?" I scream, pushing past her to the washer. I pull out the sweater, but it's already soaked through and ruined. There's no way I can fix this before Dylan comes. He'll kill me for this.

"You hadn't even taken the tags off." She glares at me. "Do you know how many people try that stuff on? It's like wearing other people's sweat."

"This is dry clean only! Not crappy used clothes from Goodwill!" I try to gently wring out the sweater, but it looks like a hideous dead rat already. "Were you going to put it in the dryer and shrink it, too?"

She looks down. "I was just trying to help. For your big date."

"By ruining my clothes?"

Finally, my parents appear in the doorway, probably startled awake by my yelling. "What's going on?" Mom asks.

"This!" I hold up the sweater. "You guys are supposed to get up when she does—you have to *watch* her like she's a little

120

kid, remember? You didn't and now I can't wear the sweater Dylan paid three hundred dollars for."

Mom comes forward, looking guilty. But it's not enough. "Maybe we can fix it. I can get the blow dry—"

"It's too late. He'll be here in like ten minutes." I squeeze my eyes shut, so angry I can't see straight. "Why did you have to be stupid today?"

"Mika . . ." Betty looks like she's about to cry. "I'm sorry."

"Sorry isn't enough!" I grab the sweater from Mom and shove it in Betty's face. My whole life has been ruined by her—having to watch her, losing my chance to intern with my parents, and now this. "You messed everything up. I'm lucky I saved the pants before they got soaked, too. No one asked you to wash my stuff! And what were you doing in my room anyway?"

She starts crying, but I don't care. She should cry.

"Sweetie." Mom gives me a stern look. "It's just a sweater. You're acting way out of line for—"

"It's not just a sweater! It was a gift. He bought it for me to wear today. Now I can't."

"That's no reason to call her stupid," Dad says. "She meant well, and—"

"You're taking *her* side?" I can hardly believe what I'm hearing. Just last week my dad wanted to get as far away from his mother as possible, and now I'm in trouble for yelling at her? "Just because she's crazy doesn't mean she can get a free pass for everything she screws up! If you'd put her in a home this would have never happened. None of this."

Dad glares at me. "Mika, you're this close to getting grounded."

121

"You need to apologize," Mom adds.

I shove past them all. "Forget it. You don't understand."

This time I do slam my door, and it takes everything in me not to scream. Betty picks the worst moments to be nuts. I have just enough time to get dressed before Dylan gets here, and half my outfit is ruined. He'll take one look at whatever shirt I wear and get mad.

I lay the sweater out flat on my desk, hoping that I can salvage it so I can wear it later. Maybe if we need to go out on another fake date. But the ribbing is stretched weird, and I can't get it to go back. Putting my head in my hands, I force myself to move on. There's nothing I can do but find something to go with the pants. I pick out underwear and get dressed save my shirt. Then I proceed to go through everything I own, hoping something will work.

Problem is, nothing is better than that sweater. Even if it wasn't me, it was beautiful and perfect and all my clothes look like they come from a completely different world than these pants and shoes.

Because they do.

I end up settling on a lacy purple tank with a cream cardigan that I wore to a benefit for the Aquarium last year. It's the nicest combo I have, though nothing near three hundred dollars. There's no time to do my hair, so I put it in a ponytail. An ocean-side golf course will probably be windy anyway.

Unable to look at my family, I grab my bag and head outside to wait for Dylan. At least this way my parents won't see his reaction. Too bad that won't spare me.

The silver car appears at the end of my street, and I feel like I'm about to throw up. Dylan parks right in front of me, gets out. One of his eyebrows is cocked as he takes in my outfit, and not in a good way. "Where's the sweater?"

That's when I burst into tears.

Chapter 19

I cover my face, beyond embarrassed for breaking down. The summer's stress must have finally gotten to me, because I struggle to pull myself together. "My stupid grandmother put it in the washer and it's ruined. I'm so sorry. I put it out and then showered and when I came back she'd taken my clothes and—"

His hands come down on my shoulders. "Whoa there. Calm down, you're rambling."

I risk a peek at his face. To my surprise, it's more worried-looking than angry. "You're not mad at me?"

"It's not your fault." He runs his hands down my arms, but then pulls away like he didn't realize what he was doing. "Did you seriously think I'd get mad at you over a sweater?"

"Uh, yeah." I wipe under my eyes. So much for looking nice today. "I thought you'd rip me to shreds."

He winces. "I guess I can see how you'd think that, but you still look nice. It's just a sweater."

"It was a gift, though. You worked for it, and . . . I liked it." I look at my feet, the snakeskin flats gleaming back up at me. "I didn't even get to wear it once."

"I had no idea you were so sentimental."

I give him my best pout.

His smile stretches wide, and even though we've been talking for a few minutes it's the first time I really take him in. Nice-fitting black polo, slender white slacks, leather golf shoes—he totally makes this sport look cool. "Better be careful with that pout, Mika. It makes me want to do real boyfriend things."

My eyes narrow into a glare. "You suck at flirting."

He laughs as he opens the passenger side door. "That's better. C'mon."

Dylan makes a U-turn, and then we're off towards the 17-Mile Drive, which I haven't been to in forever. Cypress Point is right near the beginning of it on the Monterey/Pacific Grove side. The Drive is yet another one of the touristy things around here, a beautiful road through forest and golf courses and coastline that lands you right near Pebble Beach and Carmel on the other side.

As I watch the houses pass by, my mind wanders to Betty crying and me yelling at her like a lunatic. This pit forms in my stomach—Dylan didn't even get mad, making my reaction completely unwarranted. Maybe my parents were right about how I was acting . . .

"Are you okay?" Dylan says.

I jump. "Oh, um, yeah."

"Lie."

I sigh, not really wanting to bring up all the stuff I'm dealing with at home. "I just . . . I guess I still can't believe you didn't get mad at me."

"Maybe you haven't noticed, but you're the one who's constantly picking fights with me." He pulls onto the main road that turns into The 17-Mile Drive. "It's not my fault I have to defend myself."

I open my mouth to argue, but then realize I can't because he's right. The last time he started it was . . . I can't remember. New approach. "It's not my fault you're always doing things wrong. Someone has to point it out."

Dylan's knuckles go white from gripping the steering wheel, but he says nothing. As the city gives way to cypress trees and the rocky coast, I buzz on a heavy helping of nerves. He turns at the Cypress Point sign, and as he slows down by the gate I feel like I'm trying to sneak into a palace.

The guard sneers at the car, but when Dylan rolls the window down the man's eyes go wide. "Mr. Wainwright! Sorry, I didn't recognize the car. Go right ahead."

"Thanks." When the gate goes up, he drives through like he's done this a million times.

I stare at him, unsure of what to think. This version of Dylan is so different. "Mr. Wainwright?"

He rolls his eyes. "They like propriety. Just you wait."

"Great." As the road opens up into a parking lot, my breaths come short and fast. There's an expansive clubhouse adorned with trees and flowers and big windows. A few people stand outside, all wearing clothes like Dylan's and sporting golf bags. Even dressed nice, it doesn't feel like enough. "Can I change my mind now? I don't want to do this."

"Too late." He parks fairly far from the clubhouse. Putting his hand on my knee, he smiles at me. "It'll be fine, okay?"

"How do you know?"

"Because the only pretend thing about this is our relationship. You don't have to lie about your life—you don't have anything to be ashamed of. Besides . . ." He moves his hand to my cheek, and I freeze. "Maybe it would be easier to see this as our first date."

I pull back, my face on fire. "Don't mess with me like that."

"Do I look like I'm messing with you?" His face is completely serious, and I keep waiting for him to give away the joke. He doesn't. Olivia can't be right. He can't actually like me. With a frustrated sigh, he finally looks away. "Don't bring your bag or phone. I wish I could've bought you something nice, because London really will tear that sack to pieces."

"Oh, okay." I look at my striped messenger bag. It's been my favorite for years, but suddenly it seems beaten down. I try to stuff it under the seat.

He shakes his head. "Mika, *no one* will steal that. Promise."

"So either you're hitting on me or being mean?"

"I find it very hard to be just your friend." He opens the door and gets out, leaving me in a confused daze. I signed up for fake girlfriend duty—now it seems like he did this in hopes that I *would* become his girlfriend. Maybe we don't fight as much as we did at first, but I never would have seen this coming.

I force myself out of the car. Dylan has the trunk open, and when he shuts it I see the bag of golf clubs at his side. He throws them on his shoulder and motions for me to follow.

"Those look a lot nicer than my dad's," I say, deciding I should at least be nice to him today. I'll have to figure everything else out later.

Dylan slows his pace so I can keep up. "My dad only let me take two bags when he kicked me out. This was the second one. Funny how fast you figure out your priorities when your whole life gets reduced to so little."

"I didn't know you liked golf that much."

"You never asked." He grabs my hand then, and I don't fight it. I might even enjoy it a little. "Once dreamed of going pro, but I never got to practice like I wanted."

"Okay, you're never allowed to mock my fish again—your interests are lamer."

"Golf is not lame." He pulls the clubhouse door open, waits for me to go in first. "You'll see after today."

The lobby alone is pristine. Everything looks like it's made from the best possible material. People mill about in groups, mostly old guys, a few women, and even fewer teens. Pretty much just London and Brock, who are already heading for us.

When London sees us holding hands, her face turns sour. Dylan leans in, his breath tickling my ear. "I'm whispering to you because it'll piss her off. It'd be even better if you laughed."

I do, surprising myself as much as Dylan. But it's funny, and I can't help it.

London can't muster a smile as she stands in front of us. "So you guys are actually together."

"I already told you that." Dylan smiles at me, and all my nerves are gone. This won't be so bad—messing with her is shockingly entertaining. "I'm sure your mom mentioned it, too. We ran into her the other night."

She clenches her jaw. "I'll check in. Should I get a caddie, or will Mika do it for us?"

Dylan tips his chin up. "Get a caddie. He can help you with your swing."

London whips around so fast her long brown hair almost hits us.

"Burn!" Brock's laugh is loud enough to make everyone look at us. He pats Dylan on the back, having no problem checking me out in front of him. "She's even hotter in normal clothes. Feel free to come to me when you get tired of this loser. I'll be your sugar daddy."

Dylan shoves him. "Back off."

"No thanks," I say. "I prefer guys who at least have the decency to check me out when I'm not looking."

Brock lets out another deep laugh. "Now you two make a lot more sense."

"Yeah, we do, don't we?" Dylan squeezes my hand, and it feels like he's not saying that to Brock but to me. I have no idea what I should do with that, so I study the floor. It's a really nice floor.

London returns with keys and an older man wearing a visor. I assume he's the caddie. "We're ready to go."

"Great." Dylan snatches one of the keys. "Mika and I will ride together. You guys can take the other cart."

Chapter 20

Cypress Point lives up to every rumor I've heard. The early morning fog still lingers on the grass, making the place look like it's filled with magic. Cypress trees dot the landscape, and I can hear the ocean beat against the rocky cliffs. The sun will soon burn off the mist, but I suspect that will only improve the view.

Dylan and I drive behind London's cart, so she can't watch our every move. It's odd, seeing him so at ease. He totally belongs on a golf course, and it's nice to know something makes him happy. I'm used to him being miserable.

"So what do you think?" he asks.

"It's gorgeous. My dad wanted me to take pictures, but I told him no. I didn't want to look lame."

He smiles. "Just wait 'til the sixteenth. It's legendary for a reason."

"You really like this, don't you?"

He glances at me. "Why do you ask?"

I shrug. "You seem like a different person out here—not a complete and total jerk."

"I'm not a jerk. But maybe I have been acting like one lately." He reaches to put his arm around me, and I notice

London has turned around to observe us. "So sue me if I haven't handled this recent string of life changes perfectly. I'm not you."

I gulp, thinking about Betty and my own graceless moments. "If you're implying I'm perfect, you're wrong."

"We can debate that later." He pulls me closer, and I catch the clean scent of his soap. There's no denying the physical chemistry—his proximity definitely gets my heart racing. The other stuff is still way up in the air. "Right now we have to talk strategy. London is gonna pull out the dirt fast. You can't be fazed by it."

I raise an eyebrow. "What kind of dirt?"

"Her first tactic will probably be the 'Dylan is a player' route, but you already know my history there. I'm not about to apologize for it; we all go through phases. I got it out of my system."

"You're seriously chalking that up to a phase?"

"Moving on—she'll hit the money sector next, imply that you aren't good enough for me. But that's crap because my father really did disown me, though everyone thinks he's bluffing. I might still have his last name, but I'm poorer than you."

"Really?" I didn't know it was that serious, and it sends up a warning flag. "What did you do to make him so mad?"

He cringes. "Let's not go there just yet."

I don't have time to push the topic because we're at the first tee. Dylan goes for his clubs, and Brock comes up to me with a too-wide smile. "You're not playing, right?"

I nod. "I'm pretty horrible at golf."

131

"Maybe I can teach you." He puts his arm on my shoulder, and I look back to Dylan, who seems to have overlooked Brock's role. "I'll take you to the driving range to practice."

And there it is. London hasn't given up on Dylan at all. She fully intends to use this day to her advantage. Brock will distract me—she'll have Dylan to herself.

"Dylan!" London calls from where she stands with the caddie. "Come over here for a second."

He pulls me away from Brock, leaning in to whisper. "I'll be right back. Do not go anywhere with him. You think I'm a player? Brock is worse."

I nod. "I can handle him."

He smiles. "And you were afraid you couldn't do this."

I roll my eyes and head back to Brock, who does seem genuinely interested in me. Either he's a good actor or that's why he agreed to London's plan in the first place. "Actually, I'd rather watch Dylan than learn. I haven't seen him play golf yet. Is he good?"

"Oh, he's amaz . . ." He stops. "Not very good. Barely better than London."

I look over to them chatting with the caddie. "Did London want to be a pro, too, then?"

Brock nods. "Dylan and London have always golfed with each other—they've known each other since they were kids. Way before we all went to school together."

"You went to school with Dylan?" If he has more information on Dylan, maybe I won't mind making friends with Brock after all. "Where?"

"Stevenson. They came for the golf. Their parents both live in Silicon Valley."

"I see." Stevenson is a boarding school in Pebble Beach, way up there when it comes to California private schools.

Dylan jogs back to us, clearly nervous about our conversation. He takes my hand. "London's going first. Come watch."

"Your parents live in Silicon Valley, huh?" I say as he drags me closer to the tee.

He leans in. "You are *not* leaving my side. Got it?"

"If you insist."

"I do." He looks at London, who's trying to focus on her shot but keeps glancing at us. She swings her club over her head, and at that exact moment Dylan grabs me by the waist and pulls me close.

"You missed!" Brock says. "I can't believe you missed!"

London fumes at the sight of Dylan and me. He gives her his most crooked grin, and that's when I realize he did that on purpose. She smooths her hair and takes a deep breath. "I didn't miss. That was a warm up."

"You were at the tee." Brock folds his arms. "Are we playing for real or not?"

"Fine, whatever." She puts her head down, and this time she hits the ball. It soars into the air—I have to admit I'm impressed by how far it flies. Thanks to my dad watching every major golf tournament, I know at least that she hit the fairway, the clean-cut grass not the rough outer bounds of the hole, right in the middle.

Brock hangs his head. "Damn."

London looks right at Dylan, cocky as ever. "Your turn."

He lets go of me, pulls out his driver, and places a golf ball on his tee. Then he stands there, waiting. "Feel free to say your snarky comment now, London, before I swing."

She glares at him. "Just so you know, Mika, Dylan doesn't have girlfriends. He gets what he wants and moves on."

"Maybe he'd stick around if you weren't so eager to give him what he wanted," I blurt out before I can think.

She gives me a look that could melt my face off, but says nothing.

"See, London?" Dylan approaches the tee, looks out at the fairway, and barely takes another moment to prepare. His swing is full of power, and the golf ball flies way past London's, landing dead center of the fairway. He smiles at me. "Mika is in a whole different league."

At his words, everything *snicks* into place. I can barely stand I'm so shocked. I fought it so hard, but Dylan was right. There's no way we can be just friends—and I don't think I want him to be my enemy.

London groans. "Whatever. I still don't buy this."

She can't have him. It makes me sick just thinking about it. Not because he doesn't like her, but because he's *mine*.

"You know what, London? I don't think it's up to you." I walk past her, heading right for Dylan. I put one hand on his neck and push up to my tiptoes, kissing him on the cheek. "That was an amazing shot."

His whole face lights up, and his arm slides around my waist. "Thanks, babe."

Chapter 21

"So does that mean we really get to make out all day?" Dylan says as we get in the golf cart to head for the fairway.

"No." I shove him. But when he puts his arm around me, I let myself settle into his side, try to feel what it could be like if we got together for real. "You said this could be our first date instead. I don't make out on first dates."

"I can live with that." He seems to be driving slower than necessary. "Do you mind telling me what changed?"

"I'm not sure. There are still things I don't like about you . . ." I bite my lip, trying to find the right words. "But at the same time, I think I could like the person you're becoming. We'll see."

"Your honesty is painfully endearing."

"Thanks?" I lean my head on his shoulder, liking the feel of it way too much.

We stop near Brock's ball, which is way behind London's. But Dylan doesn't get out. In the silence I can feel his nerves. "Is it weird that I like how you see all my faults?"

"A little." The words come out flirtier than planned.

"I'm gonna play horribly today—you're too distracting." When Brock's done with his shot, Dylan puts the cart back in drive, and we follow the group to the next golf ball.

My affectionate display seems to have staved off London's barrage for now. They play in relative silence, save the caddie giving several tips to Brock about the course. I keep waiting to get bored, but the view is too stunning to allow it. The sun glistens on the water, waves crash onto the rocks, and the breeze is just enough to keep me cool.

And then there's Dylan. I would never tell him, but he makes golf sexy. Every time it's his turn, I wait for the way he flexes his forearms just before he swings. He watches the ball fly, his eyes narrowed and breath held. When it lands where he wants, he flashes me this hopeful smile. When it goes slightly off course, he purses his lips and shoves his club in the bag.

I've never seen him so passionate, and I find it ridiculously attractive.

After nine holes, or what they call "the turn," there's a pavilion with refreshments and bathrooms. I'm happy for the break, and it seems like we'll have to wait anyway because the group in front of us is also resting.

"What do you want?" Dylan asks as we follow London to a table. "We still have maybe a couple hours, so you should eat something. Don't you dare look at the prices."

I sigh. "What do they have then?"

He puts his arm around my waist—he's had no problem taking advantage of that. "Sandwiches, fruit, chips, yogurt, cheese platters . . ."

"Ridiculously expensive French wine?"

That gets me a chuckle. "Of course. But they won't let you have it."

136

"I guess water will have to do, and I need to see this cheese platter."

"I'll be right back." He heads for the vendor, leaving me with Brock. London has gone to the bathroom, and I'm happy I don't have to face her on my own.

Brock smiles as I sit next to him, but it's not that skeevy look he first gave me. He doesn't seem so bad, really. I think I'd like him if I knew him better. "You know, London told me to try and woo you."

"I figured as much." I try to look serious. "Maybe I'm wrong, but I don't think she likes me."

He lets out a big laugh. "She doesn't like any chick Dylan looks at, so him having a girlfriend for the first time must piss her off like nothing else. But I've decided you're good for him."

I raise an eyebrow. "He's never had a girlfriend?"

"Nope. Total player, but no one cared cuz he's freaking loaded. Or was." I glare at Dylan, and Brock laughs again. "You got him whipped—I can tell."

"I don't know about that. So are you his best friend?" I ask.

Brock shrugs. "I guess you could say that, though he's always kept to himself. We were roommates for four years, though, so I've learned how to put up with him."

"You poor thing."

He gives me an approving smile. "Right?"

Dylan shows up with a huge platter of cheese, crackers, and fruit. "Don't eat it all, Brock."

"You know I freeload with discretion." He grabs a handful of grapes.

"Wow." I look over the various cheeses. "I don't recognize half of these."

"Here, this is my favorite." Dylan grabs a slice of a white, flaky-looking cheese and puts it on a cracker for me. "It's a sharp Cheddar made in Sonoma."

I take it and pop the whole thing in my mouth. It's *really* sharp, but in a good way. I grab a strawberry to balance it out with sweetness. "Mmm. What next?"

Dylan stares at me. Or rather my lips. "Yeah, no more strawberries for you. I'm already three strokes off my game."

"Here, Mika." Brock slides all the strawberries over to me with a wide smile. "I need to win for once."

We're about half way through the cheese platter when London finally shows. She glares at me the entire time she's in line for food, and I have a feeling most of her bathroom break was devoted to her next plot. I wish she wouldn't bother, because I'm having fun otherwise.

"So, Mika . . ." London sits next to Dylan with her yogurt. "We don't know very much about you. What do your parents do?"

I almost choke on the cracker in my mouth, and Dylan hands me my water bottle, whispering, "Told you."

When I can breathe again, I say, "They're marine biologists— they're the head researchers at the Monterey Bay Aquarium. I hope to follow in their footsteps one day."

"Dude, cool," Brock says.

London doesn't seem as impressed, but it's her smug smile that scares me more. "Interesting. So they deal with slimy creatures all day? Do they smell when they get home?"

My stomach twists, and I can't help thinking of Clark saying his own brother won't visit his "flea hole." Try as I might, I feel as small and insignificant as she wants me to.

Dylan's hand finds my knee, and I know he's saying not to let it get to me. "My uncle said Mika's parents got a big grant from Stanford they're working on. They must have a lot of respect for her parents' research." He looks at me, and I can feel his respect down to my bones. "Your parents make an impact on the world. I think they're awesome. Ours just hoard money."

"Thanks." I put my hand over his, in awe that he could make me forget all of London's insults. "Seriously."

London looks like a little girl about to have a tantrum. "Are you ready to go yet?"

"Ready when you are." Dylan pulls me towards our cart. "She's really starting to piss me off."

"Why is she like that?" I ask as we head for the tenth hole.

"I told you I was her trophy." He sighs, and I think I see regret in his expression. "It wasn't always like this. We used to be friends—we grew up together. Like, next-door neighbors and everything. I was never good at making friends, but I liked playing with her because she wasn't my friend for the money.

"Our fathers went into business before we were even born, made a bunch on their first venture, and I guess I always saw her as the same as me. She was rich, too. She didn't treat me like royalty for it."

It's hard for me to picture this version of London. He makes her sound like a sweet kid. "How did it change so much, then?"

He shrugs. "We got older. She didn't want to be friends anymore, and then our parents started talking about how we should get married. I was twelve. I just wanted a friend, but it became a power play to keep all our families' money together. London thinks that's a great idea, but there's no way in hell I'd date her or marry her."

"You'll just hook up with her," I blurt out. He gives me a death glare, and I kind of feel bad for laughing. "Sorry! You left yourself wide open. I do feel a little bad—that kind of pressure sucks. I had no idea people still thought marriages like that were a good idea."

He shakes his head as he parks by the tee. The guys in front of us are just about done. "Don't worry about it. Now you know just how drunk I'd have to be for that to even sound like a good idea."

He has a point. "When did it happen?"

"Two years ago. She got me slammed, and when I woke up the next morning she was there. I was pissed. She tried to use it as leverage—said we had to date now. I told her I'd have had a lot of girlfriends if it worked that way."

That makes me feel a tiny bit better. "I'm sorry. That's not cool."

He kisses my cheek, and I back up. His smile is full of mischief. "Sorry, when you listen to me like that I can't help myself."

My face must be bright red. "You're only getting away with it because of the deal, you know."

"Oh, I know." He gets out and grabs his clubs while I try to steady myself. Today has been pretty incredible, but I can't let myself fall completely under his spell. At this rate I really will be making out with him by the end of the day.

140

I didn't think Cypress Point could get more beautiful, but it's hard to believe the back nine holes are real. It feels like we're floating on the ocean, the water is so close. Seals sunbathe on the rocks and bark at each other. The cypress trees reach out in their jagged angles, almost like they were created to block the golfers' best shots. When we finally reach the sixteenth hole, I stare in awe at what I see.

The ocean.

There's no fairway, just water and rocks and a distant green on the other side. I look at Dylan, who seems pleased with my reaction. "Pretty cool, right?"

"Yes." I point to the ocean. "And you can actually hit the ball over that?"

He laughs. "Most of the time."

"This hole is my nemesis," Brock says, which is when I realize they've pulled up beside us.

"You have to get past the fear," London says. The caddie carries her bag for her, sets it up, and suggests a club. She takes her swing, and the ball goes invisible as it blends with the sky, but soon enough it hits the green, rolling to a stop very close to the hole. "See?"

"Wow," I can't help but say. "You're really good."

She sneers at me. "Don't try."

"She's being *nice*, London." Dylan goes to the tee. "At least have the decency to fake it back."

She scowls. "You know what I'm gonna miss, Dylan? Your parties. Has he told you about the last one he threw, Mika?"

His eyes go wide. "London . . ."

She smiles at this. "Ahh, he hasn't. Are you afraid of what poor little Mika will think of you when she finds out?"

His chest moves up and down, and he practically growls, "You have no right to tell her. That's my place."

"So I shouldn't tell her you stole your dad's company credit card and threw a massive party at the Iron Man house?" She looks right at me, savoring this. "I heard it cost over five million dollars—I bet that's probably more than your family has made in their whole lives."

Five million. The number doesn't sound real. How can you even spend that much in a month let alone one day?

"Stop!" Dylan yells.

London puts her hands on her hips. "Why? If she's really your girlfriend, she should know how you flew our entire school to San Diego, paid off a bunch of celebrities to entertain us, hired a top Parisian chef. Alcohol, drugs, sex. It was pretty awesome . . . at least until your dad found out."

Five million keeps repeating in my head. He only mentioned her other tactics to distract me from this one. He knew it would bother me that he threw away so much money.

Everyone waits for me to say something. I don't have any words as I stare at Dylan. He seems defeated, and I feel the same. I'm sure he had reasons—I hope he had reasons—but right now it doesn't feel like there's anything he could say to make me understand.

"What's with all the staring?" I finally say. "Golf."

Dylan takes his place, but he doesn't have the same energy as before. He hits the ball, and it soars right into the water.

Chapter 22

When we get in the golf cart, there is no handholding, no arm around me, nothing. I hate it, and yet I need it. Everything feels so messed up. That kind of money could have sent me to any college in the world. It could have paid for Betty's medical care. It could have been used for my parents' research. Actually, probably all three.

"Can I at least explain?" Dylan asks.

"What's there to explain? What London said was true, wasn't it?"

His jaw tightens. "Yes. But I—"

"Don't." I say it quickly, having already decided how I need to handle this for my own sanity. "The more I think about it, the more upset I'll get. I've already thought of a million ways I could have used that money, and if you start explaining right now it won't be enough. It might never be enough."

"It's not like I'm proud of it." His voice is pained. "You said you'd give current-me a chance."

"I did." I rub my eyes, a headache coming on. "But I've been slammed with information. This party . . . I didn't realize you were *that* rich or messed up. I need to think, okay? Can you let me do that?"

"For how long?"

"I don't know," I snap.

We don't talk after that, and there's this weird pain in my chest I can't quite identify. London flits around triumphantly—I can't take her comments right now, so I stay in the cart. Dylan doesn't play well on the last holes, but what makes me sadder is that he doesn't seem to care anymore. He's not mad; he's resigned.

By the time we get back to the clubhouse, the silence feels like a wall. I can't think of anything to say that wouldn't lead to me yelling at him, and I don't want to fight now that I know how good it could be if we didn't.

Five million dollars.

Now that I've exhausted the "What could I do with that kind of money?" route, I'm left wondering what kind of person has a credit card with a five million dollar allowance. Just how much money do his parents have? His world is so different from mine I can't picture it.

What does he see in me? Am I some novelty? I don't like that idea one bit, but it feels plausible.

When we get back to the car, I grab my phone. There are twenty-three texts waiting for me, and I'm grateful for the distraction. At least until I start reading some of them.

Olivia: *OMG, Shrey told me everything. U better make out w/him.*

Shreya: *We are dying to hear what happens.*

Olivia: *Call us! Where r u?*

I give up after that. I can't deal with having to recount today. I hate today. It made me want someone I shouldn't want—it

144

made me both like and hate him more. Which doesn't even make sense.

Dylan pulls up in front of my house, letting out a long sigh. "I only did it because my dad—"

I plug my ears. "Stop it!"

He pulls my hands away from my face. "Let me explain!"

"No! I already know what I'll hear: excuse, excuse, excuse. It's not like you spent five million on saving babies from cancer—you *threw a party*. You wasted it." I try to get free of his grip. "See? I'm ready to rip you to pieces."

"Go ahead. I never said I didn't deserve it." He squeezes my hands, puts my fingers to his lips briefly. "I know I messed up, but I lied about you being my girlfriend because I wanted it to be true. After today, how it felt to be with you . . . don't cut me off. Please, Mika."

I pull away, even though my body screams not to. "That's my decision to make."

He glares at me. "There's really nothing I can say to change your mind, is there?"

"No."

He leans back in his seat, looking like he wants to punch something. "I hate myself so much right now."

"Don't say that." Sighing, I shoulder my bag. "I'm sorry, but I have to be okay with this on my own before I can think about more. Don't ask. I'll let you know."

I get out before he answers, rushing into my house in hopes that he doesn't follow. The second I shut the door, my dad is right there ready to pummel me with questions. "How was it? Is the view as incredible as they say? What was sixteen like?"

145

I roll my eyes. "Epic, yes, and stunning."

"Honey." Mom's tone isn't nearly as sweet as the term. "Isn't there something else we need to discuss first?"

Dad's shoulders slump. "Oh yeah."

This morning comes rushing back, and I groan. "I'm really tired. Can we do the lecture later? I totally overreacted and I'm sorry; please let me go to bed."

By the way she looks at me, I think Mom knows my day didn't go well. "I guess we can discuss it later if you apologize to Betty now. This has been hard on all of us, but that kind of behavior isn't acceptable. I didn't raise you to treat your elders like that."

I want to snap back at her, tell her that I shouldn't have to treat Betty like I treat my *Obaachan* or *Ojiichan*, who are real grandparents. But instead I head to where Betty sits in front of the TV, engrossed in an infomercial for acne medication. She smiles at me when I sit down. "Look at those before-and-afters! Isn't that amazing?"

Her innocent expression knocks all the anger out of me.

She forgot I yelled at her.

To her, I'm just a nice girl sitting next to her on the couch. Not the mean one who called her stupid because of her disease. As I look into her hazel eyes, I think I finally get it. This isn't some act she puts on to annoy us—Betty has Alzheimer's.

She *will* die from it.

Why does that suddenly sound horrible to me? I may not like everything about her, but I don't want her to die. There are good things in her, too, like how she helped me pick my outfit when I went shopping. She has a heart, though she hides it fiercely. Or maybe she's forgotten how to show it.

"We should order that stuff," she exclaims, and my heart warms with more affection than I ever thought I could feel for her.

That conversation I had with Dylan comes flooding back—about being kind to a goldfish even if they could only remember three seconds of time. This morning I treated Betty like she didn't matter as much as my sweater, like her feelings weren't real because they'd be gone in a few hours. That makes me a pretty cruddy human being.

"I'm sorry for being mean to you this morning," I say. "I shouldn't have gotten mad at you for trying to wash my things. I know you were trying to help."

She nods slowly, like she's trying to remember what I said. "It's okay. I should have asked."

"I promise I'll be nicer to you from now on." And I mean it.

"Me too, now *shh.*"

I don't feel like I deserve kindness from her, but I can't protest because she's already back to her infomercial. It doesn't seem like enough, for her to forgive me so quickly. I turn to my parents. "Can I rest now? It was a long course."

Dad frowns. "You should have taken pictures."

Mom looks like she's trying to maintain her patience. "Yes, sweetie. We'll call you for dinner."

I head to my room, change into comfy yoga pants and a tank top. It feels good to be in clothes I belong in, clothes I don't have to worry about ruining. Lying on my bed, I watch my fish swim. My eyes keep coming back to Dill, the one I bought the day I met Dylan. He's already gotten bigger, and he's always happy to see me when I come home.

Now I understand why Dylan asked me what happened to a goldfish that was born at the top of the waterfall, if they were turned to dragons, too. That's how he sees himself—a goldfish who's never had to fight the current and had the world given to him. I still don't know the answer to his question, though. Does he get dragonhood just because he was born up there?

He sure doesn't deserve to be one.

But if your family has five million to drop, how can you not be a dragon?

I'm missing something. But I'm too tired to find the answer, so I let myself doze off. I don't wake up until I hear my phone ringing. Olivia. I hit "accept." "Don't even say his name or I'll hang up."

"You're no fun. Shreya and I are dying over here."

I rub my eyes, still trying to wake up. "The fact that I don't want to talk about it doesn't tip you off in any way?"

"Fine, fine. Subject change—we've decided to meet up with Shreya's brother tomorrow. You in?"

That piques my interest. "Pavan? Won't she get disowned for talking to him?"

I swear I can hear Olivia smile, and I get the sense that she's set one of her devious, Shrey-and-Mika-would-never-do-this-on-their-own plans in motion. "Not if her parents don't find out."

Chapter 23

Olivia's apartment smells weird, and I figure it's travel funk because all their suitcases are still in the living room. She plops down on the sofa, looking exhausted but tanner than ever. Even her warm brown hair looks a few shades lighter from all the sun. Stretching out her annoyingly long legs, she says, "Sorry it's so messy, Mom's still sleeping. Jet lag sucks, but Tahiti was worth it."

Shreya takes the recliner. "Haven't you rubbed it in enough? *The beaches are incredible! The food! The dancing!*"

"*And the guys, oh, the guys!*" I add in my best Olivia impression.

She smiles. "I haven't even told you what Waka and I . . ."

"No boys. I'm sick to death of boys." I push her legs off the couch to make room for myself. Despite my rampant jealously over her trip, I am happy to have her back. She makes life a little more normal.

She frowns. "No offense, but you really need to make out with Dylan. Work out all that tension."

Shreya cringes. "Jeez, Olivia."

"Yeah, Olivia," I say. "Keep your dirty mind to yourself."

"Whatever. You can't tell me you haven't thought about it." Her eyes glint with mischief, which is a rather common occurrence. "Shreya showed me his picture online—he's totally up my alley. Maybe I'll go after him if you—"

"No!" I say, and when they laugh I realize that was the exact reaction she was looking for. "That's not funny."

She glares, and I get the sense she's actually mad at me. "At least tell us what happened yesterday, so we know why we have to deal with cranky Mika on a day that's supposed to be happy."

Her words cut. She's telling me I need to think about Shreya today, not my own problems. "Maybe later, when I've wrapped my head around it. When are we meeting Pavan? And how did you orchestrate this without Shrey's parents finding out?"

Olivia sighs, seeming appeased by my change in subject. "We called him on my cell, so Shrey's phone is clear. Then we worked it out that he'd call her through his fiancée's number so her parents don't recognize it."

"I feel like they know." Shreya pulls her knees up. "I told them I was going to lunch with you guys to celebrate Olivia coming back, but I swear my mom can read my mind."

I frown. "It'll be okay. He's your brother—you shouldn't get in trouble for wanting to see him."

"That doesn't mean I won't." Shreya bites her lip, and it makes me feel bad for not being there like I should. Between Betty and Dylan . . . I've been a sucky friend. "We're meeting him and Rachelle, his fiancée, at Bubba Gump's."

"Good choice. Your parents would never go there. Or anyone else we know." Bubba Gump's is a seafood place on Cannery Row, just about as touristy as you can get. "Should we get going?"

Shreya nods. "I know it's just Pavan, but I'm still nervous to meet Rachelle. I hope she doesn't think I hate her. After that night, I wouldn't blame her for thinking my whole family is crazy. I wish that wasn't her first impression. Thanks for coming with me. I need the moral support."

"Of course," Olivia says at the same time I do. She flashes me a grin, punching my shoulder. "Jinx!"

We take Olivia's beat-up Volkswagen bug. I'm still not sure how she keeps it running, but she's determined to drive it until the mechanics say it's impossible to revive. It takes some time to find a parking spot along the crowded Cannery Row, which is a narrow street on its own, but add in a crap load of tourists and you're asking for an accident.

Pavan and a blond woman I assume is Rachelle stand right outside Bubba Gump's, along with a bunch of other people waiting to get in. He smiles wide, and to my surprise Shreya bursts into tears. They hug, and it both breaks my heart and makes it soar.

"I missed you, kiddo!" Pavan says.

Shreya shoots him an embarrassed look. "Don't call me that."

He laughs and introduces us to Rachelle. She seems like a lovely person, her smile genuine as she says, "Thanks for helping Shreya come today. We never meant to cause so much . . ."

Rachelle looks to Pavan, and her face cracks a little. He puts his arm around her. "Let's not dwell on that. We're having fun today with my sister."

Shreya seems a little shy, but also happy Rachelle seems to not have hard feelings about what happened. "I know my parents reacted . . . well, I'm sorry, and I want to get to know you."

"Please, don't apologize. Pavan warned me it might not go well." Rachelle looks like she's about to break down at the words, and I wonder if she blames herself for everything that happened. She recovers with a beaming grin. "I can't wait to get to know you, too. I'm an only child—I always wanted a sister."

It takes about thirty minutes to get into Bubba Gump's, but the time flies as we chat with Rachelle and Pavan. Shreya seems more comfortable by the time we're led to a table. But for some reason I'm the opposite, like my skin is covered in ants. It's not until I sit down that I realize someone is staring at me from a nearby booth. My eyes go wide as their faces register.

London and her mom. Plus two little boys jumping around like wild animals. They remind me of the kids who come into AnimalZone and bang on my fish tanks, which almost makes me feel bad for her.

"Crap, crap, crap," I mutter as a wide smile breaks out on Mrs. St. James' face. She waves me over, and I wish I could pretend I didn't see her.

Olivia raises an eyebrow. "What?"

"London is here with her family," is all I can get out before Mrs. St. James goes as far as to call my name. I hoped I'd never see her or her daughter again, but it seems the universe has other ideas. Stupid universe. "I'll be right back."

"Mika! I was sure that was you," she says as I come to their table. "What a coincidence! What are you doing here?"

"Just having lunch with friends," I say. "And you?"

"Oh, the boys love the Aquarium." She smiles at them as they tear the kids' menus to bits. London is on her phone, trying her best to not look bothered. "We go every Sunday in the summer."

"I see." Dylan did say they stayed in Carmel all season, but I didn't think that would mean I'd have to be on guard at every tourist attraction in the area. Of course I do, the Monterey peninsula isn't that big. There are only so many places to go while on vacation.

"Where's Dylan?" She looks past me to where my friends sit.

"They had a big fight yesterday at the course," London says matter-of-factly. "They probably broke up. You know Dylan."

Her mom nods like she's not surprised. "I'm sorry, Mika. This must be uncomfortable. I didn't know."

That thing inside me flares again. I'm not sure if it's jealousy or protectiveness, maybe both. "We didn't fight or break up. I'm just out with my friends. Dylan and I still do our own stuff. My boyfriend isn't my whole life."

"I'd watch him closer if I were you," London says.

"I trust him." The words feel funny on my lips because they're truer than I thought they'd be. I'm sure he meant every word he said yesterday. It's just the relationship part that's still a lie . . . a lie I'm maintaining without Dylan asking. I kind of want to punch myself.

She lets out a short, sad laugh. "Good luck with that."

"I don't think I'll need it, but thanks anyway," I snap back.

London purses her lips, seeming to crumble right in front of me. I was not expecting that reaction. Her mom places a hand over her daughter's, frowning, and I get the sense that London's been through a lot more than I'll ever know. "You can go now, Mika. You might not care or understand, but this issue is difficult for my daughter."

I can only muster a nod, because I do feel bad, but then she also called me an "issue." Like my presence in Dylan's life is a problem. That hurts. I sit down at the table with my friends, dazed.

"What was that about?" Shreya asks.

I shake my head. "Let's focus on—"

"No," Olivia says, seeming angry that I interrupted her carefully-planned lunch with my drama. Because I can control where London shows up. "Tell us what your boyfriend's ex had to say."

"He's not my—"

"You have another boyfriend?" Pavan asks out of nowhere. "I swear Shreya mentioned you just broke up with one."

"A few months ago, yeah." I gulp, knowing Shrey and Olivia will tear me to pieces later. There's officially no getting around telling them what happened. "Dylan is . . . I don't know. It's complicated."

Pavan smiles at Rachelle. "Complicated I can understand."

She blushes, and I can tell they're crazy in love. "Sometimes complicated is worth it, though."

"And sometimes it isn't," I say, still completely unsure which category Dylan fits into.

Chapter 24

"Hello, Arlingtons!" Joel struts into our house like he owns the place, and we smile. After the weekend by ourselves with Betty, he is a more than welcome sight. Excessive happiness included. "Did you miss me?"

"Yes," we say in unison.

"It's so good to be appreciated." He comes to Betty, who's currently scowling at her oatmeal. "Hi, Betty! Do you remember me?"

She appraises him, and then recognition hits. "You're the one who took my clothes off!"

Joel looks at us, the smallest hint of wariness under the smile. "So it's gonna be that kind of day, huh?"

"Good luck," Dad says as we head out for work.

My parents wave to me as I unlock my bike from the porch, and then they are off to their research in the bay while I get to go to work and see Dylan for the first time since Cypress Point. Lucky me.

No matter how hard I try to stay calm, my stomach knots the moment AnimalZone is in sight. This is why dating co-workers is a horrible idea. I want to call in sick, but going home would only make me feel bad for wasting Joel's time. And it's not like I can avoid this forever, so I take a deep breath and open the back door. It's quiet as I clock in. My eyes run over the break room, looking for signs of Dylan. There's a black hoodie draped over one chair, and I gulp.

Heading for Aquatics, I tell myself this isn't a big deal. We weren't dating to begin with, and I still don't know if I like him enough to be serious. When I round the corner, there he is scrubbing one of the tanks. Without my asking.

He doesn't notice me, his entire focus on the glass. His brow pinches, and he bites his lip as he tries to get rid of the scummy water line at the top of the tank. It's adorable, and it reminds me how easy it was to be with him at the golf course, how much I liked him. The thought makes me feel like I'm giving in, so I force it down. He won't get off easy just because he's doing what he's supposed to do.

"Make sure the corners are spotless," I say.

He looks up, surprised. Then the smallest smile flits across his face. "Yes, ma'am."

I want to say I'm *not* a "ma'am," but that would mean starting a conversation. I head for the island to check the supplies we keep there. Clean nets, food, bags for purchased fish, live crickets for the reptiles in the next section over. Everything seems to be in perfect order, which means I have nothing to do but wait for customers.

Easy enough, except the silence is weird. It used to be normal, but a month of bickering with Dylan and now the quiet feels heavy. I'm keenly aware of him nearby, though I try my best not to look at him.

156

"Dylan," Clark calls as he rounds the corner. "Order of food just came in. Help me unload."

"Yes, sir." He walks off without so much as a glance my way, and I'm surprised by how much I don't like it.

I locate items for people, clean up gravel a kid spilled, and help Old Lady Miriam with a price check—except the whole time I keep waiting for Dylan to reappear. Then I hate myself for being so stupid. I asked for space, so it shouldn't bother me that he isn't around.

There's a lull in customers, so I fill my time by scribbling goldfish drawings on a notepad. Fish are fun to draw, so flowy and open to interpretation. Too bad Shreya would never approve of a goldfish sand sculpture. She thinks I already do enough fish-related stuff.

"That doesn't look like work," Dylan says.

I jump and spin around, not having heard him coming. "Don't do that!"

He smiles. "But you're so cute when you're surprised."

Turning back around, I hope to hide the blushing. "You still have two tanks left to do. Don't think I forgot."

"I know." He leans next to me, and I can't decide if it's too close or not close enough. "Speaking of tanks, when should I come clean yours?"

I pause mid-drawing, the thought of Dylan in my house too much. "You don't have to do that."

"That was the deal. And you made good on your end, so it's the least I can do for putting you through that." He sighs, and with it I can feel the words he bites back. "I promise I won't bother you, so when?"

I retrace the outline of one goldfish over and over, unable to figure out what I want. But a deal is a deal. "Thursday. After my shift."

"Works for me. Uncle Clark should be fine with it, since I'll still be working." He grabs the notepad and stuffs it in his pocket. "You're setting a horrible example wasting time like this. I'll have to keep it."

I glare at him as he goes back to cleaning tanks, but force myself to say nothing. He's trying to get a reaction, like he'll take fighting with me if he can't get affection. It'll annoy him more if I remain silent. I should still be mad at him, though it doesn't feel like I am.

After my shift is over, I practically run to clock out, happy to get away from my conflicting feelings. I need *saag* and Shrey and some *Princess Bride* like hardcore. But when I go to unlock my bike, I notice something in the basket. Something with a bow tied around it. I grab the note tucked under the ribbon and read it.

I know it's not as nice as the sweater, but it made me think of you. —Dylan

Picking up the box, I open the lid to find a teal blue shirt with a little cartoon goldfish on the front. Under the fish it says: *Stupid? I'm not the pet who pees on your bed.* At which point my heart threatens to melt.

The t-shirt might not cost three hundred dollars, but I love it more because it fits me. How can he already know exactly what I like? Punk.

* * *

It's weird to see the Shades of Bombay kitchen minus Pavan. Shreya's other two brothers seem more frantic as they try to fill orders. Their father is livid with them, yelling stuff I'm glad I don't understand. I never noticed before, but I think Pavan was the chill one who evened out the tempers around him.

Shrey cringes as she comes over with my *saag* when their other waiter clocks in. "Sorry for the crazy. Dad won't hire a new cook, but keeping up is impossible without . . ."

Knowing she can't say his name, I nod. "Thanks for this. Work was rough."

"Am I allowed to ask why?" She glares at me, and I feel guilty that I still haven't told them what happened on Saturday.

I sigh. Time to give in. "Because I don't know what to do with Dylan."

As I launch into the story, it reminds me just how wonderful and horrible that day was. Shrey lights up when I tell her Dylan wants us to be more, but by the time I get to the five million dollars she looks as confused as I feel.

She puts her hand to her mouth, thinking. I continue to stuff my face. She takes a piece of *naan* and nibbles on it. "How do you spend that much money in one night?"

"I know!" I let out a frustrated grunt. "But more importantly, what kind of person thinks that's okay? His parents are freaking loaded, but he had to have understood how much money that was, right?"

She nods. "How could you not?"

I lean back in my chair, wishing I could stay here instead of having to watch Betty. "It's not the money that bothers me anymore—it's the fact that he *knew* what he was doing. He

159

wasted that money *on purpose*. It wasn't like he got carried away. How could I be with someone who'd do that?"

"*Did* that," Shreya corrects. "You think he'd still make the same choice if he could do it over?"

"I don't know . . ." I want to point out he's already spent his whole paycheck like it was nothing. Except he spent it on me, so I don't know how to feel about it. "I'm in way over my head here, Shrey."

She puts her hand on mine. "You should probably let him explain."

"Yeah." I get up, my stomach twisting from all the food. "But I still need to think about it."

"Do you?" Her look is skeptical. "Or are you afraid of what this could be?"

I narrow my eyes. "Don't get all deep on me."

She laughs. "We're on for Saturday, right?"

"As you wish."

I pedal home, trying my best to focus on anything but Dylan. The ocean breeze, the gulls squawking, the warm summer sun. By the time I get home, I'm ready to put my energy into taking care of Betty—I need to make up for what I said to her—instead of worrying about my own problems. At least until I open the door and hear her screaming like a crazed animal.

Chapter 25

"You're going to hell and you'll burn forever!" Betty screams over and over. I almost want to go back to Shades of Bombay, but I can't leave Joel hanging. He probably has another person to care for in the afternoons, and he shouldn't have to deal with more of this than he has to.

"Now, Betty. That's not a very nice thing to say to someone." I have to hand it to Joel, he sounds completely unfazed by the outburst.

"I don't care! You're going to hell!"

I reluctantly round the corner. Joel smiles like this is totally normal and gives me a hug. "She's been an *angry* one today. I tried to calm her down, but she finally caught on to my orientation."

I wince. "I'm so sorry."

He waves it off. "Patients lose social rules quickly. Women who used to be prim and proper start swearing like sailors. Those who had few reservations to begin with let it all hang out, you know?"

"Oh, yes, I know. How do you keep it from bothering you?"

He shrugs. "Mostly I feel sorry for them."

Finally, Betty notices I'm in the room. Her eyes go wide and she pulls at my arm. "Get away from him, Mika!"

I pull back. "Why?"

"Because!" She points accusingly. "He's . . . he's a homo-sapien!"

Joel and I bust up laughing, to the point that I have to lean on the wall to keep from falling over. Joel wipes at tears as he continues to giggle. Betty's indignant glare only makes it more priceless.

"I hate to break it to you," I say. "But we're *all* homo-sapiens, Betty."

Her jaw drops. "I am *not*!"

"You are. Homo-sapien means human."

She frowns, thinking about it for a second. "That's really what it means?"

I nod.

"Oh." She glances at Joel, seeming apologetic, but then goes to the couch to watch her usual afternoon blitz of talk shows. I stare at her in wonder—she can go from a moment of complete crazy to totally normal in seconds. Every day with her is like sticking a quarter in a slot machine. Sometimes you hit the jackpot, others you lose money.

Joel is still laughing. "Can't wait to tell that one at the dinner table."

I snort. "Me, too."

He sighs, for once showing some of his fatigue. "She'll probably be a beast for the rest of the day, maybe longer than that. From nostalgia last week to cranky this week, it seems."

"I think I prefer nostalgia." At least that way I could learn about her past. Now that I've decided to be better to her,

162

I'd like to understand why she is the way she is before she forgets everything.

"Yes, me too. At least when they're happy memories."

"Can I ask you something?"

He raises his eyebrows. "Of course."

I hesitate because it will show how my attitude has changed, but I'm curious. "It just seems like this job would be hard to do all the time, watching people go through this over and over again. Why do you do it?"

"So you're starting to get it." He smiles at Betty, a surprising amount of love in his gaze. "For people who don't see Alzheimer's up close, it's easy to forget about. The patients forget, so people forget them, right?"

"That's . . . sad."

"It is." Joel's face changes then, and it's the first time I've seen a hint of sorrow there. "But when you watch someone you love go through it—you never forget. I watched my grandmother suffer from it for eight years, and now my mother has been diagnosed with early onset. It could be me one day, too. I guess it's my own little crusade to bring some joy to all the sadness."

I smile, feeling bad for giving him a hard time. "Well, I'm glad you're here. Thanks for answering my question."

"Anytime, sweetie." Joel gathers his things, briefs me on what Betty ate, and then he's off.

Betty wastes no time living up to Joel's warnings—she doesn't like *anything* today. She doesn't like the TV shows or the sound of the aquariums or the entire contents of both our fridge and pantry. As patient as I try to be, she doesn't seem to notice or care. When she throws the remote at me, I just about lose it.

"Okay, no more TV," I say.

She folds her arms. "Everyone is mean to me. You shouldn't be mean to sick people."

I clench my jaw, trying to remain calm. I promised I would be better at this, and the over-achiever in me will not fail. "If you don't like anything on the TV, let's watch a movie, okay?"

Betty doesn't speak, but her posture relaxes the littlest bit.

I take the opening and head for our movie drawer. "I have the best movie—you'll love it."

"What's it about?" Her voice has softened, and I pray this will turn the day around because cranky Betty is way more exhausting than nostalgic Betty.

"You'll see." I put in *The Princess Bride*, figuring it's better not to give her a summary. She'd probably complain that she doesn't like those kinds of movies and it'd be over before it even began.

Betty looks as unconvinced as the boy in the opening scene, but says nothing. I hope this is a good sign. She seems excited when Westley and Buttercup fall in love. That's when I realize I made a critical error in choosing this movie. And sure enough, her face turns sour when Westley leaves.

"I don't like him. He doesn't really love her," Betty says. "He left her, and then he's stupid enough to get killed."

"But he left to earn money so they could get married," I point out.

She shakes her head. "If he really loved her—if she really loved him—would the money have mattered? They could

164

have gotten married without money. All you need is a marriage license and a priest, for Pete's sake. They're stupid."

I open my mouth to argue, but nothing comes. Betty is right, after all. "You get hung up on abandonment, don't you?"

"All the Arlington women are cursed. Men always leave us—my mother, my grandmother, even perfect beautiful Gracie couldn't escape. You won't either." Her expression is grim, but I try not to let it affect me.

"I don't believe in curses, and my mom and dad are still together."

She gives me a side-glance. "You've never had a boy leave you before?"

I shift in my seat, uncomfortable with the truth. "No."

She looks surprised. "Really?"

"Really." I always make sure to leave first, to not get so attached that separating will hurt. Because deep down, getting left behind by someone I care about is the thing I fear most. I've always made sure the guys I'm with are completely safe, the kind that wouldn't break up with me. Maybe I didn't love them, but I liked them and knew I'd be the one to leave if I wanted.

Dylan isn't like that—he's a risk. He doesn't have any history of commitment. He's here indefinitely, meaning there's no easy escape route. And worst of all, I could see myself falling for him.

"Just wait until you find someone you really love. When he leaves . . ." She sighs, her pain palpable. "You'll know the curse is real."

I don't answer, scared to reveal in any way that she might have gotten to me. Cursed. That's a bunch of crap. It's an

165

excuse she uses so she doesn't have to take responsibility for separations. She's playing the victim. I'm nothing like her . . . but then why can't I stop my heart from racing?

Chapter 26

By the time Thursday rolls around, I regret the tank-cleaning agreement. Dylan doesn't look like he's about to get punished—he's *excited*. I can feel it, no matter how hard he tries to hide his smile. There's a bounce in his step as he goes from tank to tank with his brush. He's actually really good at cleaning when he takes it seriously.

"My uncle let me borrow his bike," Dylan says as he pours the clean water into the tank. "He said I could ride home with you."

"Great," I grumble, scrubbing my own tank faster.

He deflates. "Is it really that bad?"

"I don't know." And it's the truth. I can't figure out what's real when it comes to what I think of Dylan. Sometimes I think I hate him, and I'm getting pulled in by the chemistry. Other times I'm crazy about him, and I want to be his girlfriend like I played at Cypress Point.

"That's okay." His voice is soft. "I know enough for both of us."

"Not how it works." I put away the cleaning tools, antsy to get out of here. "I usually go out to lunch before I go home. Is that okay?"

His eyes light up. "Yeah, I have a little money left."

"You're not paying for me." I pull off my apron and stuff it onto the island's shelf.

"How'd you know I was planning that?"

I shrug. "C'mon."

There's no way I'm taking him to Shades of Bombay—Shrey would enjoy that too much—so I pedal my way to Su Casa. Dylan is right behind me, which I'm not a fan of because I know he's checking out my butt. I can feel it.

"Is this place any good?" Dylan asks as we go inside. He looks uncomfortable, his eyes running over the rough interior.

"Best in the area." I shove him because people are starting to stare at the skittish gringo. "Stop acting like such a rich boy."

I order two fish tacos, and Dylan gets three beef ones. As he takes the first bite, all the apprehension fades. "Damn, that's amazing."

"Told you." The fried fish crunches perfectly when I take my first bite, the burst of cilantro and lime are so satisfying, the fresh corn tortilla comforting, and the salsa's heat tops it off. "It's sad you've lived here for so long and never eaten at this place."

He swallows before he talks. "One taco, and I'm seriously regretting it."

I try not to, but I smile anyway.

He nods at my food. "With how much you love fish, I didn't think you'd eat them for lunch."

"I can't help that other people kill them, but I can honor the sacrifice by making sure they don't go to waste." I grab a napkin to wipe my mouth, too aware of him watching me eat.

168

"Besides, I'm half Japanese—my mom snacks on dried squid for crying out loud. Loving seafood is in my blood."

He laughs. "So she's actually from Japan? I didn't know that."

"Yup. My dad went there for an internship in college and stayed longer to be with her. When they both got into Stanford for their doctorates, they moved back." Why I'm telling him this, I don't know. But it's nice to talk with him without fighting. "What about your parents? How'd they meet?"

"High school sweethearts."

I raise an eyebrow. "Seriously?"

He nods, unwrapping another taco. "Picture every cliché possible, and you'll be pretty close to their reality."

"Quarterback and head cheerleader?"

"Yup. Valedictorian and Salutatorian, too. Went to Yale together. Got married. Had a son. That's kind of where it went wrong for them, though." His eyes get sad, and I restrain myself from putting my hand on his. "Anyway, I should probably stop there. Too close to information I'm not allowed to give you."

"Right." I keep eating, though I kind of want to ask him and get it over with. Except once he tells me there's no going back. And I'm still scared to take that step.

The closer we get to my house, the more nervous I become. By the time we reach my front yard, my heart feels like it's about to explode. I thought I didn't want to explain my family problems to Dylan, it seemed like the easier option. But then I grab his arm to stop him before we get to the door.

He looks at me, confused. "What's wrong?"

I gulp. "Just so you know, my grandma . . . she has Alzheimer's. I watch her after work until my parents get home. She can be unpredictable, so I don't know how she'll react to you. It could be bad."

I can almost see the dots connecting as he nods. "That explains a lot."

"Yeah . . . It's been difficult having her around."

"How long has she been here?"

"She showed up the same day you did—it was the first time I ever met her. She and my dad had a falling out when he got engaged to my mom." I look at the ground, unsure if I want him to understand me this much. "She's . . . kind of racist and rude and she's been a total pill this week. So you've been warned."

There's a pause, and I can feel Dylan looking at me though I focus on my bike. "How can someone be *kind of* racist? It's an all or nothing category, isn't it?"

"I don't know . . ." I might have agreed before, but now that I've dealt with Betty the lines are blurring. "There's a big difference between someone who's knowingly racist, someone who is just ignorant, and those who understand. It's grayer than you might think."

"I guess." He reaches his hand out to where mine rests on my bike handle. When his fingers touch my skin, my whole body tingles. "So you've been dealing with this the whole time we've known each other? You never thought to say, 'Hey, Dylan, my sick grandmother is making my life hell, please don't add to it'?"

"That never came to mind, no." I stare at his hand on mine, telling myself to move my arm. It's not listening.

He lets out a short laugh. "Of course not. It was easier to take it out on me."

My head snaps up, my eyes meeting his. "That's not—!"

"I'm relieved, actually." He pulls back, his smile smug. "Here I was starting to think you were perfect."

I clench my jaw, forcing myself not to argue with him. He's more right than I want him to be. I probably have taken out a lot of my anger over Betty and losing the internship on him. "Let's get this over with."

We lock our bikes to the porch, and I open the front door. At least there's no screaming this time, but I can still hear Betty's cranky tone coming from the kitchen. Joel's at the table trying to get her to eat lunch.

"You're missing out, Betty." He bites into his sandwich. "Mmm, that is some quality grilled cheese. I even cut it in a heart just for you."

"I don't like hearts," she grumbles.

"Then you better eat it so you don't have to look at—" Joel sees us and smiles wide. "Mika's home! And look, she brought a *very* handsome friend with her."

Betty appraises Dylan with a sneer. "He *is* handsome."

I hate that I'm blushing. "This is Dylan. He'll be cleaning the aquariums today. Watch him a second while I get out of my work clothes?"

"Sure thing, sweetie," Joel says.

I lock my door and change as fast as I can. It's tempting to wear the goldfish shirt he bought me, but I can't bring myself to do it. Ending up in jeans and a purple tee, I rush back to the kitchen in hopes that nothing disastrous happened while I

171

was gone. To my surprise, Betty is happily eating her sandwich while Joel laughs hysterically.

"Mika, you'll have to bring Dylan home every day," he says. "He said he liked grilled cheese, and now Betty seems very hungry. I think she might have a crush on him."

"I do not!" Betty says, though she looks embarrassed. She totally likes him. Of course she does—everyone I know seems to.

"I'll be here each week to clean the tanks." Dylan looks at me. "Maybe more. It depends."

"I see . . ." Joel stands, seeming to understand his implication. "Good luck with that. See you later, Mika."

I wave to him as he goes, and then I get down to business. "I'll start you on the freshwater tanks first, since they're easier. C'mon, the stuff's in the laundry room."

We keep two fifty-five-gallon barrels of water at all times, one fresh and the other salt. I show Dylan the water pump, siphons, heaters, filters, scrubbers, etc. He seems overwhelmed.

"You're hardcore," he says. "Do your parents make you do all this?"

I roll my eyes. "They don't *make* me. I want to. It's good practice—the second I was old enough to do it on my own I gladly volunteered."

"I've never met someone who actually wants to be like their parents," he says as we push the fresh water out of the laundry room. We rigged the barrels with wheels a long time ago to make it easier.

"Now you have. Betty, my room." I motion for her to follow us, and she doesn't complain. She seems happy to stare at Dylan non-stop. I'm trying not to be creeped out by it.

172

My heart speeds up as he takes in my room. There's not much I can read in his expression except surprise. "That is a lot of goldfish for one person."

"Yup." I show him how much water to drain from each tank, then hand over the empty buckets. "You're pretty familiar with this by now, so get to it. Then you can do the koi pond and the saltwater tanks."

He nods. "This is gonna take hours, isn't it?"

"Probably."

He goes to the tank nearest my bed, where the smallest goldfish swim in a school. Putting his finger to the glass, he says, "Hey, there's the one you bought my first day at work. What'd you name it?"

I freeze. I can't tell him I named it after him. "I didn't. He doesn't have a name."

Dylan gives me a suspicious look. "But you said you named all your fish."

"When did I say that?"

"The day that fish fanatic came in and you said you'd let him have one of yours," he says without skipping a beat.

"You remember that?"

He looks at his feet. "I remember everything about every day I've known you."

The more he says things like that, the easier it is to believe he's not as big of a risk as I think. Even though I've hardly given him any hint that I might be interested, he's made his feelings crystal clear.

"I named him Dill," I blurt out before I can think better of it.

173

A huge smile breaks out on his face. "Did you seriously name your fish after me?"

"Get to work." I sit at my desk and open my laptop, beyond flustered. That was too close to admitting how I feel about him. Too scary.

"So you do think about me sometimes," he says. I don't turn around. "Gotta admit it's nice to know, what with how much I—"

"You should stay for dinner," Betty says.

"No." I check Facebook, but there's nothing entertaining. My email is empty except for spam. I try to look busy, even if I can't stop thinking about the fact that Dylan is in my room, seeing my pictures and makeup and where I sleep. Betty is being good at least. She compliments him on how well he cleans the tanks until she drifts to sleep on my bed.

It's not until she's snoring that Dylan says, "I like your room. It's really you."

"Uh, thanks?" I turn away from my computer, finding him staring at one of my corkboards full of pictures. Of my parents, friends, sand sculptures. He's smiling, but it seems sad somehow.

He points to a picture. "Where's this?"

I have to get up and come close to see what he's talking about. "Oh, that's my grandparents' house in Japan. My mom took me there when I was two—I don't remember a thing. Sucks."

"If I ever put up pictures or posters in my room, left clothes on my floor, whatever, they'd be gone within the day."

I give him a confused look.

"Maids." He sighs. "My mom doesn't like stuff disrupting the design of the rooms in our house. She's super Type A, a little OCD."

I nod, though I'm stuck on one word. "Maids? Plural?"

"And a chef, a pool guy, gardeners. My dad even had a butler for a while because he thought it might be cool. He decided he didn't like being fussed over, though. Now he just has a personal assistant."

"Weird."

"It is, isn't it? I like my room at my uncle's. If I leave something on the floor, it stays there. If I put up a picture, no one takes it down. Makes it feel like my space, not a museum." He pulls the pin out of one picture, taking it in his hand. Olivia took it of me while I was at the beach sculpting. "Can I have this?"

I watch him intently, and he watches me back. He might not be asking directly how I feel about him or what I've decided, but my answer to this question will give him a big clue. I take a deep breath. "Yes."

"Really?" His voice is full of hope.

"Yeah, really." I bite my lip, scared to say it, and yet I can't ignore my feelings anymore. Whether it's a good idea or not, I like him. So much. Most girls probably love feeling this way, but I hate it. I feel vulnerable, weak, like I have something to lose. But right now, as he holds a simple picture of me like it's worth a million dollars, I can't help thinking I might have something to gain, too. "I think you should—"

My phone rings. I almost consider letting it go, but the sound wakes Betty up and that means the moment is lost. I look at the screen, trying not to be angry at whoever it is. "What's up, Olivia?"

"Mika, oh my gosh, I have something to tell you."

"It doesn't sound like good news." I sigh, sitting on the edge of my bed. Dylan slips my picture into his pocket and picks up two buckets of dirty water, heading to the hall.

"That chick from Bubba Gump's, London?"

My eyes go wide. "What about her?"

"She was here at the spa! With her mom. They were talking about you, and not in a nice way."

Chapter 27

My stomach turns at the thought of all the things London might say behind my back, especially with how upset she seemed on Sunday. "Olivia, I don't think I want to know."

"What?" There's clattering in the background, and I imagine she's in the storage room at the spa where they keep the bottles of lotion and fancy oils. "Come on! This is serious information. I had to restrain myself from beating the crap out of her and her stupid mom."

"Is something wrong?" Betty sits up, rubbing her eyes.

I shake my head. "Fine. Tell me."

"Thank you! They were getting facials when I heard your name, so I hung around to see what they'd say. London whined about how Dylan obviously likes you, and she didn't know what to do because he's never liked anyone enough to date them."

"That's nothing new," I say, mad that I have to hear about what an "issue" I am yet again.

"I know, but then her mom told her not to worry about it. She said Dylan's going through a phase—that he thinks he wants to be in charge of his life but will realize the money is better. She said the only reason he's interested in you is because you're exotic and eventually he'll get bored. When he does, he'll come back home and realize London is the right girl for him."

I feel like curling up in a ball the more she talks. Olivia tells me they said I'm not that pretty and too flat and my clothes are cheap. Their words shouldn't bother me—London is jealous—but at the same time this conversation is all my fears rolled into one. "I'm so sick of people calling me exotic. What the hell does that mean, anyway?"

"They're saying you're Asian without saying you're Asian. Pretty much they are thinking racist thoughts but not saying them out loud," she says. "If they order drinks, I'm spitting in them."

I squeeze my eyes shut, hoping that will stop the tears. "Go for it."

"Believe me, I will." There's a pause. "Are you okay? Maybe I shouldn't have told you. I can feel you worrying from here."

I let out a long sigh. "I'm not feeling great."

"Aw, just look at it this way—they're scared because he actually does care about you a lot. That's good, isn't it? Shrey told me about your date . . . I think you like him a lot more than you're letting on."

"See you tomorrow, okay? I need to watch Betty."

She gives me a frustrated sigh. "Fine. Call me, okay?"

"Yeah." I hang up, my heart a mishmash of ugly emotions. I tell myself not to believe what London's mom said, but it repeats over and over in my head. What if Dylan does leave? Why *does* he like me?

"Who's calling you exotic?" Dylan's voice comes from behind, and I turn to find him leaning on the doorjamb.

"Spying on me, huh?" I stand up, force myself to brush off Olivia's news. "Since you're done in here, I'll show you how to do the koi pond. C'mon, Betty, let's go outside and help Dylan."

She gives me a knowing look. "If you say so."

I show him how to scrub off the excess algae and clean the filter, then comes the water replacement. Betty sits on the porch, watching us and complimenting Dylan more. I keep pointing out spots he missed. He goes back to them without complaint, but eyes me with what I think is worry. "You never answered my question."

"Because you don't need to know." I fold my arms, staring at the pond. "You missed over there."

He moves the long scrubber to the right spot. "I have a feeling it has something to do with me, though, because you were nice and now you're prickly again. The only thing that happened in between was that phone call."

"It's just . . ." I glance over my shoulder, and sure enough Betty is looking on intently, as if we're more interesting than a TV drama. "Can't really talk about it right now, okay? We have an audience."

"When *can* we talk about it, then?"

I chew on the inside of my lip, thinking. I can't stand to wait any longer, like what Olivia relayed pushed me over a cliff. London can't have him. Not ever. Dylan's knowing smile and thoughtful conversations and perfect gifts are mine. "Can you meet me somewhere after my parents get home?"

"Anywhere."

179

"The beach where Shrey and I made the dragon, then. I'll try to get there by seven."

He smiles. "You mean Lovers Point?"

I glare at him. "Time for saltwater tanks."

"As you wish." The words give me goose bumps.

After Dylan leaves, time slows to a crawl. I keep looking at the clock, wondering why it's not six yet. It should be. Betty flips through channels, frowning at everything. I put on *The Princess Bride* again—she always ends up liking it if she can get past the part where Westley first dies.

Finally, my parents show up. I tell them I'm going to the beach, but can't bring myself to mention that Dylan will be there. Maybe if things . . . I'll think about it later. Right now I need to go. I need to see him. I can't pedal fast enough—there are too many lights and cars and tourists in my way. When I get to the beach, there are plenty of people soaking in the pleasant evening sun.

Scanning the shoreline as I walk down the cliff steps, I spot him sitting at the water's edge. He's changed into different clothes, shorts and a royal blue shirt. He watches the water, his face set in a serious expression. I wonder what he's thinking about, if he's as antsy as I am. Then he turns, and he finds me immediately.

When he smiles, all I can think is that I need him and he is mine and no one else can have him. How I could ever think differently, I don't know.

"Hey," he says as I sit next to him.

"Hey." I want to touch him, to give in without any explanation at all. That's how I know I'm ready to hear the whole story—it

180

won't change how I feel about him. He's not that person anymore. I'm sure of it. "So are you gonna tell me?"

"If you want me to," he says tentatively.

"I do."

He gulps. "Okay, here goes nothing. It all began when I started doing well in the Junior PGA tournaments—a lot of coaches were saying I had a real chance at going pro. There were even pro golfers offering to teach me, but my dad had other plans. He didn't want me to be a pro. He wanted me to go to college and take over his investment firm.

"I never wanted to, and for a while I kept going to my tournaments and figured he'd drop it. But then I started getting calls telling me I wasn't allowed to play. They don't just un-invite people, by the way. The Junior PGA doesn't have any score requirements to participate."

My brow furrows. "You mean . . . did your dad tell them to stop letting you play?"

"More like *paid* them to stop me from playing. I was pissed, but he didn't care. He said I could play all the golf I wanted for fun, but no way would I be professional. I was his heir—according to him my only choice was the company.

"So I started doing stupid stuff to get back at him. He couldn't make me go to college if I failed my classes. He couldn't stop me from being labeled a bad boy no one wanted their daughters around. If I ruined my chances in high school, then I could do what I wanted."

"That's horrible logic," I say.

He smirks. "I know. Looking back, it all seems stupid, but here's the worst thing: it didn't stop him. I never did an

181

assignment, never turned in my papers, failed tests, and yet somehow I would always end up with a passing grade in all my classes. I never even applied for college, but I still got an acceptance letter from Yale."

That's when my jaw drops.

"He paid everyone off. To me, it was his way of saying he didn't care what I wanted to do. He was going to *make* me do what he wanted. The Yale thing . . . that's when I cracked. So, yeah, I took a company credit card and maxed it. If there's one thing my dad cares about, it's money. Losing that much, I finally pissed him off enough for him to realize I wouldn't go along with his plans."

"That's when he kicked you out?" I ask.

Dylan shakes his head. "He was going to force me into the military, said I needed to learn respect. He threatened to press charges for the party I threw, since there were drugs and I'd technically stolen his card. So it was prison or military, but then my uncle stepped in and here I am."

I stare at the ocean, taking in the information. It makes sense. I still don't think it was right, but I get how someone like Dylan could crumble under such expectations. He doesn't seem like the kind of guy who'd survive in a suit and tie, stuck in an office. Maybe he had everything, but the price was too steep.

"So do you hate me now?" he asks, which is when I realize I haven't said anything for a while.

"No. It's just . . . sad. Maybe I want to do what my parents do, but they wouldn't get mad if I chose something else."

"You're lucky. Not everyone has such understanding parents."

I nod. Though they expect a lot from me in their own way, they are pretty understanding. "I have one more question."

"Okay."

It sounds so stupid in my head, and yet I have to know. "Why do you like me?"

"What?"

I wrap my arms around my knees. "I don't understand why you would. First we fought a lot, and then it started to change. Sometimes I wonder if maybe I'm some new toy to play with."

"Mika, in all honesty, you're the first girl I *haven't* seen that way. It kinda freaks me out, actually." He comes a little closer. "Fighting or not, everything hurts less when I'm with you."

My heart, how it flutters. "When did it happen?"

"It started when you bought that fish."

I look at him, surprised. "The first day we met? When you flipped me off and yelled at me?"

He winces. "I'm trying to forget that part. But yeah, when you said everyone deserves a real home, it hit me. I've had a lot of things, but I've never had that. You always say things that make me think, and you don't pander to me. I really like that. You're also hot, but that's not very romantic, is it?"

I smile. "Not really, but it's nice to hear anyway. You're not so bad looking either."

"Oh yeah?" He raises an eyebrow. "Does that mean I can kiss you now?"

"Hmm, yes." I grab his arm and pull him close. When my lips meet his, I'm glad we're in a public place because, wow, he's a good kisser. I might be tempted to do a lot more if there weren't people around.

He pulls away first and runs a hand through his hair. "Damn. Where'd you learn to do that?"

"Shh." I tug him back to me, buzzing from the sensation of his lips on mine. He puts his hand on the back of my neck, and I wrap my arms around him. Who cares how many people are out here? I'm kissing him all night.

After a while I realize someone is calling my name. It's annoying. I'm busy. But it's getting louder, and I finally look up. My eyes go wide as I take in Olivia and Shrey standing maybe ten feet away, hands on hips.

Chapter 28

There's a long moment before anyone talks. Dylan and I stand as they close the remaining distance. What am I supposed to say? Shreya and Olivia have these smug grins, and somehow I know they're thinking, "I told you so." I hate when they're right, but, well, I'd like to get back to kissing Dylan.

"Finally," Shreya blurts out.

"Seriously!" Olivia blatantly checks out Dylan, and then looks back to me. "He's even better looking in person. How did you keep your hands off *that*?"

Dylan laughs like this is the funniest statement he's ever heard. "Your friends are awesome. Who's the tall one?"

"Olivia," I grumble.

"Nice to meet you." He goes to shake her hand. "You were the one on vacation in Tahiti?"

She nods, seeming star struck by him.

I grab his hand just to make sure she doesn't get any ideas. Not that she would, but I can't escape this need to make sure everyone knows Dylan is mine. Especially now that I've decided to go all in. "How'd you know she was in Tahiti?"

Shreya raises her hand. "Might have mentioned it on the phone."

Olivia waves her hand. "That doesn't matter right now. We have a problem—a big problem."

I finally realize that they tracked me down for a reason. I don't have my phone . . . they must have asked my parents where I was, which means this could be pretty serious. "What?"

Shreya shrinks. "I slipped up."

"Huh?" Then it clicks. "Wait, you mean about Pavan?"

She nods. "I left my phone in the kitchen while I was serving, and he called from Rachelle's number. My mom answered it even though it was just numbers, and she flipped. But that's not the worst part . . ."

Shreya's face cracks as she folds into herself. Without a second thought, I put my arms around her shoulders. Olivia finishes the story for her. "Shrey tried to lie and say she always hangs up, but she said she hadn't talked to Pavan *or* Rachelle. Her parents never asked what his fiancée's name was, so they knew she'd seen him again. They kicked her out."

"Oh, Shrey, I'm sorry I didn't have my phone." I hug her tight.

"I still can't believe they actually kicked me out. What am I gonna do about school? Why does it have to be like this?" She sniffles into my shoulder.

"I don't know, but we'll figure it out." I look to Dylan, who seems slightly uncomfortable with the turn of events. "I have to go."

He nods, his smile sad. "Of course. Take care of Shreya."

Shreya pulls away from me, seeming embarrassed about crying in front of him. "Sorry for ruining your date."

He shakes his head. "Mika was out of control anyway. It was good you interrupted."

"Hey!" I punch his shoulder.

He grabs my arm, pulling me in for a quick kiss. "What were you saying?"

"Uh . . ." Why can't I remember? His lips should not be able to do that to me. "Don't do that!"

He laughs. "See you later."

As he walks off, I try to focus on Shrey and Olivia, but my eyes drift to Dylan constantly. He keeps looking back at me, and it makes everything real.

"Mika!" Olivia snaps her fingers in my face. "Jeez, is he really that good a kisser?"

I shake it off. "Yes, but this is more important. I'm here. I swear. Do you need a place to stay, Shrey? My house is yours, you know that. My parents would totally understand."

She bites her lip. "But you already have Betty to deal with . . ."

"You're not someone 'to deal with'—you're my friend! And you don't have Alzheimer's last I checked."

Olivia sighs. "I wish I could put you up, Shrey, but our apartment is so small. I don't think my mom would go for it. She's touchy about her personal space, especially after having to massage people all day."

"C'mon, my house. You can sleep with me!" I say, laughing. "My bed's big enough. I'm pretty sure Dylan won't mind."

Shreya tries not to smile. "I feel like I'm imposing. Maybe I should stay with Pavan and Rachelle."

I frown. "Where's he living now?"

"Salinas. At Rachelle's place."

"Salinas!?" I shake my head. "No. That's like thirty minutes away, and you don't have a car. We'd never see each other. Inconceivable!"

Olivia purses her lips, eyeing Shreya thoughtfully. "I can see why you'd want to be with family, but we'd really miss you if you moved."

"I can't just stay at Mika's house forever, though!" She wraps her arms around herself. "I still have a year of high school left, and now I don't have a job. Maybe your family would let me stay a few weeks, but almost a whole year?"

I hate that she's right. My parents are nice, but I still don't know how long they'd be able to handle such a full house. "We don't have to plan your whole future right now. It just happened, and maybe they will change their—"

"They won't!" Shreya stomps her foot. "Stop saying that. You don't get it. Not every family is accepting like yours! My parents told me I was dead. To never come back." She bursts into tears.

This time Olivia gives the hug. She looks at me, seeming upset with the way I'm handling this. But I don't know how else to deal with it. Shreya's right—I *don't* understand. I can't fathom why marrying a sweet, white girl is such a huge problem. My friend shouldn't have to deal with this. No one should. I feel like I'm living in a different century.

"There's only one thing to do," I say.

"W-what?" Shrey says through her sobs.

"Buy a butt load of ice cream and watch movies all night, duh." I hook my arm with hers, and Olivia does the same on the other side. "There are no rules saying we have to handle this like adults."

"First we raid her room," Olivia says, seeming to have brushed off whatever was bothering her. "While we're at the not-being-responsible thing."

"Good idea!" I laugh, trying to lighten up an impossibly heavy situation. "Your parents are at the restaurant anyway. It's like breaking and entering, but not. We can feel deviant without actually doing something illegal!"

Olivia nods. "That's the best kind of crime."

Shreya snorts through her tears. "You guys are so stupid. I love you."

"Of course you do." I make an exaggerated seductive face, and by her laugh I know I must look ridiculous. But at least she's smiling. The rest we'll have to figure out later.

Chapter 29

The next morning, Betty glares at Shreya from across the table. Shrey tries to ignore it, but I can tell it bugs her. Though I'm trying to be nicer to Betty, it's hard to get used to her increasing lack of manners. Trying to laugh it off like Joel is better than being mad all the time.

"Mom, eat your oatmeal," Dad says.

She jumps out of her death glare. "Oh. But who is that strange girl?"

He sighs. She's asked this four times since last night, and it seems like his patience with her is gone. "Shreya is Mika's friend. She's staying with us because her parents have the same problem you had with Yumi—so they kicked her out."

"I didn't kick you out!" Betty says indignantly. "You left all on your own."

"After you told me you'd never see me again unless I broke up with 'that Japanese girl,' though you used a bad word. I didn't break up with her, and so you stopped talking to me. Except when you needed money, of course."

"Who else could I call? Jenny still lives off me, for crying out loud." Betty frowns. "It's just not right, mixing."

190

I roll my eyes, the sting of her words gone now that I know she's a broken record. "Here we go again."

Dad pinches the bridge of his nose. "I can't wait for Joel to show up."

"Sorry, Shreya," Mom says, cringing. "I'm afraid our family issues are hard to hide lately."

"Don't worry about it," Shreya says. "It's oddly comforting."

Mom smiles at her, and we continue eating breakfast in pleasant silence. Last night we worked out that Shreya could stay at least through the end of the summer. My parents seemed wary about committing to more, but I still hope things will miraculously work out before we have to decide what happens then.

"Mom," Dad repeats, his voice sharp. "Eat your oatmeal."

"Okay! I'm not a child." Betty takes a bite and makes the sourest face. "It's cold. And bland."

He gets up and throws Betty's bowl back in the microwave forcefully. Mom sips at her orange juice, looking embarrassed. "Shreya, what are you doing today? Should I tell Joel you'll be here?"

"Oh, umm . . ." She looks down, the air suddenly uncomfortable. "No. I think I should look for a job. I'll come back when Mika does."

My mom nods. "Sounds like a good idea, but you can stay here if you want to. We just need to let Joel know. He's wonderful. You'll like him."

"He's super happy," I say. "But it works for him."

"I don't want him to help me shower," Betty grumbles.

Shrey raises an eyebrow. "That's okay. If I get out I think I'll feel better."

"I think so, too." I get up and put my cereal bowl in the sink. "You ready to go?"

Mom tilts her head. "So early?"

I shrug.

"To see Dylan?" Shreya asks.

"Dylan?" Mom's eyebrows pop up, and she stares me down. "The boy you went to Cypress Point with?"

"Shrey!" I bite my tongue, knowing I've already given myself away. May as well get it over with. "Okay, we're dating. Now you *all* know. Happy?"

Shreya winces. "Sorry."

I slip my messenger bag over my head. "It's fine. I was gonna tell them anyway, after last night."

"Please tell me that doesn't mean what I think it means," Dad says.

"No. Gosh, Dad, I haven't known him *that* long." I feel the need to bolt, since I don't want to hear what Betty has to say about this. We've already been to "no mixing" territory enough for one day. "Shrey, you ready?"

"Yes." She follows me outside, and as we enter our lock combinations, she says, "I messed that up, didn't I?"

"No." I purse my lips. "I don't care that my parents know, but Betty . . ."

"Ah." She guides her bike down the porch stairs. "She's not any better than my parents. I'm starting to get why Pavan never told them—it wouldn't have mattered if he told them when he started dating Rachelle as opposed to marrying her."

"Maybe not. Who knows?" We pedal slowly down the road. "So where're you gonna look?"

She sighs. "Probably some restaurants. I do have three years' serving experience. That's a lot for our age."

"It is. You're really good at it."

Her smile is sad. "It'll be weird to work at a different place, though. I never thought I'd work anywhere else. I love that restaurant."

"Me, too." I hate to see her so down. Not wanting to make her cry, I search for a subject change. "Hey, should I ask my boss if there might be a job for you? I'm pretty much his favorite employee."

She looks surprised. "But is he hiring?"

"I don't know. It's not like we're well staffed. Even with Dylan the checkout lines still get backed up."

She seems to be on the fence. "You're already giving me a place to live. You'd get sick of me if I worked with you, too."

"Psh!" I kick her bicycle playfully. "When have I ever been sick of you?"

She doesn't answer.

"That's what I thought. I'll just ask, okay? Or maybe you'll want to work somewhere else. I won't be offended if you don't want to work with me."

She glares at me. "Go ahead and ask, then."

"Fine. I will." I smile, and she rolls her eyes.

Shreya and I split up when AnimalZone is in sight. I round the corner to the back of the store and see Dylan outside leaning by the door. I try my hardest not to smile as I come to a stop in front of him. "That excited to see me again, huh?"

"Yes." He kisses me. "I *really* like that I'm allowed to do that now. I've wanted to since I accidentally tackled you on the beach."

193

"I wanted to murder you that day." I get off my bike, and he immediately pulls me close. It makes me want to cuddle up with him on a couch.

"I know. It was hot."

"You're weird."

"And?"

"So what were you thinking that day?" I ask. "Because you looked absolutely miserable."

"I was. You hated me, and I deserved it." He pushes my hair from my face. "Also, I thought a lot about the goldfish legend you told me. That dragon you guys made—which was awesome, by the way—it was about to push out of the water like in the story."

"Yeah?"

He nods. "When you told me that story, I couldn't stop thinking about it. It's not like I've had to work for anything, so it was like I got dropped in the pond, you know? Like I just got handed dragonhood."

"I thought about that after Cypress Point," I admit. "But I didn't find an answer."

"When I saw your sculpture from the cliff, it hit me. Dragons have to learn to fly—they can't sit in the spring forever like they're still koi. They have to fight for that dream, but in a different way. They have to decide where they want to fly and why. That's when I decided to go for you, even if I didn't have much of a chance."

He is so sincere, and his words carry so much meaning. I can't believe a sculpture I made impacted him so much, and I love the idea of dragons needing to learn to fly. Of all the places he could soar off to, I like thinking he's decided to fly to me.

194

I kiss him. I shouldn't—we need to get to work—but I can't stand not to when he talks like that. The chemistry is insane, like nothing I've ever felt before. He pushes me up against the wall, and I run my fingers down his back.

"Let's skip work and keep doing this," he whispers between kisses.

"We should go inside." I slip my fingers into his belt loops and pull him closer. All the repressed attraction has come back to bite me—I can't get enough of him.

His lips stretch into a smile on mine. "You're sending very mixed messages."

"Mm-hm."

That's when the back door swings open. Supervisor Clark freezes at the sight of us in full make out mode, and I want to die.

Chapter 30

Dylan whispers in my ear, "We need to find a private place next time."

I shove him back, trying not to look completely mortified. Turns out getting caught by your boss is way more embarrassing than getting caught by your parents—I do have experience there—especially when the guy you're making out with is his nephew. Though I search for words, none come.

Clark clears his throat, clearly uncomfortable. "Well, I'm glad you two have . . . resolved your differences, but maybe you could save that for after work?"

"Yes. Of course," I manage to get out. "Sorry."

"Sorry," Dylan repeats.

"We're open, so." He nods towards the door, and I head inside without another word.

"Why are you always embarrassed about me?" Dylan asks as we head to Aquatics. "He was trying to set us up anyway."

I put a hand to my face, which still feels warm. "I'm not embarrassed about *you*. He's my boss! There's a line, you know? It's like seeing a teacher outside of school, and you have no idea how to interact with them that way."

196

He laughs. "Okay, fair enough."

"Besides," I say as I hand a tank scrubber to Dylan. "I was supposed to ask if he might be hiring, and there's no way I can look him in the eye now."

"Hiring?" Understanding crosses his face. "You mean a job for Shreya?"

I nod, heading for the goldfish guppy tank. It always gets the dirtiest, and the water needs to be super clean to keep them alive. "Not that she's desperate, but I thought I could at least ask."

"Is she okay?" He takes the tank next to mine, filled with small blackmoors and other fancies.

I purse my lips. "No, not really. You can imagine what she's going through, having been there."

"Yeah . . . it's not pleasant, even when it's what you want."

I sigh. "I don't know what to do. I'm trying to be upbeat and positive, but it doesn't feel right. Nothing does."

"Just be there for her. My uncle's been hard on me, but he's been a huge support, too. It'll be easier if she knows she has someone she can rely on."

I look at Dylan. He's focused on the tank, and I can't help thinking how much he's changed since that first day. "You know, you're pretty smart when you want to be."

His eyes meet mine, and he smirks. "Another compliment? This is weird."

"It is, isn't it? Should I balance it out by saying that uniform looks horrible on you?"

He laughs. "No one looks good in this, not even you."

My eyes narrow.

"It's probably best, though. Otherwise I'd be in big trouble." He glances at my butt and frowns. "Those pants do not do you justice."

"Stop!" I smack him with the scrubber. "I was supposed to be insulting you, not the other way around."

He stares at the wet mark on his shirt. "You did not just get dirty fish water on me! You'll pay for that."

I can tell he wants to kiss me, and I force myself to back up. We need to be professional at work. That'll be way harder than I thought. "Get the siphons. Because we're *working*."

"Working. Right." He sighs, but heads for the utility closet a few aisles down. I take the time to center myself. We can do this. It's not like I need to kiss him all the time. That's just the fun, new part. All these work hours I can spend getting to know him.

When he gets back, it seems we've both cooled off. He siphons the tanks I've already scrubbed, saying, "We need to go on another date. Preferably one where London is not present."

I smile. "She did put a damper on things."

"When can you go?"

"Hmm . . ." I scrub the tank, wanting to say the most immediate time possible. But there's someone else I need to think about. "I should take care of Shrey this weekend. She got kicked out because her brother is in a relationship like ours and she supported him—it might hurt that it's easy for us."

He nods, seeming sad. "I didn't know stuff like that still happened. Aren't we supposed to be past that crap?"

"You'd think." I move to the next tank. "My parents went through it, but I never thought I'd see it happen to someone my age."

"So maybe next weekend?"

I roll my eyes. "One track mind much?"

"I just want to hang out with you. Is that so wrong?"

Smiling, I say, "I think that could work, on a Saturday when my parents are home so I don't have to work around Betty. And you're still cleaning my tanks on Thursday, right?"

"Of course." He smiles, and for some reason I get the sense he has plans.

"What are you thinking?"

He shrugs. "Since we went golfing first, we should go to the Aquarium. You can talk fish all day. Then we could go to dinner wherever you want, since you clearly know the good places to eat."

I bite my lip as a surge of affection hits me. "That sounds great."

"Next Saturday then? At, like, three?"

"Should work," I say, trying to restrain my giddiness. "I'll meet you there."

When my shift is over, Dylan walks me to the back. I give him one peck, and he frowns. But his uncle has his office door open, and I'm not risking another ambush. I probably should talk to Clark about job openings, and yet I can't bring myself to do it. It's not like Shrey needs a job right away. Maybe next week. Then I'll have a few days for the shame to subside.

"Lunch?" Dylan asks.

I wince. "I should find Shrey."

"That's fine." He hugs me. "See you on Monday."

This pang hits me in the gut. Monday seems like forever away, and I have no way to contact him except for Clark's home number. "You need to get a cell phone."

"Seriously. Next pay check."

Ugh, too long. "We should go buy it together."

He smiles. "I like this plan."

"See ya." I reluctantly pull back before I get too mushy. It's just two days—what is wrong with me? I've never been this sentimental, at least I don't remember being like this with my other boyfriends. I liked being around them, but when we were apart I rarely missed them. I've only been outside for a minute, and I swear I miss Dylan already.

I pedal faster, this need for him freaking me out.

Shrey and I didn't discuss lunch, but I know where she'll be. I crave curry when I'm down, and she craves pizza. That means I'll find her at Round Table, her favorite place. I don't know why she likes it so much, but she could eat a whole vegetarian pie on her own.

It's only five minutes away by bike, so I figure I'll surprise her if she's there. The place is old, usually dirty, and the epic fantasy mural on the wall screams 80s cartoon. But there Shreya sits, stuffing her face and crying.

"Didn't go well?" I sit across from her.

She scrambles for a napkin and wipes at her eyes. "How'd you know I was here?"

I give her the look. "What else do you crave when you're down?"

"Right." She takes a long sip from her root beer. "No one was hiring—they've filled all their summer spots. I'm screwed."

"Hey, it was only the first day." I take a piece of her pizza, even though she glares at me for it. "It's not like you went everywhere in the whole city. We'll find something."

She nods, though she doesn't look convinced. "What did Supervisor Clark say?"

I cringe, feeling even worse now.

"You didn't ask him?"

"Well . . ." I should say it fast, like ripping off a Band-Aid. "He kinda caught me and Dylan kissing, and I was so embarrassed I chickened out."

Her eyebrows go up. "You were making out at work? You, Miss Responsible?"

"It was technically *before* work, but he came out back and found us and I wanted to disappear. I swear I'll ask on Monday. I'm so sorry I didn't—I didn't know it would be hard to find something."

She laughs to herself. "That's fine. But what's gotten into you?"

"What do you mean?"

She grabs another piece of pizza. "You've always been so, I don't know, calm and in control. Dylan gets you all flustered."

I want to argue, but her saying his name gives me this fluttery feeling. It's freaky. "Is it that bad?"

"I don't know. Isn't that how it's supposed to be? Now that you've given in, it seems like you're happy." She takes a bite. "It's okay to be happy, Mika. I might be miserable, but I still want you to be happy."

I smile. "This is why I'll never get tired of you, punk."

She rolls her eyes, and I kick her shin. "Hey!"

"I know you don't want me to say it, but I still think it'll be okay. We'll make it work out."

She nods. "I don't want you to say that, but keep doing it anyway. Maybe someday I'll believe it."

"You will." In the meantime, I will hope for her.

Chapter 31

It's Thursday, and I still haven't asked Clark if he's hiring yet. Shreya says it's okay, but I can tell from her eyes she's lying. I'm making the make-out ambush too big a deal, but it's impossible for me to hold a conversation with my boss now. So much for time making it less awkward—the more I put it off the harder it becomes.

"Should I ask him?" Dylan says as we stand in the break room after my shift.

I eye Clark's door, chewing the inside of my lip. "No, then he'd know how embarrassed I was."

Dylan snorts. "Because he can't tell by the one-word answers and crazy blushing."

"Shut up."

He pulls me closer. "Then do you want me to come with you?"

I put my head on his chest, the smell of him intoxicating. "Can we just go to lunch?"

He sighs. "If you don't ask by Monday I will."

"Deal. Where should we eat?"

"Hmm, I'll think while I'm changing." He pulls away.

I tug him back. "You're changing?"

Laughing, he nods. "I don't want to spend all afternoon in this uniform, so I brought extra clothes this time."

"So I have to go to lunch wearing this alone?"

He kisses my cheek. "Don't worry, you'll be with me so no one will notice anyway."

I shove him, and he runs off to the bathroom. Leaning on the wall, I try not to smile. I shouldn't laugh about his cockiness, but something about it has changed since we got together. Or maybe I understand now that he's kidding—he doesn't really think much of himself at all.

Dylan comes out wearing gray plaid shorts and a dark purple t-shirt. He totally pulls off purple. "I think I need tacos."

"Mmm, yes." We bike to Su Casa, and this time Dylan buys my food despite my protests. "Why do you always want to pay?"

He shrugs. "I don't know. Maybe it's habit. Maybe I just like buying things for you—it's funny how you get mad."

"Why is that funny?"

"No one ever stopped me from paying before. They expected it." Something clicks as he thinks about it. "But you always resist, even over something as small as a few tacos. I guess it's a nice reminder that you're in it for me, not the money."

I roll my eyes. "What money?"

"When you say that, it makes me want to buy you everything."

"You better not!"

"I'll try." He unwraps his taco, and we eat. We take our time biking to my house, soaking in the summer sun. On the less busy roads, we pedal side by side. There is much flirting.

As we put the bikes on my front porch, I say, "You probably shouldn't act like we're together around Betty. I have no clue how she'll react."

His brow furrows. "I don't want to hide it just because she has a problem."

"Well, I don't want to get berated all afternoon." I sigh, knowing he has a point, but hoping he'll go along with this anyway. "Look, she has a big problem with people 'mixing'. She can really fly off the handle about it. Since I don't know what mood she'll be in, please do this for me. I don't want to deal with her losing it and calling me names."

He glares at the door. "It bothers me that anyone would have a problem with us just because of that."

I hold in my sigh. Dylan has probably never had to deal with any kind of prejudice. I can't imagine what it's like, but I take his hand and stand firm. "If she wasn't sick, I wouldn't ask, okay? But she is, and I worry about her. Since she's gotten here, her memory has already gotten worse. She could think we're my parents or that you're her dad or something weird and I can't predict the triggers. It's easier this way."

"You really care about her, don't you?" he asks.

The question takes me off guard, but the answer is even more surprising to me. "Yeah, I guess I do. When she first got here I didn't understand what she was going through, but now that I do I feel like it's wrong to hate her for something she can't control. Maybe if she could, she'd change her mind now. But she can't."

"Fine, I'll do it because it means so much to you." He gives me a long kiss. "Guess I'll have to wait for our date for more of this."

I narrow my eyes. "That's why you're really mad, isn't it? You can't just kiss me all afternoon."

"Let's go inside." He pulls me towards the door, avoiding the question. We're met with laughter inside, and I'm relieved. Joel, Shreya, and Betty lounge on the couch watching what I'm pretty sure is *Monty Python and the Holy Grail*. Dad loves that movie, but I still don't get why. *The Princess Bride* is way better.

Joel stands when he sees us. "Mika, did you know Betty can quote this entire movie?"

"Really?"

"She does an uncanny impression of the Black Knight."

I smile, wondering if this is why Dad likes the movie. Did they watch it as kids? Suddenly I'm picturing him, Uncle Greg, and Aunt Jenny huddled around an old TV in a run-down trailer watching this with their mom. Maybe not all his memories are bad ones. "So she was okay today?"

His smile cracks for a second. "She talked a lot about her father abandoning them. We put in the movie to distract her."

"Huh." I look over to Betty, still laughing with Shrey. "She's mentioned that before, but I don't know anything about it."

He nods. "Better figure it out now before she forgets entirely."

"Yeah." The thought is sobering. It feels like there's a clock ticking away my chances of getting to know my grandmother better. "Well, I guess I'll see you tomorrow."

"Of course, sweetie." He looks back and forth between Dylan and me, his smile sly. "You two behave yourselves."

My eyes go wide—he sure picked up on that like a bloodhound.

Dylan laughs. "I'll try."

206

I smack him, hoping Betty didn't hear. "Shh. Get to work."

"Psh, taskmaster."

He heads to the laundry room, and I sit down next to Shreya on the couch. She doesn't look away from the TV, and I know I'm in trouble. "Let me guess, you still haven't asked."

I hang my head.

"It's been a week."

"I know. I'm a horrible friend."

She sighs. "You're not. I wouldn't be mad if I had more options, but this job hunt is a huge fail. If I don't have a paycheck soon I won't have a phone. Plus, I wanted to give some kind of rent to your parents."

"Shrey, you don't have to do that," I say.

She purses her lips. "I feel so useless."

"You're not." I put my arm around her. "I swear I'll ask tomorrow."

"I'm asking on Monday if she chickens out," Dylan says as he wheels the fresh water barrel to my room. "I got your back, Shrey."

He disappears, but she still smiles at the hall. "He's really sweet, Mika."

"Who would've guessed, right?" I bite my lip, torn between staying here with Shreya and going to my room with Dylan. But I can't leave her with Betty like that, especially when she's been here all morning.

She elbows me. "Go."

I look at her, surprised.

She rolls her eyes. "Your angst is suffocating. I'll watch Betty."

I give her a big hug. "You are the best friend in the whole entire world."

"Pretty much."

Tiptoeing to my room, I peek in. Dylan is hard at work scrubbing my tanks, then he pauses to look at my pictures. He puts his finger to one and sighs happily—I have never felt so wanted in my life. I step inside and shut the door behind me.

He jumps, but when he sees me he smiles. "What're you doing?"

I shrug. "Making sure we have privacy."

He drops the scrubber, and we meet in the middle. He wraps his arms around my waist, his lips urgent on mine. It's been way too long since I've kissed him like this, and I plan to get my fill.

Chapter 32

It's hard to focus on our sand sculpture when I have a date with Dylan in a few hours, but I try anyway. Shreya needs these days at the beach more than I do—she's in her element, carving her side of the Taj Mahal like a pro. Last Saturday we made a coiled cobra, and the battered remains of it stand about fifty feet away from us.

"Lots of people today," I say. We've gathered a crowd that presses down on us in a thick circle. "I think we're getting famous."

She smiles. "Maybe we'll have to move beaches, throw people off."

I laugh. "Yeah, if they keep crowding in on us like this."

"Can you people back up?" Olivia calls from her perch on a towel next to us. "You're in my sun!"

The crowd thins at her command. I don't know how she does that, but she's always had a dominating presence. She turns so she's on her stomach, grinning at us. "That better?"

"Yes, thanks." Shreya doesn't take her eyes off the sand, the wall needing to be perfect to support the heavy domes on top.

"Do you need to be tanner?" I ask Olivia. "You're about as brown as a white girl can get."

"I like the sun! Leave me alone. I don't need another Mika Skin Cancer Lecture."

I laugh. "Oh, fine."

Time passes slower than ever today. I love being with my friends, but at the same time I'm so excited for this date I can barely contain myself. It's nice to spend so much time with Dylan at work, but it'll be even better to do fun things with him, to hold his hand and wear normal clothes and not be interrupted by customers. I've already planned to wear the fish shirt he bought me, plus my best jeans. Casual but cute. Perfect for the Aquarium.

"Mika," Shreya says.

I look up, wondering if that wasn't the first time she said my name. "Yeah?"

She snorts. Crap, she obviously had to repeat herself. "What do you think of this arch? I swear it's not centered."

I tilt my head, analyzing the middle one. "I can't tell."

She gets up and walks away to get a better view. I follow her. The sculpture is starting to look like the Taj Mahal, and will look even better when we carve in the details. "Maybe it's fine."

"I think it is. Once we do the one on the left it'll look right." I nudge her. "Too bad you can't make money off this, because you're really good at it."

She nods. "Well, we make a good team. If only we could travel to competitions. I'll do the other arch—you're losing focus every second."

"I am not!"

Olivia laughs. "Mika, you are so head over heels it's not even funny. Though how could you not be? Dylan's gorgeous. You should bring him around more so I can at least enjoy the view."

I roll my eyes. "I'm trying to be a good friend here. You guys are important to me, too, and I know you don't like me bringing my boyfriends along."

"That's not true," Shrey says, digging into the sand to make the third arch.

"We just didn't *like* your other boyfriends." Olivia pulls out a water bottle from our cooler.

I laugh. "You never said this while we were dating!"

Olivia shrugs. "Not really our place to tell you who to date, is it? But I like Dylan. He fits with you, and he's funny."

"I agree," Shrey says. "So stop tiptoeing around us."

"Fine." I try to focus on the sculpture, but it doesn't work. I can't stop thinking about the fact that my friends approve of Dylan. Because if they like him, then it means this is more serious than I might be ready for. With my other boyfriends, I knew my friends wouldn't like them, and that made it easier to find a way out when I wanted.

With Dylan, I don't *want* a way out.

I set down my carver, my hand shaking too much to do the fine detail. I've put myself in a place where I'll be the one losing if we break up—I don't like this feeling. If he left . . . I can't even think about it. I knew I was taking a risk liking him, but I'm in so deep I could drown.

"Mika?" Olivia says. "Are you okay?"

I try to shake it off. "It feels like things are getting serious so fast, and you guys liking him . . . it's just weird."

She throws sand at me. "That's how it's supposed to be! Just chill out and enjoy it. Both of us would love to be in your situation, you know."

Shreya nods shyly. "In time, yes."

I get the sense they've been talking about me when I'm not around. It doesn't feel like they're jealous, but something feels off. Shreya and Olivia usually tell me everything. Right now I'm sure that's not the case.

"You're right. Sorry." I take a deep breath and force myself to listen to Olivia. Why should I be afraid? Dylan hasn't kept his feelings secret. I hold on to that, savor the truth of it, and smile. "I better get going. I need to shower and look nice."

"Have fun," Olivia says. "And don't worry, I'll take care of Shrey all day."

"I'm not a dog!" Shrey throws a plastic trowel at her.

Olivia laughs. "Should I get a collar?"

When I get home, I can hear screaming even before I get inside the house. The words become clearer when I come through the front door. "Don't come near me! Go away! I hate you. I hate you. I hate you."

"Mom . . ." Dad's voice is mock calm, the kind of calm you use when you're scared but trying not to be.

"Don't talk to me! You have no right to be anywhere near me—especially with that whore next to you. How could you bring her here after all you did to us? Go to hell! I wish you had died!"

I peek around the corner, afraid of what I'll see. Betty looks wild, pulling at her hair so hard I'm afraid it'll come out. Tears stream down her face even though she's so angry my parents keep their distance. She's had some bad moments, but this is the worst I've seen and it scares me. This isn't just some forgetful moments or rudeness. She actually looks full on crazy.

"Mom . . ." Dad holds out his shaking hand. "I think you have me confused for someone else. I'm your son, Stanley."

"I don't have a son!" Her words are so shrill I worry she'll lose her voice. "How could I have a son?"

"Who do you think I am?" he tries.

"You know who you are!" She grabs a heavy vase from the table, and my mom gasps. "I know what you did! She said you were dead but I *knew*. Gracie didn't believe me, but I KNEW. I found the letter you sent Mom!"

"You think I'm . . . your father?" Dad asks.

"OF COURSE YOU ARE!" Betty throws the vase at him.

Dad grabs Mom, and they duck just in time. The vase shatters on the coffee table behind them, sending shards all the way to where I hide. That's when I step out—my sandals crunch over broken glass as I scream, "Stop it!"

Betty doesn't stop, but instead points at my dad like she's telling on him. "He left her. He left the US. He left his country. And for what? An ugly Oriental whore he claimed to be in love with! I HATE HIM. We lost everything because of—"

Her face crumples as she clutches her chest, and despite the horrible things she said I'm horrified to see her hit the ground. I run over to her, put my hand on her shoulder. "Betty? Are you . . .?"

213

When her eyes meet mine, all I see in them is terror. She's not okay. Mentally or physically. Not even close. I'm no doctor, but I'm pretty sure she's having a heart attack. My parents pick themselves up from the floor, and I wonder if I look as scared as they do when I say, "Call 911."

Chapter 33

I haven't spent much time in hospitals, but as my parents and I huddle in the waiting room I'm positive I want to spend as little time here as possible. This place reminds me too much of my parents' lab, except instead of studying fish they study humans. Dying, sick humans.

What if Betty dies?

I keep thinking about it no matter how hard I try not to. The EMTs rushing into our house, using the defibrillator, getting her on a gurney and saying all these things that sounded like she was already gone. Maybe it's been hard to have her around, but I never wanted her to die. Who's horrible enough to wish someone dead?

She can't. She just got here, and I need to know if what she screamed about was true. I think it is. It explains everything, why she's so hard on the outside but still like a child inside. Why she pushes people away although she wants them so badly.

My stomach rolls as I imagine her somewhere in this awful place on an operating table. Please, please let her live.

A doctor in sea green scrubs comes through the big double doors. He looks over the waiting room and zones in on us. "Are you the Arlingtons?"

"Yes." My dad straightens his glasses. "I'm Stanley."

"Your mother, Elizabeth Arlington?"

Dad nods. I wish the doctor would get to the point already.

"She's in surgery now. I'm afraid we won't know the extent of the damage until it's over, but we do know it was a major heart attack. I pulled her records and noticed her cholesterol and blood pressure were quite high." He puts his pen to the clipboard. "Now, the EMTs said you described a stressful event taking place when this happened. Could you provide me more information?"

My dad takes a deep breath. "You probably saw in her records that she's been diagnosed with Alzheimer's. When I came into the room with my wife—after having been gone only a few minutes—she started screaming. We figured out that she had mistaken me for her father, who she did not have a good relationship with. She threw a vase and just after that collapsed."

It sounds so . . . not intense in summary. The doctor clearly doesn't find it that horrific, but I'm still reeling. Her anger was so palpable, her sorrow as real as if her father had left yesterday.

The doctor finishes his notes, seeming satisfied. "The stress must have aggravated an already dangerous situation. I'll have more for you after she's out of surgery."

"How long will that be?" Mom asks.

The doctor purses his lips. "Hard to say, not knowing how much has been damaged. I would guess at least six hours to be on the safe side. Standard bypass is around four."

Since Betty fell I haven't looked at a clock, but my stomach sinks when I see it's already a quarter to three. Dylan. He'll be waiting for me, and I have no way to call him.

I push two on my phone—the speed dial for Shreya. She doesn't pick up. I try three—Olivia. Nothing there either. I sigh. Of course I can't get a hold of them. Either they're still at the beach sculpting and too far away to hear their phones, or they've gone somewhere else to spend the afternoon. Maybe a movie. Or the spa. Olivia has gotten us in there for free a couple times.

There's only one other person to call, and I'd rather not. My finger hovers over Clark's home number. I take a deep breath and press it. Each ring makes my heart pound, and my mind races through what I'm supposed to say.

Turns out I don't have to say anything, because he doesn't answer either. He must be at the store, so I call there. Nothing. Again. I hang up at the voicemail message. This isn't something for voicemail.

Well, I tried. What else can I do but call again later? I don't have his email, though he probably isn't allowed to check it anyway. I lean back in the seat, already exhausted. The doctor finishes with my parents, and then it's quiet for too long. I'm not sure any of us know how to deal with death well. Dad never even told me his Aunt Grace died, and Mom's grandparents are *still alive*. I've talked to both sets of them online, even though they think the internet is weird. I guess I would too if I was a hundred years old.

"What are we gonna do?" I finally say. "We just sit here?"

Mom frowns. "I'm sorry, you had your big date, huh."

I shake my head. "This is more important, but what do we *do*? There's nothing we can do for her?"

Dad sighs. "We can be here. That's about it."

"It doesn't seem like enough." I feel like we did something wrong, like maybe if we had taken better care of her this wouldn't have happened. Maybe if I was nicer to her from the start, or if I'd tried to learn more about Alzheimer's, or if we'd taken her to the doctor every week. I don't say any of this out loud. My parents already look stressed.

"It is enough." The bump in my dad's throat bobs, and it seems like he's holding back tears. "No one's ever been there for her, I don't think. Not even me. Sitting here, even if she doesn't know we are, would mean more to her than anything."

I nod, tears pricking my eyes. "Is what she said true? About her dad?"

He shrugs. "Maybe. She told us he died in the war. I never thought to question it. But if he really left like that . . . well, it makes sense. It doesn't excuse her behavior, and yet I'm glad I understand it better."

"This isn't the first time she's hinted at it," I admit. "I should have told you sooner. I'm sorry, I didn't think anything like this would happen."

"Whoaaa . . ." Dad leans forward, his hazel eyes locked on mine. "Do you think this is your fault?"

I look down.

"Mi-chan, none of us could have seen this coming. We've done our best to take care of her, and her health was already poor. Her disinterest in food has actually been kind of helpful for her weight, but it didn't help fast enough."

"And we can't control what she remembers or how she reacts," Mom adds. "We didn't do anything differently. She was fine all morning."

I try to push back the guilt. "Yeah, I know. It's just . . ."

"Just what?" Dad asks.

I bite my lip, my head and heart filled with a jumble of emotions. The right words seem impossible to find. "It's like, I know she's kind of a horrible person . . . but at the same time I feel sorry for her and I wish she was better and I really, really don't want her to die. I . . . I . . ."

I love her. She was no one to me at first, but now I care about her more than I ever thought possible. She's my grandmother. And as hard as it is sometimes, I *like* having her around now.

A tear escapes, at which point my mom puts an arm around me. "Sweetie, none of us want her to die. I hope we taught you better than that!"

I wipe at my face, trying to keep it together. "How can I dislike someone so much and yet love them at the same time?"

My dad chuckles. "I think that's the definition of family."

Mom slaps his knee and calls him stupid in Japanese. "I think it's okay to care about someone, even if they've made bad choices in the past. We've all come to understand Betty more in taking care of her, and with that comes compassion. I never thought I'd be glad we let her stay, but I am."

I nod, feeling a little better.

Dad puts his elbows to his knees. "Sure would have been nice to know this stuff about her a few decades ago, though. Could have saved me a lot of trouble."

"Why do people keep secrets like that?" I picture my grandma as a little girl, finding out that her dad was never coming back. And not because he was dead, but because he just didn't want to. She's carried that pain with her forever, and it seems like it impacted her life in all the worst ways.

"Everyone has reasons," Dad says, and I wonder if he's thinking about the things he keeps to himself. "Sometimes it's too painful to think about. Or they're ashamed. Or they want to forget."

"Sounds like excuses, like running away," I mumble.

Dad smirks. "We are fight or flight creatures. It might not be the best way to cope, but sometimes it's the easiest."

"Yes, this is so easy." I grab a magazine, suddenly angry. It could have been different. If my grandma would have talked about it, gotten help, something. Did any of this have to happen? I don't know; I just wish things didn't have to be this way. I wish I would have known her before she got sick. I wish she had had a happy life, and my dad, too. So many wishes. Nothing I can do to change history.

The hours tick by, one then two then four then six. We take turns getting food at the hospital cafeteria, making sure there's always one person around in case the doctor returns. The food isn't as bad as I've heard, or maybe I can't taste right in this haze of waiting.

Dylan hasn't called, though I tried getting ahold of him a few more times. I thought he might at some point. The Aquarium closed at six, and I hate to think he waited all that time and is now seething somewhere because I ditched him. It's past nine. If he hasn't called by now . . .

That's when my phone rings. It's him.

Chapter 34

"I tried—"

"Am I some joke to you?" he says over me. "I'm starting to think you enjoy messing with me."

"Dylan," my voice cracks despite my best efforts. "My grandma had a heart attack. I'm at the hospital, and she's still not out of surgery. I tried to call your uncle at home and the store, but he didn't answer. Olivia and Shreya never called me back, either. I'm sorry."

He doesn't answer for so long I wonder if I lost him. "Well, I feel like a huge jerk now."

I smile a little. "Told you you need a phone."

"I'm beyond convinced. Sorry I jumped to conclusions." He sounds genuinely worried now that he knows I didn't intend to leave him hanging. "Do you need anything? Should I come?"

"What?" My heart about jumps up my throat. I look to my parents, who are pretending not to listen. "Um, I don't know."

He'd be face to face with my mom and dad, something I usually avoid at all costs. And then there's the undeniable fact that him being here would turn this relationship from "we really like each other" to "this is serious." Hospital waiting rooms, rides to the airport, helping with a move—those are all things that suck, things you only do for people you care about a lot.

"Well, are you staying all night?" he asks.

"I'm not sure. We don't even know if she'll make it yet. There . . ." I have to push the words out. " . . . might be nothing to stay for."

"That's it. I'm coming." His voice is resolute. "I'll bring some blankets in case you guys need them, and food. I'm guessing you're at Community Hospital, right?"

This is the part where I could tell him not to come. If I tell him where we are, that's basically saying I want him here. Which means I want him this involved in my life, my family. Maybe I'm overthinking it, but it feels big to me. And yet at the same time I know my answer.

"Yes. A few blankets would be great. The seats are kind of gross and not comfortable."

He laughs, and the thought of him smiling makes everything a little better. "What kind of food should I get?"

"One sec." I put my hand over the phone and look to my parents. "Dylan wants to bring us food—what do you want?"

Dad raises an eyebrow. "Really?"

"Yeah."

Mom tries not to smile—as if her excitement might make me chicken out—and fails miserably. "Tell him to get some burgers and fries from wherever you want, Mi-chan. Can't mess that up, and it'll keep us full. We might be here a long time."

"Okay." I tell him, though it seems weird to eat fast food while waiting for someone to get out of heart surgery.

222

"My uncle says he's sorry he didn't answer and is letting me use the car so I can get whatever you need. I'll be there soon." He hangs up before I can say goodbye.

I hold my phone to my chest, trying not to show how relieved I am that he's coming. A weight lifts off me, like I don't have to hold all this on my own anymore. It's both terrifying and awesome.

"So." Dad straightens his glasses. "Am I allowed to ask him about Cypress Point tonight?"

Mom smacks his arm. "Honey."

"What?" He holds back a smile. "I just want to know what's off limits before he gets here. I'm being considerate."

I roll my eyes. "He loves golf. Yes, stay on golf. Do not get anywhere near what I was like as a baby or child."

Mom smiles. "We promise. At least for now."

It doesn't take Dylan long to get here. His eyes light up when he sees me, and I have to restrain myself from running over and hugging him. He sets the bags and blankets on the coffee table in front of us. "You must be Mika's parents. I'm Dylan."

Dad stands, trying to be intimidating. It doesn't work with his thin frame and general nerd-like appearance. He holds out a hand. "Nice to finally meet you. I'm Stan, and this is my wife, Yumi."

"Nice to meet you, too." He glances at me, his smirk mischievous. "Sorry it wasn't sooner—Mika is slightly ashamed of me."

I glare at him.

He laughs. "See? She's worked hard to teach me how to be a decent human being."

223

My parents give him a puzzled look. Then my dad asks, "What does that mean?"

Dylan's eyes go wide, as if he just realized how that might sound. "Oh, nothing seriously bad. I'm not like a pimp or drug dealer. Just a selfish rich boy out on his own for the first time."

They both breathe a sigh of relief.

"Get over here before you put your other foot in your mouth," I say, pointing to the seat next to me.

"Yes, ma'am." He sits and takes my hand tentatively.

"So you're out of high school?" Mom starts passing out food. It has been a few hours since we had dinner, and I'm more than ready for some stress eating. Especially now, with my parents and Dylan in the same place.

"Just barely." He reaches for a blanket and puts it around my shoulders. The gesture makes me blush, and I hide my face in the soft fabric. "I'm staying with my uncle, working at the pet shop while I figure out what to do next."

"You don't have plans yet?" Dad does not seem impressed by this.

Dylan purses his lips. "Well, my father had plans—I did not agree with them. Now I'm trying to decide if I should go for the pro golfer thing or if it's too late. I need to get in touch with some of my old coaches and see if they still think I have a chance. If not that, then I'll go to college and play—"

"You're good enough to do that?" Dad barely hides his skepticism.

Dylan shrugs. "I was at the top of the Junior PGA until my dad stopped me from playing, and now I don't get to play as much as I'd like. But when I do, I have a plus-seven game average right now. That's not in tournament, though."

Dad's eyes go wide. "That's pretty good."

The big swinging doors *swoosh* open. The same doctor from before comes straight for us, and my heart pounds twenty thousand times a second. My parents stand, but my legs won't follow suit. The doctor's face gives away nothing, and I don't know what I'll do if it's bad news.

Dylan's hand comes around my shoulder, and he squeezes once. No words. It means the world.

"Good news," the doctor says. "You mother made it through surgery."

Dad hugs my mom, and I lean into Dylan. "Thank goodness."

"She's on her way to recovery, but I'm afraid she's still in danger. We had to do a quadruple bypass, and her heart is very weak. She may need to stay here longer than a normal heart patient, especially since we can't rely on her to be careful on her own with the Alzheimer's."

My parents nod, though I swear I can hear their thoughts. *How will we pay for this?* It'll already be more than we can afford, without extended hospital stay.

"When we've settled her in her room, I'll send a nurse for you." The doctor looks at Dylan and me. "Since it's after hours, I'm afraid it's family only."

"Of course," Dad says.

The doctor leaves, and about twenty minutes later our guide shows up. She hands us special bands that show we have clearance. My parents stand and look at me. I gulp. "Can you give me a second to say goodbye?"

225

"Sure. I'll text you with the room number." Mom pushes Dad forward before he can disagree.

"Thanks for everything," I say once they're out of earshot. "Really."

Dylan gently puts his hands on my face and kisses my forehead. "I'll wait here for you, okay?"

I bite my lip. "You don't have to do that."

"I want to." His hands drop to my shoulders. "They have TV here. Do you know how long it's been since I've watched TV? My uncle still doesn't think I'm ready for 'media.'"

"Seriously?"

He nods. "But I'm allowed to eat when I want now. I don't have to do chores all the time either. I got my wallet back and he's going to let me have a phone once I can pay for it myself. And if something involves you, I can get the car easy. He thinks you're good for me."

"That's a little creepy, but I guess I won't complain." I kiss him, making sure not to linger too long. "You really don't have to stay."

"Why are you always trying to get rid of me?"

"Psh. I'm just saying it could be a long time before she wakes up, and you don't have to sleep deprive yourself." I stand, pulling out my phone to text Mom. "Maybe I worry about your wellbeing sometimes."

His arms come around me from behind. "Good to know."

"I better go." I reluctantly pull away.

"You know where to find me."

I shake my head. He might be cute right now, but what if this takes six more hours? At some point he'll have to leave.

He does have his uncle's car. I head down the hall, following the directions for the room number my mom sent me. I warn them with a knock before coming in.

Mom and Dad sit by my grandma's bedside. To my surprise, Dad has his hand over his mother's. For all his anger, I guess part of him does still love her.

Never thought I'd understand that, but I do.

My grandma is hooked up to a lot of machines. She looks pale, and I might think she was dead if it weren't for the slow, steady beeping that I assume is monitoring her heart. I should step closer, but I'm scared to mess something up or startle her at the worst possible time.

But more than anything, I'm taken back by the undeniable fact that she's not just that crazy woman I met on the first day. She's my *grandmother*. Part of my family. And I love her. I never thought it would be possible, seeing how different we are, but it happened so fast.

Mom reaches out for my hand and pulls me onto her lap. I feel like a child, but that's okay right now. We watch her quietly, waiting. Time passes slowly in the dead of night. She doesn't wake. My dad's head bobs as he nods in and out of sleep, and my eyelids feel like they're made of lead.

At two in the morning, she finally opens her eyes. She doesn't say anything—is probably too weak to manage it—but she smiles.

"We're here, Mom," Dad says.

She closes her eyes, and one tear trails into her hairline.

After that, Dad tells us to go home and rest, that we'll take turns and he's first. We don't argue. I want a bed after all this.

Who knew waiting could be so exhausting? I feel like I've run a marathon.

When we get back to the waiting room, I can hardly believe what I see. Dylan sleeps awkwardly in a chair that is decidedly too small for him.

He stayed.

I'm not sure I'll ever be able to tell him how much that means to me, but I let go of any fears I had. I let myself be okay with how much I care about him, just like I let myself love my grandmother.

Chapter 35

My phone is ringing. Problem is, my brain tells me this way before I can figure out how to move my arm. I have no idea what time it is, but surely it can't be morning yet. There is so much sleeping left to do.

Again with the ringing. I reach for my nightstand, fumbling around until I find my phone. I don't bother looking at the screen before I say, "Hello?"

"Are you still sleeping?" Shreya asks.

I force an eye open. My clock says it's past noon. No wonder I'm so hungry. "Yeah, it was a rough night."

She groans. "Please stop there."

It takes a moment to figure out what she thinks I mean. "No, Shrey, ugh. I didn't even go out with Dylan. My grandma had a heart attack."

"Seriously?"

"Yeah . . ." For a moment, last night doesn't seem real. It happened—the details are all crystal clear—and yet my mind still wants to resist the truth of it. "I tried to call you and Olivia."

She sighs. "Olivia missed yours. I . . . kinda don't have a phone anymore."

"What?" I sit up. "I thought you still had time on yours!"

Long pause. "My parents must have turned it off, because I don't get service anymore."

"Oh, no . . ."

"It's okay. Olivia took me to a movie to distract me from having a total meltdown, and then we ended up visiting Pavan and Rachelle."

"Really?" She must have been really hurt if she made Olivia drive her all the way to Salinas. And neither of them called to let me know what happened? Maybe they didn't want to interrupt my date, but still. I should have been there for her.

"Yeah, and they made us stay the night so we just got back. Sorry we didn't get your call. Is she okay?" Shreya says. I purse my lips, sure Olivia had to have seen my calls. She just didn't answer them. I get the feeling I'm not hearing the whole story, but I'm too tired to push it.

"All things considered, I guess." I plop back into my pillows, fatigue outweighing hunger. "She had quadruple bypass surgery."

"Whoa."

In the background, I hear Olivia saying, "What's going on?"

Shreya parrots what I said, and then asks me, "Do you need anything? We can drive you over there or bring you food or—"

"Maybe later. You already have so much to deal with, Shrey." I can't believe she doesn't have a phone anymore. It's like my lifeline just got severed. She's always been the first person I call in any situation. Suddenly I have serious motivation to get her a job. "I need to get cleaned up and run a few errands. I'll call you guys after?"

I can feel her frowning. "Okay. Call Olivia if I'm not at your house later."

"Yup. See ya."

Throwing off my covers, I head for the bathroom to shower. I put on my goldfish shirt because I'm tired of saving it, and also maybe because it feels like Dylan is with me. The house is too quiet, and I can't believe Mom would sleep this late. When I check her bed and then the garage, I discover she didn't. She must have gone back to the hospital, choosing to "spare me" against my will.

Cereal at one in the afternoon is probably not the best choice, but I'm not sure I can stomach much more. It feels *empty* here, like a shell of a house without my parents, without my grandma complaining about her food. I don't like it, and it makes me wonder if this is how Shreya feels all the time. I have to get out of here, and there's only one place to go.

AnimalZone.

I always park my bike out front when I'm not working, heading inside like a normal customer. To my surprise, Dylan is at the register. He smiles when he sees me. "Here for another fish?"

I smirk. "No. I didn't know you worked Sundays."

"My uncle thought it would be nice to give non-family Sundays off, so it's just me and him."

"Ah." I look around, nervous about seeing my boss. "Speaking of your uncle, where can I find him?"

He raises an eyebrow. "So you're finally gonna ask, huh?"

I nod.

"Good." He comes around the cashier's counter and takes my hands. "And since I have you here, we need to reschedule

231

our date. Hopefully this time no one will get kicked out or have a heart attack."

I feel horrible for laughing. "I have no idea when I can now. I'm almost afraid to plan anything and have something happen to you next time."

He frowns. "Call my uncle's house when you can, then. We'll just do whatever we have time to do."

"Okay." I hug him, burying my head in his chest.

"Whoa, you alright?" His arms come around me slowly, which is when I realize that hug was kind of out of the blue.

"Yeah. It's just . . . I wanted to do that last night, when I saw you still waiting. But my mom was there." I breathe him in, never wanting to let go. "Thanks, for everything. You really did help."

He squeezes me tighter. "I'm glad. You seemed pretty scared."

"I was. I wouldn't have known what to do with myself if she had died."

"She'll be okay." He rubs my back in small, comforting circles. The doorbell dings, and we jump apart as a customer walks in. She gives us a disapproving glare. Dylan nods towards the back. "I think he's cleaning the bird cages."

"Okay." I head down the main aisle.

"Oh, and, Mika?" Dylan calls.

I turn. "Hmm?"

His smile is blinding. "Nice shirt."

I roll my eyes, though at the same time I wish we were back in my room with the door closed. How I've managed to resist going further with him is starting to seem like a miracle. Or plain stupidity. I'm not sure.

232

Clark is just returning from the back alley—I assume to throw away bird poop—when I enter the break room. I straighten my shoulders, determined not to chicken out this time. He seems completely normal when he sees me, though a little concerned. "Hey, Mika. Dylan told me about your grandmother. I'm so sorry."

"Oh," I say, though of course he told his uncle where he was going last night. I vaguely remember Dylan mentioning something about Clark on the phone last night. "Thanks."

"You here to ask for time off? It should be fine if you need it."

"Actually . . ." I gulp. Shreya needs this. If I want to keep her in Monterey, she needs money. "Kind of the opposite. I was wondering if you might be hiring anytime soon?"

His furry eyebrows raise. "Why?"

"It's just . . . my friend Shreya got kicked out, so she can't work at her family's restaurant. She's been trying to find a job but it's not going well." I bite my lip, nervous that I can't read his reaction under the mustache. "She just needs something part time, since school is starting in a month. I thought I could at least ask—it's totally fine if you can't hire her."

He snorts. "This is what you've been so skittish about?"

"Yes?" I say, happy to have him think that. Clearly he wasn't as uncomfortable with the make out ambush as I was.

He smiles. "If you haven't noticed, I have a soft spot for strays. Shreya's welcome to work here if she wants."

"Really?" I completely fail at hiding my excitement as I jump. "That's great! Thank you. She'll be so happy."

"Just have her call me when she decides." He heads into the office. "We'll work out the details from there."

233

"Okay, thanks again!" I practically skip out of the break room. Giving Dylan one quick kiss goodbye, I call Olivia with one hand and unlock my bike with the other.

She answers. "I'm *so* sorry I didn't call you back. I thought you just wanted to give us the rundown on your date, and I was already trying to take care of Shr—"

"It's fine, really."

"I feel like we should have been there, though."

"And I should have been there for Shrey, but it's okay. Dylan came." I get on my bike, but stay where I am. "That's not why I'm calling, though. Where are you guys? I have a surprise for Shrey."

"Ooo, what?"

"I want to tell her in person! You'll blurt it out before I can."

"Oh boo. We're actually headed to your house, thought we'd chill out some."

"Okay, I'll meet you there." I hang up and head home. Surely this will make Shreya feel better—I will have restored my good friend status and saved the day all in one fell swoop. Olivia's bug is already out front when I arrive, and I find them in my room when I get inside.

I bounce next to Shreya on the bed. "Hi!"

She gives me a funny look. "Hi. You're sure excited. I thought this was a surprise for me."

"It's mutually beneficial. So . . ." I pause for dramatic effect. "Clark said if you want a job, you have one!"

"Really?" The look of shock on Shreya's face is priceless.

"Really!" I laugh, the idea of working with my best friend too much. "Isn't that awesome?"

"Yeah. It's great." She glances at Olivia, who has an overly bright smile on her face.

"So great," Olivia says.

I'm not sure what it is, but it seems like they're not as excited as I imagined they'd be. "I thought you wanted the job."

"I do!" She smiles wider, but in my gut I know it's forced. "It's just surreal. I had no prospects and now I have an offer. Trying to take it in."

I look to Olivia, who seems to know way more than I do. It makes me squirm, like I've done something wrong. Clearly, there's something Shreya isn't saying, but I can't get myself to ask her what she's really thinking. I'm too scared to hear it.

Chapter 36

Betty looks better today. She's been in the hospital for nearly a week because of meltdowns so bad that she broke stitches, and she's not going anywhere anytime soon. The doctors told Dad to stop coming, since sometimes she sees him as her husband or father. He mopes around the house feeling guilty about it.

Now I'm the one who does the visiting mostly, because I can't stand picturing her in that stark hospital room by herself. Not when she's been alone for so long. Plus, I seem to be the only person she currently likes. They say it could be because she has no long-term memories of me.

Not sure I find that comforting.

"Can you get me more of these?" Betty holds up the funsize bag of Peanut Butter M&Ms I brought her. She's like a kid—candy instantly distracts her from a bad train of conversation. I'm armed to the nines.

"Here." I pull out another, and she snatches it. "Are you being nice to the nurses?"

She frowns as she opens the bag.

"I know it's not fun to be here, but if you can't be calm then we can't take you home. We miss you. The house is so quiet, and Joel is worried." He's come to visit her a couple times, too.

She sinks into her pillows more, looking tired. "I'm trying."

"I know."

"It's so hard. Sometimes I forget I had surgery and try to get up or panic because I don't know where I am or something hurts. I hate this disease so much."

I put my hand on hers. She's been so coherent today—and it's wonderful—but it also hurts because I've learned how fleeting it can be. Tomorrow she may not remember any of these thoughts, but more than ever I hope she does. If only she could always be like this. "I hate it, too."

"I wish the heart attack had killed me," she says in a whisper.

"Don't say that." I squeeze her hand, upset she'd even think that. "I don't want you going anywhere anytime soon."

Her eyes are sad when they meet mine. "I might not go anywhere, but my mind will. I'll be like a dead person, but still alive. Lord Almighty, what a horrible way to die. No, the heart attack should have been it."

I shake my head. "I'm glad I get to know you. And, believe it or not, I like having you around."

She smiles a little, and I wonder if that's what she wanted to hear. Someone wants her. Like Dad said, it means a lot to my grandmother. "I'm glad I was able to meet you before I went. To think I have a granddaughter who has it so together. It's a miracle."

I laugh. "I don't know if I have it together."

"You do, trust me."

She means it, I can tell by the way she looks at me. She's proud, despite all our differences, and I feel more connected to her than ever. I want to hug her, but don't dare with her condition so fragile. "Can I . . . call you Grandma?"

Her eyebrows pop up. "You want to?"

I nod.

"I guess it's all right then." She looks away, as if embarrassed by my show of affection. "Can't promise I'll remember I said that, you know."

"I know. It's okay, Grandma."

She smiles wide. "You better get going, hon. You've been here all afternoon—do something fun with the rest of your evening. I'll be fine."

I sigh, wanting to but still worried. "You sure?"

"Yes. I'm tired anyway." She pulls her blankets up. "I'll try my best to heal. I promise."

Satisfied with that, I stand. "You can do it. I'll see you tomorrow."

"I'll be here."

Waving as I leave, I pull out my phone the second I'm out of the room. May as well call Dylan. Maybe he can pick me up so I don't have to take the bus, and then we can do something for once. Between taking care of my grandma and Shreya, my time has been virtually zero. It's Friday after six, so Dylan should be home, since AnimalZone is closed.

"Hello," he says, clearly recognizing my number on caller ID. "Please tell me we get to hang out tonight."

"If you can pick me up from the hospital, yes."

He asks his uncle, but I can't hear Clark's reply. "Sweet, I got the car. I'll be there as soon as I can. Bye."

"See ya." I laugh to myself, picturing his excitement. It sure is nice to be wanted. Can't deny that.

It takes Dylan about thirty minutes to drive up in front of the hospital. When I hop in the car, he pulls me in for a kiss. "I'm glad you called, because I was this close to begging."

"Sorry it's been so crazy." I settle into the seat, feeling tired and hungry and glad that someone is around to take care of me. "She was doing better today. Hopefully it stays that way."

"I hope so, too." He pulls out of the hospital parking lot, heading in the direction of the freeway. "And how's Shreya? My uncle hasn't mentioned a call from her."

I fiddle with the frayed corner of my bag, wishing he hadn't brought that up. I've been trying to pretend it's not a big deal. "I . . . don't know. I thought she wanted the job, but she didn't seem very excited when I told her. Now that she's gone so long without calling, I'm not sure what's going on."

"Hmm." He purses his lips, seeming genuinely worried. "You haven't asked her?"

"I'm afraid to. Maybe I'm making too big a deal out of it, you know? She keeps telling me not to worry about her so much—I don't want to badger her about it. She could be waiting for the right job for her."

"But wouldn't she tell you that?" He turns onto the highway.

I sigh, knowing he's right, but I haven't had the emotional energy to deal with more than my grandma's heart attack. "Can we please not think about this right now? I want to be with you and relax. Worrying is exhausting."

He smiles. "Fine, I thought we could get dinner and buy me a phone. Maybe a movie?"

"Yes, please. Finally."

He laughs. "You don't mind the food court, do you? This whole rationing out my money thing is sinking in."

"Of course I don't. I'm too tired for a fancy place. A dark theater sounds awesome right now. I need some cuddle time."

He bites his lip. "Sounds good to me."

Dylan drives to the Del Monte Center, a much less posh shopping mall than the Carmel Plaza. But it has the most affordable theater in the area. We have dinner at the cheap Chinese place there, and it's everything I could ask for after such a long week. Salty, sweet, spicy, yum. After that, we walk hand in hand to the nearest place to pick a phone.

"I've never had to look at the plan prices. These are ridiculous!" he says, pointing to the sleek, cutting-edge smart phones. "The phone alone is like a quarter of my pay check, and the monthly fee is way more than I thought."

I can't help laughing. "Just wait until they add in all the taxes and fees."

His eyes go wide, and he pushes me away from that section. "I need money to buy a car and take you out. Goodbye, cool phones."

Dylan settles on a more affordable model, one that can text and take decent pictures. He doesn't get a huge data plan, and I'm oddly proud of him. As we head for the theater, he types with one hand and wraps his other arm around me. "Guess who's going to be my first contact."

"Hmm, your uncle?"

"Yup."

"Jerk!" I shove him away.

Laughing, he holds out the phone and says, "Do that scowl, the one where your nostrils flare." I glare at the description, and he takes a picture. "Perfect!"

My jaw drops. "No! Delete it. Take a real picture of me."

"I like this one." It's too late. My scowl is now the background on his phone. He grabs me again, and we walk as he types in my number from memory. He doesn't plug in my name, though, but *Fish Girl*.

I roll my eyes. "You think you're so funny."

"I am." His eyes flash with excitement. "Should we see if it works?"

He's so beautiful. That's all I can think as I take in the hard lines of his face and the dark brown of his eyes. They might even be darker than mine. But more than that, he's gorgeous on the inside, too. "You've changed a lot, you know that?"

"You could say that." He keeps fiddling with his phone, trusting me to guide us through the crowd. The place is busy, being Friday night and all. The movie theater gleams in front of us, and people flood in and out of it. "But it's more like I'm finally allowed to be the person I want to be, and I . . ."

He stops abruptly, his eyes now forward. I follow his gaze to a group of people not twenty feet from us. They stare right back at us, something like horror on their faces. I recognize half of them—London and her mother and little brothers. And here I thought I'd never see them again.

"Mika," Dylan says as they come over. "Follow my lead, okay?"

"Okay?" I'm only nervous because he is. I can feel it in the way he grips my shoulder as if it's a life preserver.

"Dylan, you're here," says the bleached blond woman I don't recognize. She plasters on a smile, but it seems to be holding back pain. The imposing man next to her looks like he wants to bore a hole into Dylan's head. "How have you been?"

He lets out a short laugh. "I'm doing great, Mom."

My stomach drops. Can we just run away now?

Chapter 37

London seems to enjoy my reaction immensely. I'm sure I look like a deer in the headlights. His *parents*? These are the people who kicked him out, who tried to force him into a life he didn't want. They look so . . . normal. I would have never guessed they were uber rich. Their clothes are nicer than average, but other than that they're just people out on a Friday night.

"What are you doing here?" Dylan asks.

"The St. Jameses are hosting their big summer gala tomorrow. We couldn't miss it," his mother replies. "We drove down this morning, got settled, and decided to go out for a movie."

"Ah, the gala, of course. How could I forget? Well, cool." He holds up his cell, and I can't tell if he's actually okay or an amazing actor. "I just bought myself a phone, and this is my girlfriend, Mika. We were thinking of seeing a movie, too."

"Hi." I can't seem to manage any more words.

His mom's jaw hits the floor. "G-girlfriend? Really?"

"You didn't know?" He looks to London, who seems even more annoyed than before. Her little brothers run circles around us yelling Dylan's name, so maybe I can't blame her. "I thought they would have informed you immediately. Or did you guys not believe me when I said it?"

"You don't have a reputation for commitment," London says.

"Boys!" Mrs. St. James snaps. They stop the yelling, but not the running.

Dylan shrugs. "Maybe not, but here we are, still together. How long has it been since we played at Cypress Point? A month at least."

"We were dating before that, though," I say, though it's not true. It feels true, with how much time we've spent together this summer.

"Yes, yes we were. Not bad for a guy who's never been in a serious relationship, right, London?"

She doesn't answer. I try not to smile.

His father, who hasn't said a word yet, finally speaks. "So you're happy."

Dylan tips his chin up. "Very. You can't tell?"

His father doesn't seem to like this answer, which bothers me more than anything so far. Shouldn't he be glad Dylan is happy? Isn't that what every parent wants for their child? I didn't think I was naïve in believing that, but maybe I am.

"Well, that's . . . nice." His mother appraises me—they all do—and I can tell what they see though they try to hide it. I'm a wrench in the plan. An "issue." Dylan was supposed to be miserable at his uncle's and come crawling back to them. I'm sure of it. "So your name is Mika? Not a common name. Are you American?"

Dylan's hand about crushes my shoulder. "Mom! Seriously?"

244

"What?" She looks shocked that he could possibly be upset. "My son finally has a real girlfriend—I'm curious about where she's from."

"What does it matter?" He steps forward, as if he needs to protect me.

"It's okay, Dylan," I say. "I grew up here in Monterey, Mrs. Wainwright." I almost add that I can speak English and everything, but force myself not to. "My mother was born in Japan, though. My parents met as grad students doing a marine biology internship off the coast of Okinawa."

"Oh, how charming." His mom does seem genuinely pleased by the story, though part of me wonders if she's relieved that I'm not some uneducated vagrant. "So they're scientists?"

I nod. "At the Aquarium, actually. Someday I hope to be out there with them."

This makes his mom smile wider, almost as if she approves. Even his father seems mildly impressed. "How did you two meet?" she asks.

London groans. "Can we eat now? I'm starving." In response to this, her brothers start chanting, "Food, food, food!"

"Right." Dylan's mother shakes her head, as if she had forgotten everything she was doing before she saw her son. "Do you two . . . want to come with us?"

"No," Dylan says way too quickly. "We're, uh, we were gonna meet up with some of Mika's friends. They're waiting for us."

I try not to show how relieved I am that I don't have to endure that particular brand of torture. Karma couldn't possibly allow such a thing to happen, because I have earned major brownie points this summer.

"I thought you said you were seeing a movie. Why the sudden change of plans?" London gives us a cruel smile. "C'mon, maybe Mika can recommend a good Asian place."

Dylan steps forward, livid. "Excuse me?"

"London! That's enough," her mother says, though it seems half-hearted.

"It's fine, Mrs. St. James," I say, trying not to seethe too much. But there's a big difference between ignorance and saying something racist on purpose, and London just crossed the line. Maybe she's upset about losing Dylan, but that's no excuse to go that far. "It's how the kids speak these days. First thing I asked London when we met was if she could recommend rich, white-people restaurants."

London's eyes narrow.

"We're leaving." Dylan grabs me by the waist. "Thanks for reminding me how much I don't miss this."

"Dylan, wait!" his mom calls, and I think I hear panic in her voice. It makes me wonder if she wasn't completely on board with the whole kicking-Dylan-out thing.

He doesn't wait. In fact, I have to work extra hard to keep up with his long strides. I can feel him fuming, but I don't say anything as we pass the theater and head for the parking lot.

The second we're in the car, though, he's talking. "It's like the universe hates me, I swear! I know there's not that many places to see a movie around here, but why? Why? All I wanted was one nice night out with my girlfriend."

"I'm sorry." I put my hand on his shoulder, unsure what words will comfort him.

"Don't be. It's not your fault." He clenches his jaw. "I can't believe London said that, and my mom . . . what the hell? Does that happen often, people talking to you like that?"

I purse my lips, unsure if this is the moment to get into the reality of looking visibly "other" and "mixed" on top of that. "It happens. Not every day, but yeah. I try not to think about it constantly, but people can be really stupid about the way I look sometimes."

"I'm gonna have a hard time not punching people who do that." He grips the steering wheel, putting his head to it. I rub his back in the silence, and slowly his shoulders relax. "Seriously, why do they keep showing up?"

I shake my head, surprised he doesn't see it. "Maybe they miss you?"

This earns me a nasty glare. "You saw my dad. That disapproving sneer pretty much sums up my whole life. Did you see how mad he was that I was happy?"

I can't argue this, so I put my fingers through his and bring his hand to my lips.

He keeps talking. "He's always treated my uncle like that, too. I used to think Uncle Clark was a total loser because of all the shit my dad said about him wasting his life in a pet shop. Did you know he has a business degree from Yale?"

My eyes about pop out. "Clark? Seriously?"

Dylan nods. "They were supposed to handle the business together, but he walked away. My uncle is just as smart as my dad, and yet all I ever heard was that he's the laziest soul in the world. But you see how hard he works—and he loves that store so much. Now that I've lived with him,

247

I'm positive he's the only person in my family who *isn't* miserable."

I think about it for a second. "So I guess Clark figured out a long time ago that money doesn't buy happiness, huh. Kinda like you're doing now."

"Yeah." Dylan leans his head back, squeezes my hand tighter. "Not only that, but he knew all along that happiness was more valuable. Now that I've had it, I wish my whole family could feel it. I think they've forgotten what it means to be happy. They wouldn't act like that if they could remember."

When he talks like this, I never want him to stop. "Maybe someday you'll be able to convince them how important it is."

He smiles. "I hope so."

Leaning my head on his shoulder, I say, "Let's delete that part of our night and go to my place for a movie. My couch is more comfortable than theater chairs anyway."

He starts the car. "Good idea."

When Dylan and I step inside my house, I can hardly believe what I smell. The spices . . . there's no mistaking the scent of Shades of Bombay. But it can't be—my parents wouldn't dare venture there with all that Shreya's going through.

My mouth waters as I round the corner to the kitchen. Mom, Dad, and Olivia sit at the table, bouncing like excited children. Shreya stands in the kitchen, one hand stirring what I can only assume is curry and the other holding our home phone. She speaks in Hindi, so I assume she's talking to Pavan.

"Mika! Dylan!" Dad smiles ridiculously wide. "Isn't this great? Shreya wanted to make us dinner for letting her stay with us."

"She really didn't have to," Mom says, though it's clear they've both missed Shades of Bombay as much as I have. "But she was determined. She's been on the phone with Pavan all evening."

"And she dragged me through an Indian market all afternoon," Olivia says with a smile. "Doesn't she look happy?"

Shreya's back is to me, but there seems to be an energy to her that's been missing since her parents kicked her out. She gets off the phone, and when she turns around she's smiling. "There you are! No wonder you were late."

"Sorry about that," Dylan says.

She shakes her head. I'm not sure why her mood has changed so drastically, but I'm happy for it nonetheless. "No you aren't."

He grins. "True."

We sit at the table though it hasn't been long since we ate. Olivia asks, "How's your grandma?"

"Better," I say. "She was really coherent today and felt bad about having to be there so long. If she has a few good days we'll be able to take her home next week."

"Let's hope," Mom says. "Hospitals aren't cheap."

I sigh, not even wanting to think about how much we could lose over this.

"No stress on Friday night." Dad eyes Dylan. "We have more important things to discuss, like when Dylan will take me to Cypress Point. You'd get major boyfriend brownie points, just saying."

"Can I go?" Olivia asks. "I wanna meet a hot rich boy, too."

I thunk my head on the table, but Dylan laughs. "She and Brock would get along well."

"Too well," I mumble.

"Probably. Anyway, I'd be happy to take you sometime, Mr. Arlington. I haven't golfed enough this summer, that's for sure."

"Yessss." Dad pats my shoulder. "You can't break up with him—I've been trying to find this hookup for *years*."

"Do you know how creepy that sounds?" I ask. Something clinks on the table, and when I pull my head up I'm greeted with a huge bowl of *saag*. "Shrey, it's magnificent."

"Seriously," Olivia says. "It was worth driving to Seaside for the ingredients."

Shreya rolls her eyes. "I hope it tastes good. I had to ask Pavan for details because I rarely make it, and you don't have a tandoori or even a grill so the *naan* didn't come out great."

"It's wonderful," I say through a mouthful of bread. Spooning *saag* onto my plate, I dip the *naan* in this time. Perfection.

"Wow, you should be a chef." Dylan takes another bite. "This is just as good as what you brought to AnimalZone for Mika."

Shreya lights up. "You think?"

We all nod in agreement.

"I was hoping to hear that, because . . ." She pauses, looking at us like she's about to make a big announcement. I brace myself. "Pavan and I have been talking about sticking to our strengths and opening a restaurant. He would be the chef and I could run the house."

It clicks. "Is that why you haven't called Clark?"

She shrinks a little. "Yeah, sorry. I'm still not sure what'll happen, and I didn't want to commit when Pavan might need me."

"Don't worry," Dylan says. "I'm sure my uncle considers it a standing offer."

"Why didn't you tell me sooner?" I ask. "I was kind of worried, honestly."

"Yeah, Shrey," Olivia says through her teeth. "You shouldn't have put it off for so long. See how well everyone handled it?"

Shreya doesn't reply. Clearly Olivia knew about this before I did. I'm willing to bet this idea sprung up the same day my grandma had her heart attack. Did Shreya think I couldn't handle the news with everything else I've been going through? Or was she afraid I'd get mad that she didn't want to work with me? I hope she doesn't think I'm that petty.

My parents decide to catch a late movie, since they don't often get the chance with Betty here now. Shrey, Olivia, Dylan, and I settle in the living room and skim through Netflix movies. We end up on some B movie thriller, but I don't care because Dylan's arm is around my shoulder and mine is around his waist. Shrey and Olivia don't seem annoyed at the cuddling, which is a bonus.

About half way through the movie, Dylan says, "Hey, could I use your laptop for a sec?"

I give him a suspicious glare. "Are you allowed?"

"Not technically." He bites his lip, which is when I realize something must be bothering him. "But it's important. After what happened tonight . . . I can't think of any way to make it clearer to London."

"London?" Olivia's eyebrow arches. "You saw her tonight?"

"Ugh, yeah. It was ugly." I stand up, heading for the hall. "I'll be right back—Dylan can fill you in if he wants."

After a quick check in my mirror, I grab my laptop and go back to the living room. Dylan takes it from me and opens

251

Facebook. He logs out of mine and into his. I figure he'll look through all the wall messages Shrey saw during her cyber-snooping, but he types in my name and sends a friend request. Then he goes to his profile and clicks on the relationship section.

"Whoa whoa whoa." I pull my laptop from him, my heart pounding. "Are you serious? This is what you wanted it for? No way. I can't handle the lameness."

"I know it's kinda stupid." His eyes are soft, almost worried. "I've never done this before, but I don't want her or anyone else questioning us again. Even if it's lame, London will take this seriously."

I don't know what to say, but I can feel Shrey and Olivia watching. They know I'd never do this on my own. I've never changed my relationship status, even when I was with my other boyfriends. It felt so . . . stupid yet official, which would make it harder to untangle when it ended. But I want everyone to know Dylan is mine, too. I especially don't want London thinking she has any chance. There is nothing clearer or more public than this, so I take a deep breath and hand him back my laptop. "Okay, let's do this."

"Holy. Crap," Shreya whispers at the same time Olivia curses.

Dylan changes his status to "in a relationship" and identifies me as the one he's with. Then he gives it back to me so I can login and approve his requests. The friend one is easy, but my cursor hovers over the relationship approval. It's crazy how nervous this makes me. "I've never done this for anyone, you know."

"I know." He takes my hand and puts it to his chest. His heart pounds at my palm. "I'm nervous, too."

"Here goes nothing." I take a deep breath and click "approve."

252

Shreya and Olivia stare at me like they're not sure who I am anymore. Can't say I blame them.

I lean into Dylan, watching as my feed explodes with shocked responses. We log into his profile so we can watch the chaos unfold on both sides. There are a lot of excited congratulations on mine, and many crying girls on his. I hate to admit it, but this makes me extra happy.

"If London doesn't get it now, she never will," I say after a few minutes.

"Seriously. Thanks for humoring me." He leans down and kisses me, and I'm pretty sure I've never been so happy in my life.

Chapter 38

After another week of slow recovery in the hospital, the doctors finally give my grandma the all-clear. I just have to make it through a work shift before we pick her up—Mom and Dad are meeting Dylan and me at the hospital after. I'm so excited I can barely take it. How we lived without her, I'm not sure. Now it feels like she's always been here.

"Are you sure you don't want to come?" I ask Shreya as I slip my shoes on.

Shrey shakes her head. "Pavan is picking me up for lunch. We'll be scouting possible restaurant locations."

"Sounds fun." I grab my bag. "So you'll be okay?"

She smirks. "Yes, Mom. Being with my brother makes things feel a little normal."

"That's good. Are you staying with him tonight?"

She bites her lip, as if she's scared to tell me. "Yeah. You don't mind, right? They really like having me around."

"Of course I don't. It's not like you'll be gone forever. I'll live. Barely."

She smirks. "You're gonna be late."

I look at the clock. "Crap!"

When I get to AnimalZone, Dylan is unloading an order of fish gravel from a truck. He gives me a disapproving glare. "You think you can be late because you're dating the owner's nephew? Tsk."

"Yes, three whole minutes late. I'm clearly taking advantage."

He nods at the door. "No seriously, you better get in there. My uncle needs help."

"Going." There are a few early customers, and Clark scrambles between them. I stride up to the one with a little dog in her arms. It has a neon pink bow in its stringy hair, and it glowers like it wishes me dead. "Can I help you, ma'am?"

"She needs dog food," Clark says. "Thanks, Mika."

I take the lady to the right aisle and try to stay patient as she describes her precious dog's dietary needs. This is not my area of expertise, but I know which brand Clark recommends the most often, so I go with that. She seems pleased enough, and when she checks out the place is deserted again.

Clark sighs. "I swear that always happens when there's only one person here."

"It's like retail law or something," I say.

He nods. "Your friend never called me. Did she find something else?"

I wince. "Kind of. She might be helping her brother open a curry house. I guess it all came up after I told her."

"I'll just have to see if I can get someone else." He straightens the merchandise by the register. "I really do need another hand around here."

"Sorry." It would have been fun to work with Shreya, though I know she'll be happier in her element. "I'll keep an eye out.

School starts in a few weeks—I'm sure I'll run into someone who needs a job."

"Sounds good."

Dylan appears from the back room, heading for us with a big smile. He grabs me by the waist right in front of his uncle. I swear he likes to embarrass me. "So today's the day. Are you excited?"

I smile. "I am. I miss having her around."

"Sounds like it's been a hard recovery," Clark says.

"So hard. I hope being home will help reduce her outbursts, though we'll still have to be extra careful. Our home aide even said he'd come extra the first week she's home."

"That Joel," Dylan says. "Heart of giddy gold."

"Totally." I pull away from him, pointing to Aquatics. "Now, to the tanks!"

He smirks. "Drill sergeant."

"She's perfect for you," Clark says, smiling like a proud father.

"I know." Dylan takes my hand and drags me to the tanks. Work always flies by now. It might be only a week since we saw his parents, but we've spent almost every second possible with each other since. I can't believe there was a time when I couldn't stand him.

After work, Dylan hooks my bike to the back of his uncle's car. I barely sit still as we drive to the hospital, the thought of my grandma being okay and coming home overwhelming. We could have been having a funeral, but she's still here. We have time. Not as much as we could have had, but I'll take what I can get.

Mom and Dad are waiting for us in the lobby, and after a quick greeting we head for my grandma's room. I knock on the door and then open it. When she sees me, a big smile spreads across her face. "I get to come with you today."

I nod. "Are you feeling okay?"

"Just super." She looks down, seeming embarrassed. "But I need help dressing. The nurses told me not to try it alone. They don't want me to fall."

"You have good nurses."

"Boys." Mom points to the door. "If you'd give us a minute."

My dad and Dylan leave. We help Grandma pick out the clothes she wants from a bag my parents brought. When Mom helps her out of the gown, I can't help staring at the long scar down her chest. It's not fully healed, and it reminds me just how close it was. We help her with the loose shirt and pants, and then I fluff her hair while Mom works on her makeup.

"I wish I had daughters," she says.

"You do have a daughter—Jenny," Mom says.

Grandma frowns. "She doesn't count. She never did stuff like this for me. All she ever did was drugs and men."

"What's the first thing you want to do when we get home?" I ask, knowing Aunt Jenny isn't a good topic to linger on.

"Hmm . . ."

Mom stands, heading for the door. "I'll get the boys."

"I want to eat. The food here is terrible." She pats her hair, as if she's unsure about how it looks. "It will be nice to have dinner together again."

I smile. "What do you want to eat?"

"Oatmeal."

I cram my lips together so I won't laugh. Her and oatmeal. There has to be something behind it. "Why do you like oatmeal so much?"

"Oh, my sister Grace makes the *best* oatmeal." She licks her lips just thinking about it, and everyone else comes in while she imagines whatever this amazing oatmeal was. "She would cook it on the stove and mix in nuts, brown sugar, and cinnamon. Then she'd stir in a handful of raisins. Mmm, it was heaven in a bowl."

"I remember that," Dad says softly. "Aunt Grace would make that for me when I visited her. No wonder you always complain about ours not tasting good."

"We'll have to try making it that way," I say.

A nurse comes in to take us through the checkout process. She gives my parents several forms to fill out, and then says she'll be back soon to talk about specific care needs. I sit on the small bench while we wait, and Dylan takes the spot next to me.

"You look tired," he says. "And nervous."

"Yes to both." I let out a long sigh. "But it's almost over. I'll finally be able to relax soon."

"You do need a break." He places his hand over mine, squeezes once, and then whispers, "I know a way I can help you chill out."

I try not to smile, but fail miserably. "And what would that be?"

"What are you doing?" Grandma's voice is stern, and when I look up so is her face. Her eyes are on our clasped hands.

I pull my hand away and stand. No, no, no. "It's nothing, Gran—"

She's not looking at me, but at Dylan. "Why are you holding hands with a girl like that? Did you go blind, son?"

Dylan balls his fists. "I don't know what you're talking about."

I wish I could telepathically beg Dylan to let it slide just this once. If she gets mad now . . . My grandma steps in closer. "You know exactly what I'm talking about. I told you a thousand times that mixing with other races is unnatural. You won't be seeing that girl ever again."

"That girl?" Dylan sounds as if he's about to burst. "You mean your own granddaughter?"

She looks horrified. "I don't have a granddaughter, and if I did she wouldn't be an ugly Jap like that."

I cringe at the words.

Dylan stands. "Don't call her that!"

I stand between them, my heart pounding a thousand times a second. This can't be happening. Not now. She needs to stay calm. "Dylan, now is not the time."

Mom and Dad try to get my grandma's attention, but her eyes are trained on us. Dad attempts to pull her away—she slaps him back.

Dylan grabs my shoulders, so angry I can feel him shaking. "Did you not hear what she just called you? That doesn't bother you?"

"It does! But—"

"No, don't say it's okay because she doesn't know, because she's sick. That's not right."

"You shouldn't touch her," Betty says. "That's what's not right."

I gulp, trying to hold back the tears and silently pleading with him to let it go. She'll freak out any second, I know it.

And who knows what will happen in her condition? "It's fine. Let's go."

"It's not." Dylan spins me around and keeps me next to him with a firm arm. "Mika is the most amazing person I've ever met, and I refuse to let you talk about her like that. You should apologize."

Betty's eyes go wide, and she points at Dylan. "How dare you disobey me! How dare you choose that . . . that whore over your own mother!"

"Mom! We're not reliving this memory anymore." Dad grabs her by the shoulders, and that's when all hell breaks loose. My grandma screams and flails like a wild animal. Mom runs for the bed and hits the emergency button, while Dylan pushes me towards the door.

As Mom ushers us outside, Grandma's screaming continues. Nurses rush down the hall while Mom says, "Dylan, if you'd take Mika home. I'll call you when we find out what the doctor decides based on this."

"I don't want to go," I cry.

Mom puts her hand on my cheek, her eyes haunted. "I know, but I think you also understand you have to. Today you two are your father and me—I prayed you would never have to hear such horrible things, Mi-chan." She looks to Dylan. "Thank you for defending her like you should."

He nods once. "C'mon, Mika. We need to go."

I let him take me, though inside I can't stop seething about how he treated my grandma.

Chapter 39

I stare out the window as Dylan drives me home, because if I look at him I'll lose it. My anger bubbles and boils, threatening to spill over any moment. He parks in front of my house, and when he goes to unbuckle his seatbelt I say, "You're not coming in."

"Mika . . ."

I open the door and shove it closed as hard as I can. His door opens and closes, but I don't turn back. "Leave me alone!"

"I don't think that's a good idea."

I can feel him behind me as I fumble over my keys. Finally, I get the right one and unlock it. I try to shut the door on him, but he pushes back. I dig in my feet. "I really don't want to look at your face right now. I'm so mad I could hit something, and it might be you."

"Get mad. That's fine," he says with a growl. "I'm plenty mad myself, but you're not running away from me. I won't let you."

I give a frustrated grunt, letting the door open. He stumbles in as I stomp to the living room. I'm half tempted to throw something like my grandma did the day she almost died. "How could you do that to her? I told you she needs to be calm.

261

You *knew* how fragile she was, and you went off like it didn't matter if she died or not!"

He throws his arms up. "What was I supposed to do? Let her call you horrible names and not defend you in the slightest?"

"Yes! That is *exactly* what you should have done."

He gives me a look that clearly says he thinks I'm crazy. "How can you say that? I don't care who's calling you names—you should never have to just take it."

"She is *sick*, Dylan." I pinch the bridge of my nose, trying not to cry at the thought. "She didn't even know who she was talking to—she thought we were my parents."

"That makes it okay? You don't find it disturbing that she said those same things to your mom and dad?"

"I do!" I wrap my arms around myself, trying to keep it together. Part of me knows he's right, but I'm so worried about my grandma nothing else matters. "I know she's not a perfect person. I know what she did to my family with her crazy beliefs—trust me, I know."

He puts his hands on his hips, my words seeming to frustrate him more. "Then why do you let her get away with it?"

"Because . . . look, I tried to be mean to her, but it made me feel like a shitty person. I swore to myself to treat her better." I close my eyes. I refuse to cry, not right now. Crying during a fight means you lose. "She's my grandma—she's part of who I am whether I want it or not. What she did, who she is . . . her actions made some of me. And as much as I hate lots of the things she does, I still love her.

"She's had a hard life, and now she's dying of an incurable disease that will slowly rot her mind until she can't function

262

at all. There's no cure for Alzheimer's—there's nothing I can do but watch." I put my hand over my mouth, the thought of losing her raw as ever.

"So excuse me if I want to keep her as long as I can, if I want to learn as much as possible about her before she forgets it all, if I want to make the rest of her life comfortable and happy and full of the love she never had. Maybe she doesn't deserve it, but does that give me a pass to be cruel to her?"

Dylan's shoulders slump, and the fight in his eyes fades. "Why do I care so much about someone who makes me feel like a horrible person constantly?"

I roll my eyes. "You aren't."

He sighs. "Look, I get where you're coming from. I promise. But you have to understand my side, too. Because I don't think I did the wrong thing, and neither did your mom."

"You're really gonna start that way?"

He holds up his hands. "Wait, okay?"

"Go ahead."

He takes a deep breath. "I know you love your grandma and won't do anything to harm her. Even when it hurts you. But to me, all I see is someone I care about being called horrible names, and a woman I barely know telling me I shouldn't be with you.

"Mika . . ." His eyes meet mine, and they are sad and full of longing all at once. "You know how I used to be. You get that I didn't give a shit about anyone but myself. It sounds cheesy, but you're the first person I've ever really cared about. You make me so happy I want to spend every second with you. There's no way I could have let her think I agreed with her.

263

"I'm sorry, but I will always stand up for you, especially when you can't stand up for yourself. I have to—you mean everything to me."

I scrunch my lips together to stop them from quivering, because he means more to me than any guy ever has. "Why do you have to do that?"

"What?" His voice is quiet.

"Why do you have to make me want you so much, even when I'm mad as hell?"

He smirks. "Does that mean I'm forgiven?"

"Yes."

He strides over and grabs me, picking me up as our lips meet. His kisses are hot and urgent, but mine are even more so. This summer has brought me so many things, and Dylan might be the best of them all. As scared as I am to admit it, I've fallen for him. Deeply.

I entwine my fingers in his hair, wrap my legs around his waist, allow myself to let go of everything else but him. His hands run up and down my back, hover at my bra strap as if he's thinking about unhooking it. I want him to, think about whispering for him to just do it already because I can't imagine wanting anyone as much as I want him.

He moves to my neck, and I breathe in his ear, "You're so hot."

"Mika, I'm about to lose it." His fingers slip under my shirt. "You better get off me if you don't want that to happen."

"My room." I kiss his earlobe, so far gone he doesn't even know. "Now."

He doesn't waste any time carrying me through the hall. He sets me down just inside, and I reach past him to shut the door. And lock it. He breathes hard, his eyes all desire as they run over me. It makes me adore him even more, knowing how much he wants me back.

I need to take his clothes off right now.

"I don't have any . . ." he says as I go for his shirt.

"I do. In my nightstand." I pull it over his head, and when I take in his bare chest I can hardly get air. I put my hands on his stomach and kiss him again.

He guides me to the bed and stops just short, looking me straight in the eye. "Are you sure?"

"Have I not made myself clear enough?" I take off my own shirt. "Yes, I am sure. Very, very sure. Thanks for being such a gentleman, but let's do this."

He laughs, low and soft. It's so hot I can barely function. "Okay, then."

Dylan pushes me onto my bed, and it's over. His weight on me feels more right than anything in the world. His fingers on my skin are magic. This has never felt so good, and in that moment I know we're not ending this anytime soon.

And I'm totally okay with that.

Chapter 40

I slip back into my clothes while Dylan is in the bathroom, though part of me wishes we could do this for the rest of the night. Sure takes my mind off all the other crap I'm dealing with. When he comes back—strutting around in his boxer briefs like he owns the place—I can't help but smile. "You look ridiculous."

"I do not care." He gets back in my bed, pulling me close. "You were right. It's way better when you're crazy about the person you're with."

"Feel free to say I'm right as much as you want."

He laughs. "As long as we do that every day."

I scoff. "We're lucky my house was empty for this long."

"I know, I know." He kisses my forehead, and I want to stay like this forever and ever. "Wishful think—"

My phone rings, and I scramble for it. The second I see my mom's number in the window, my heart starts pounding. Please don't tell me they're on the way home right now. I hit "accept." "Hi, Mom."

Dylan hops up and grabs his pants.

"How are you doing, sweetie?" she asks.

"Better." I hope she can't tell why over the phone, though she does have an incredible radar for this stuff.

There's a long pause. "You were responsible, right?"

I sigh. How does she do that? "Of course."

Dylan gives me a curious look.

"Good." She clears her throat, and I hear Dad in the background asking her something. "Nothing, hon. Anyway, Mika, the doctors finished their tests, and it looks like Betty didn't damage anything during her episode. They're going to monitor her for another hour, and then we should be able to bring her home."

"Really?" I ask, surprised. After all that screaming I thought for sure Grandma would be stuck there for at least a few more days. Maybe the nurses are tired of her.

Mom laughs. "Yeah, they said this last week she did well, so things have healed faster. I think that's thanks to your visits."

"Psh."

"It's true. You've really been there for her. I'm proud of you for taking care of her, despite how hard it's been. You're a wonderful daughter. I'm lucky to have you." She sniffles, and it shocks me because Mom is not a crier.

"Thanks, Mom." I'm not sure what else to say, so I change the subject. "So you'll be home in a couple hours?"

"Probably. And, Mika . . ." Her voice gets quieter. "I'd make sure Dylan is gone by then, otherwise your father might pick up on things."

"Good point. See ya." I hang up. "They'll be home with her in a couple hours."

His face lights up. "That's good, right? She's okay?"

I nod. "But you better go so I have time to clean and calm myself down. My mom totally knew. She tolerates it pretty well, but my dad will get weird."

He frowns.

"Don't give me that face." I give him one more hug. "I'll see you tomorrow."

"I was just hoping you'd say we had time to make out more before they got home."

I shove him away. "Get out of here, dork."

He laughs as he grabs his shirt, and watching him put it on almost makes me reconsider.

As I sweep the floor and do the dishes, I'm keenly aware that I grin at random times. This will be a dead giveaway, especially since I'm supposed to be upset over what my grandma said to us. So I pull out my phone and text Olivia. *What r u doing?*

Her reply is immediate. *Drowning myself in reality TV. Why? Wanna come over?*

Ur not w/Dylan?

He just left. Need to talk this out before the fam gets home.

Ooo! Coming!

I can always count on Olivia in these situations. When she arrives, her smile is blinding. "Does this mean I can finally tell you about all my exploits in Tahiti?"

I laugh. "Yes."

"Good." She drops her bag by the front door, slips off her shoes, and heads for the living room. "I've been dying to talk, but Shreya goes pale if I even hint at it. So how was it? I'm betting he's amazing—he has 'experienced' written all over him."

I bite my lip. "Help me clean while we discuss the details."

"Fine. As long as I get to tell you about Waka."

I hand her cleaning spray and paper towels. "You first then."

And off she goes, regaling me with tales of warm nights on the beach making out with hot Waka, while her mom had her own fling with a wealthy businessman. Those two—talk about the apple not falling far from the tree. I think that's why Olivia's never had an ounce of shame when it comes to intimacy. A lot of girls at school call her names, but she just feels bad for them because "they don't know what they're missing."

Once we can't talk guys or clean anymore, we plop on the couch and turn on the TV. It's been about two hours, so my family will be home soon. Olivia picks a vampire drama, and we watch in tired silence.

"We need Shrey," I say after a few minutes. "I don't like her being in Salinas. Feels like we're missing something."

Olivia sighs. "I know, but she seems excited about starting a restaurant with Pavan. It's nice to see her happy about something, don't you think?"

"I guess." I stretch my legs out on the coffee table. "Though it'd be nicer if her parents would get over the whole thing and stop being stupid."

She smirks. "If only."

That day at the beach, when Shreya first told me her parents didn't want her marrying certain people, comes rushing back. She said this stuff should be simple, but it isn't. I think I get that now, having dealt with my grandma almost all summer. There's nothing simple about how it feels to love someone who directly opposes who you are or what you believe.

"Olivia?" I say.

She turns her attention to me, seeming cautious. "What?"

"Is Shrey really okay? It seems like she's not telling me stuff, like with the restaurant they're starting. You knew about that, didn't you?"

Olivia cringes, and that's all I need to know I was right. "Yeah, it happened the day her phone got cut off. She really freaked out, Mika. I think before that she hoped her parents would come around, because they were keeping a method of getting in contact, you know?"

I nod slowly. "Why hasn't she told me any of this?"

"I don't know . . ." Olivia bites her lip, which means even now she knows more than she's saying. "Look, it's not my place to tell you. I think you need to talk to her about—"

The garage door opens, and I reluctantly pull myself away from whatever Olivia was going to say. My grandmother walks in first, seeming cranky as she looks around. It only makes me smile wider as I hug her. "Welcome home, Grandma."

She pats me on the back. "It looks clean."

"I polished everything just for you."

"Thanks, sweetie," Dad says as he and Mom come in. He notices Olivia on the couch. "Thank you, too, Olivia."

She stands, seeming ready to go now that they're home. Or maybe she's ready to escape my questions. "No prob! I'll catch you later, Mika."

"See ya." After she waves goodbye, I turn back to Grandma. "How are you feeling?"

"I'm tired. I'm going to bed." My grandma pushes me to the side and walks towards the hall. At least it seems like she remembers where to go. I worried it might be a hard adjustment after being in the hospital so long.

"I'll help you into bed." Dad follows her. "The doctors said you still need to be careful."

"Oh, fine," she grumbles.

Mom heads for the cupboard, seeming concerned about me. "Should I make you some tea?"

"Yeah. Make enough for yourself, too." I lean on the counter and watch Mom put water in the kettle.

She looks exhausted, but she still smiles. "If you insist."

"I do." As she pulls out cups and tea bags and little cookies, I can't help thinking about what happened at the hospital. The words my grandma screamed . . . "Did Grandma really yell at you like that?"

Mom pauses, then looks at me. "It was much worse than that, Mi-chan. I insisted to your father that we should visit his mother to tell her we were engaged. He didn't want to—we got in a big fight about it—but I eventually won."

"So we're going there tonight, huh?" Dad leans on the counter next to me, sighing heavily. "I really hoped we'd never tell this story."

"I know," Mom says. "But she deserves to know."

My dad has never looked so sad. "We went to Vermont, Mika, though I knew what would happen. Yumi thought she could win my mother over, but she's the most stubborn woman

271

alive. This disease has actually made her more agreeable, if you can believe it."

"Wow." I can't picture her being surlier than now.

"I was surprised your father came from such poor circumstances. He was always careful to look clean and polished." Mom pours the water into the teacups and sticks the bags in. She hands one to me. "He never told me he had a hard childhood, but I could handle that fine. It was Betty's reaction to me I wasn't prepared for. She called me awful names and told me to get away from her son. And then . . ."

Mom takes her tea and drinks. It doesn't stop me from noticing her hands shake. Dad puts his arm around her trembling shoulders. Then he looks at me, a flicker of anger still there. "My mom hit her with a lamp. Can you imagine that? She picked up the nearest thing and swung right at your mom's head. I had to wrestle her to the ground and take the lamp before she did it again. Your mom was bleeding badly. I rushed her to a hospital, and that was the last time I saw my mom until she showed up here."

Mom pulls back her hair, revealing a scar I've never seen before. "Fourteen stitches. We thought about pressing charges, but then we'd have had to see her and deal with her in court. Plus, we were still poor grad students. We didn't think it was worth it."

My mouth hangs open as I watch Dad protect Mom even now. He kisses her scar, holds her close as they relive that nightmarish day. I had no idea it was that bad. "No wonder you didn't want her around."

Dad sighs. "I wasn't about to risk the safety of my wife or daughter, though I know cutting her out of my life was cruel.

What else was I supposed to do? I had to protect you guys—you mean more to me than anything."

Mom leans into him more. "That's why I love you."

I go over and hug them, feeling luckier than ever that they stayed together through all that. They wrap their arms around me, and I don't think I've ever felt so close to them in my life.

Chapter 41

"More sugar," Grandma says for the fourth time. After hearing what she did to Mom, I watch her closer than ever this morning. I know I should be angrier with her about it, but what's the point? She won't remember. I'd only be punishing myself. So while I'm on my guard, I'll still care for her as she is right now.

I'm pretty sure the oatmeal is more sugar than anything else, but I comply with her request. I'm determined to figure out how to replicate the stuff my great aunt Grace used to make. It's not going particularly well. I give her the spoon again. "How's that?"

Grandma blows on it and takes a bite. Her face scrunches as she judges the flavor, and I expect yet another complaint. "It's edible."

"Edible? Does that mean I can get you a bowl?"

She nods. "It's not right, but you can't cook well enough for it to be perfect."

I pour the oatmeal in a bowl, trying not to laugh at her dead serious assessment. "I can't cook *at all*."

"It shows."

"Mom," Dad snaps from the kitchen table. "Be nice. She's trying."

She sits next to him with her bowl in hand. "She'll never get it if I don't tell her when it's wrong!"

"It's fine. I have no pride in my cooking skills." I'm just glad she's here, that we're all around the breakfast table as a family again. With Mom tapping at her smart phone, Dad shoving down cereal before it gets soggy, and Grandma griping about the food, it feels like her heart attack never happened.

The doorbell rings, and I jump up to get it. When I open the door, there's Joel with a big smile on his face. "Mika! It's been too long. How's my Betty?"

"Better. Still weak, and the doctors said she needs to stay as calm as possible." I let him in.

"Of course, that's easier said than done."

"I know, right?"

He struts ahead of me and waves excitedly when he rounds the corner. "Betty Arlington, don't you ever scare me like that again, young lady! I don't want you going anywhere for a long time."

Grandma gives him a curious look, but doesn't seem too upset about Joel being here. "Sorry?"

"You're forgiven."

While Joel distracts her with stories about his other patients, my parents grab their work things. Mom catches my eye and motions for me to follow them into the garage. I don't know why, but I feel like I'm in trouble. "What is it?"

Dad straightens his glasses. "This might upset you, but your mom and I were thinking you probably shouldn't bring Dylan here for awhile. Just in case she has another bad reaction."

"Oh, yeah, of course." I try to act cool, but all I can think of is what happened yesterday. "I was already planning on that, actually. He'll understand."

Mom smiles. "I'm sure he will. Have a good day, sweetie."

"You, too!" When they're gone, I rush around the house getting ready for work. I wish I could wear anything except my uniform, but at least I'll get to see Dylan for four whole hours. I pedal extra fast on my way to AnimalZone, not even embarrassed that I'll be early and obviously excited to see him.

I park my bike in back and run my fingers through my hair. My heart pounds as I clock in, picturing the smile on his face at the sight of me. But when I get to Aquatics, he's not there. I check the register, frowning when he's nowhere in sight. He has to be here somewhere if the store is open.

Finally, I break down and head for Clark's office. He sits in front of the computer, rifling through bills. He jumps when he sees me. "Oh, there you are, Mika."

I raise an eyebrow. "Where else would I be?"

He offers a small smile, but something seems off about it. "So your friend never called me. Does she not need the job anymore?"

My brow furrows. "I told you, she wants to start a restaurant with her brother."

"Oh, right!" He fiddles with the papers on his desk. "Sorry, guess I forgot."

He must need another employee more than I realized if he's bringing this up again. "I mean, she might change her mind, but she doesn't have a phone because her parents cut hers off. It's hard for me to stay in contact with her lately."

"Sounds familiar," he says.

"Yeah, I guess so." I purse my lips, suddenly feeling weird asking him. "Speaking of the help, where's Dylan?"

"D-Dylan?" His voice cracks, and he pulls at his collar.

I frown. "Is he sick or something?"

He gulps. "Not exactly."

The warning bells start going off, but my boss is the last person I want to freak out in front of. "What do you mean by 'not exactly'?"

He sighs, and with it his face falls into something part-sadness part-anger. "I don't know how that punk expected me to do this. It's really not fair to either one of us after all that's happened this summer."

"What are you talking about?" The panic is rising, rising, rising, like a tide coming in too fast. "Did something happen to him?"

He takes a slip of paper from his desk and holds it out to me. "I'm so sorry, Mika."

I take it, trying not to show how scared I am. It's the kind of paper you write a grocery list on, and I imagine this was written in their kitchen at home. I don't want to read the words, but I force myself to:

Uncle, I'm going back to apologize. I have to do it now before I chicken out. Tell Mika for me. Bye.
—Dylan

Chapter 42

"He must have left in the middle of the night," Clark says when I don't answer for who-knows-how-long. "I found that this morning. He took all his stuff and my car. I never thought he would do this . . . he seemed so happy."

I shake my head. "You're misunderstanding what this means." He has to be. Dylan wouldn't just up and leave the same day we . . . "He wouldn't steal your car and never come back. That's not who he is anymore."

"Are you sure?" He doesn't seem convinced, and I'm not sure if it makes me mad or scared. "I hate to say it, but he doesn't exactly have the best track record."

"I'm sure," I say, though my mind is racing in all different directions. He wouldn't leave me after all we've been through. Or was it just a game to him? No, it wasn't. The way he defended me from my grandma yesterday wasn't a lie. No one could be that deceitful. "There has to be an explanation. He'll call. He probably just didn't want to wake me up in the middle of the night. And it's not like San Jose is that far away. He probably just wanted to clear the air with his parents, and he'll be back tonight."

Clark purses his lips, thinking it over. "That doesn't sound impossible. I sure hope you're right."

"I'm right." I have to be. I don't know what I'll do if I'm wrong. "I'll get to work now."

When I'm not checking my phone, I scrub and vacuum and brush and help every customer that comes through the door, but the day still goes by much slower without Dylan to talk to. How I ever did this alone baffles me.

I'm tempted to call him, but I also don't want to look needy just because he's gone for one day. It's been three hours and I still haven't gotten a phone call, so I decide I'm allowed to at least send a text. It takes me a few minutes to settle on: *Did you get there safely?*

That's neutral enough. Shows I care but I'm not freaking out. I hit send and wait for a reply.

Nothing. For a whole hour.

He doesn't have time to send me one line telling me he's okay? I tap at my phone, waiting and wondering why he decided *now* was the time to go see his parents. When we saw them at the mall, he still seemed furious with them. But he *did* say he wished they could be happy. Maybe he really does miss them.

Shaking myself out of it, I focus on fish tanks. There's something soothing about watching fish swim. They're graceful and quiet, in a world all their own. They're so . . . not enough to keep me distracted from the fact that my boyfriend just up and left in the middle of the night for a reason I can't understand.

I pull up my text window again. *Are you okay? Starting to worry.*

I send it before I think too much about how needy I might sound. But he was driving in the middle of the night, and San Jose is almost three hours away. What if he fell asleep at the wheel and got hurt? Because he wouldn't just go home without contacting me. He wouldn't leave me like that. I'm sure of it.

Why does Shreya not have a phone right now? I need her to tell me this is okay. I need her to talk me off the cliff while I stuff my face with curry. Except I can't go eat curry thanks to all her family drama.

The second I get off work, I'm desperate enough to call Pavan. He answers cheerily. "Hello, Mika. You looking for my sister?"

"You had her for a whole day." My voice is decidedly whiny. "You better give her back to me."

His laugh is hearty. "We're actually just about to leave for your house."

"Good. See you soon, then." I get on my bike, but then can't decide where to eat. Another text, just in case his phone is on vibrate. *When are you coming back? I wanted to go out with you tonight.*

I end up going home. Joel raises his eyebrow when I enter the kitchen, where he's making lunch. "You're early."

"Yeah, I didn't want to eat anywhere." I'm starting to not want to eat *anything*, but I don't say that. "Those grilled cheeses sure look good, though."

He laughs as he grabs more bread. "You're very subtle."

"It's a talent." I stare at the clock, hoping Shreya comes soon. Then I check my phone, wishing it would ring or beep or something. Shouldn't Dylan at least text me back? What's so hard about typing a quick message so I don't totally lose it wondering what that note—

Grandma puts her hand on my knee, which was bouncing a hundred times a minute. "You're shaking the table, girl."

"Sorry," I say, though I don't like her calling me "girl." Maybe she's having a hard time remembering my name.

"You okay?" Joel asks as he sets our plates in front of us. "You seem . . . nervous."

"I do?"

His eyes narrow. "I should warn you—I'm *very* hard to fool. So if you plan on lying to me, don't bother."

"I wasn't." I sigh, trying to let some of my nerves go with it. There's no reason for me to be this wound up. Everything is probably fine. I'll feel silly if I worry too much and then find out it's nothing. "It's not a big deal. If I find out it is, then I'll be sure to tell you. I don't want to stress anyone out."

"You promise?"

"Of course." The doorbell rings, and I hop up. "That must be Shrey! Finally."

I practically tackle her after I open the door, never happier to see her in my life. She laughs as she hugs me back. "You'd think I was gone for a year with that welcome."

"I told you I can't live without you. There's so much I need to tell you—you have no idea." I pull her towards my room, and I think I hear Joel complaining about me not eating the food he made. But this can't wait any longer. I have to tell Shrey before I explode with panic.

By the time I'm done recapping the hospital freak out, what happened after, and the note Dylan left for Clark, she stares at me with wide eyes and no words. I pull Dylan's note from my pocket, and she reads it a few times. Finally, she says, "It has to be a misunderstanding. If he didn't like being here, why would he write a note at all? Wouldn't he just leave?"

"True! Yes." I pace my room, this odd energy coursing through me. I have no idea what it is, but there's no way I can sit. "Excellent point. So I shouldn't worry, right?"

"No, but you should just call him," Shreya says. "You've given him plenty of time and texts to reply to. You're his girlfriend—you don't have to apologize for wanting to hear from him."

"You're right." I grab my phone and call his number. My hand shakes as I put it to my ear. Shreya leaves the room while it rings.

"Why hello, Mika," a voice says. A female voice. "Or should I say Fish Girl?"

I can't breathe, and I have no idea what to say except, "London."

"You slept with him, didn't you?"

When I don't answer immediately, she laughs and laughs.

282

Chapter 43

I should be cussing out London, defending myself, demanding to speak to Dylan. Something. But all I can do is listen to her laugh and wonder why the hell she's answering his phone. Is she in his house? His room?

"The second I saw that dumpy car in the driveway I knew he must have come home," London says when she finally stops snickering. "And sure enough, I was right. Didn't I tell you, Mika? Dylan doesn't have girlfriends."

"You don't know what you're talking about." I want it to sound strong, but instead I sound squeaky and weak.

"Oh yeah? So you didn't sleep with him?"

I don't answer again.

She scoffs. "You thought you were so much better than me, that you somehow changed him. You were a game, like all the other girls—a tougher game, sure, but still a game. Once he won, he did what he always does. He got bored and moved on. I think you should get over it, too."

Her words feel like burning hot acid dripped straight on my heart. Not because I believe her, but because she's saying everything I'm afraid of. I force the lump in my throat down, determined not to show my weakness. "You're full of crap. Dylan's not like that anymore, so let me talk to him."

"He went golfing with his dad, didn't even bother to bring this cheap-ass phone. His mom called me over to play tennis, and I just happened to hear it ring."

"You're lying." I can't fall for this. London hates me, she's obviously trying to scare me away. "Give him the phone."

"He's gone. I swear."

"Let me talk to him. Now," I growl.

She sighs. "Clinginess is not a very attractive quality. You really can't get the picture?" I hear someone else in the background. It sounds like another woman. Then London says, "I'll be right there, Mrs. Wainwright!"

No, was that really her, or is London pretending? Maybe Dylan actually is out golfing with his dad.

"I gotta go, but let me give you some advice, Mika," London says. "Dylan is beyond charming, but you need to accept this before you hurt yourself more."

The way she talks, it feels like she pities me. I wish I could punch her. "I don't need to accept anything. He's coming back—and he'd talk to me right now if you weren't such a bitch."

"Are you that dense?" She takes a deep breath. "Dylan isn't coming back. He came home to tell his parents he was sorry for what he did, and they forgave him. He doesn't belong at his uncle's dirty old pet shop—he has much bigger things to do in his life. Do you understand?"

I grit my teeth. "He said he didn't want what his dad forced on him. He said he hated his life."

"Maybe he did. But then he saw how much it sucks to be poor, and now he's learned his lesson. I guess I should thank you for helping him see the light, but if you really care about him you'll let him go. It might sound harsh, but there's no place in his life for a girl like you."

"Like me?"

"Yes. Please don't call him again." London hangs up without even a polite farewell.

I immediately call back, ready to unleash my best swearing on her. She can't possibly think I'd fall for that. She doesn't pick up, and I call and call until I get the message that his phone is off. I let out a frustrated grunt. "You think that'll stop him? He'll call me back, bitch! He has my number memorized and he can find a phone."

I know he will. He'd never do that to me.

Four days pass without a single text or email or phone call from Dylan. I've called so many times I've lost count. I try to remain strong, but as I sit on my bed and stare at my phone I don't know what to think. He lives in a huge mansion—there's no way he can't find a phone or get internet access. Whether London told the truth or not, her words are beginning to hurt.

Am I being clingy? Did I miss some big sign that he didn't actually care about me? Because I was never so sure about a guy in my life.

Part of me still wants to believe she's lying. Maybe he'll still call. Maybe she's hatched this elaborate scheme to keep us apart now that he's come home. Except I realize that sounds way crazier than admitting I was his summer fling and now he's back to his fancy life in his mansion surrounded by power and money. It's not like I'm in some TV drama—that really is the most logical explanation.

Shit, I *am* being clingy.

Dylan is gone. I just don't want to believe it. But after so long without a single word how can I keep believing? Isn't that called denial?

There's a tap at my door, and then Shreya peeks in. "Still nothing?"

I start sobbing. It's like all the times I wanted to cry in the past several days were saved up for this moment, and I fall into my pillows weeping uncontrollably. Shreya's weight makes the bed creak, and her hand squeezes my shoulder. "Oh, Mika, I'm sorry."

"I . . . I . . . don't think he's coming back." I'm not sure she can understand what I'm saying, but I can't control myself.

She doesn't say anything, which has to mean she agrees. That feels like the final proof. She rubs my back as I let the reality of Dylan being gone hit me. I have no idea how I'm supposed to stop caring about him as much as I do. His arms should be around me if I'm crying this much. Shreya isn't enough. No one is enough.

Then Grandma pokes her head around the door. "What is all that racket?" she says in a very grouchy tone. "Did someone die?"

I wipe at my face with my already-wet sheets. "Grandma . . . he left me. My boyfriend left me."

Her face fills with a deep sense of understanding, and she rushes to my side. She pulls me into a tight hug, stroking my hair. "Oh, sweetheart, I'm sorry. I'm so, so sorry."

I hug her back. She may not be perfect, but she of all people understands what this feels like. "It hurts so much."

"I know. I told you it would if you really loved him."

That makes me cry harder. Maybe I really am cursed.

"You," Grandma says, and I assume she's speaking to Shreya. "Make her some tea. Something soothing."

Footsteps sound down the hallway.

"I don't want tea," I say.

"But you need it." She makes me lie down, and she pulls the covers up to my chin. "You also need to sleep."

I sniffle and cough. I must look like a mess. "How did you handle people leaving so many times? It's the worst."

She purses her lips, and in her eyes I see more wisdom and understanding than I have in a while. Thank goodness she's coherent today, because I'm certainly not. "You say to yourself, 'Today I will let myself be the most miserable creature on the planet, but tomorrow I will get up and keep going.'"

"How can I?"

She takes my hand. "It won't be easy, but you do it anyway. That's all I got—I'm not sure I handled any of it right."

Maybe she didn't, but I'm glad to have her here right now. "Do I really have to get up tomorrow?"

She snorts. "Well, maybe you can have two days in this case. Since it's the first time."

Shreya brings me tea, and Grandma makes me drink it all though it doesn't sit well in my stomach. Before I know it, I'm spent from all that crying, but I can't rest when I'm almost positive I'll never see Dylan again.

* * *

It's dark when I wake up, and Shreya sleeps next to me. My eyes are swollen and my head pounds. I glance at my clock—almost midnight. Though I don't want to get out of bed, my bladder forces me to. By the time I'm done, I know I won't be able to sleep more. I can't stop thinking about what London said, about how much I miss him and want to pretend it's all a horrible joke.

I grab my laptop and head for the living room. Putting on *The Princess Bride*, I hunker down on the sofa with a blanket and do exactly what I shouldn't do.

Open Facebook.

Check my status.

It still says we're in a relationship, which gives me a weird sense of hope that I immediately despise. I almost change it myself, but I can't. I'm not ready for it to be that final, for people to know how much pain I'm in. Besides, if he really wants out, he should be the one to change it.

I try to watch my movie, try to feel better because at least Westley and Buttercup still make it. But I keep checking my status, imagining Dylan in his giant mansion, one click away from breaking all ties with me.

Chapter 44

The next day, I do what Grandma says. I get up. I get dressed and eat and go to work even though it's the last place I want to be. My smile is fake, but the customers don't seem to notice. Clark can't look me in the eye, but I'm fine with that.

"Hey, Mika," he says about half way through my shift. "How about you take the rest of the day off?"

I sigh. "Do I look that depressed?"

He cringes. "It's Friday, thought you'd like a longer weekend."

Hell, I want to leave anyway. I'm way past pride at this point. "Thanks, I guess. Longer weekends never hurt."

"Um, one other thing."

"Yeah?"

There's a long pause, and I'm really hoping he doesn't bring up his nephew because I'm poised to attack anyone who even thinks of that jerk. "I'd hate to lose you, but if you don't want to work here anymore, I understand. Say the word, and I'll put up an ad, okay?"

"Oh." I'm struck by how extremely considerate of him this is, and how *in*considerate the rest of his family is. "I haven't really thought about it, but if it gets too . . . Well, I'll let you know."

"Okay."

I don't want to go home so early, but I don't want to be anywhere else, either. So I pedal slowly, trying to think of something to distract myself with for the rest of the day. I got nothing. Besides, I'll be trapped in the house with my grandma in a couple hours anyway. May as well spend my time staring at Facebook, waiting for him to officially break up with me.

Stopping in front of the mailbox, I check to see if we got anything. There's a bunch of junk mail and one letter addressed to me. It's from my school.

My class schedule.

I stare at the envelope, hardly able to believe it's time for school again. My junior year feels like it happened years ago, and the thought of classes and homework and tests doesn't mesh with what my life has been like this summer. I feel too old for school, as if in one season I officially turned into an adult.

When I open it and look at my schedule, it seems like nonsense. Do I really have to do this in a week?

Sighing, I push my bike up our path. Maybe it's a good thing. School is a distraction, and I need one of those. It could help me get back to normal, to start making this summer a distant memory.

"Mika! You're home early!" Joel exclaims when I open the door. And not in an excited way. But Grandma is at the kitchen table in front of a game of checkers, and nothing seems immediately out of order.

I narrow my eyes. "Can you be more suspicious?"

He bites his lip, glancing at the hall. "I told them they should tell you, but they wouldn't listen to me."

"What are you talking about?"

He gives me this pitiful look. "You better go see. In your room."

I hurry down the hall, which is when I hear the music in my room, accompanied by voices. When I push the door open, I freeze. Olivia and Shreya stand by my bed, where they are packing a suitcase. Shreya's suitcase.

"What the hell?" I say, and they both turn. The look on their faces is pure shock, and I can't help but feel a deep sense of betrayal.

"M-Mika," Shreya sputters. "What are you doing home?"

"What are you doing packing up and leaving while I'm at work? Were you even going to tell me?"

"I was on Monday, but then Dyl . . ." Shreya looks at her feet. "I didn't want to add insult to injury."

Olivia cringes. "She should have told you sooner, but you've just been going through so much—"

"And you thought doing the *exact same thing* he did was the way to go?" I shouldn't be yelling, but I'm so angry and if I don't scream I'll cry. "You were going to disappear and let me discover you ditched me, too?"

"I'm so sorry," Shreya squeaks. "I should have thought about that."

I fold my arms. "So what, you're going to Olivia's because you can't handle all my crap anymore?"

They exchange a glance, and I get the feeling it's much worse than that.

"Actually . . ." Shreya gulps. "Pavan found a restaurant to rent in Salinas, so I need to be closer to help him get it ready."

I stare at her, horrified. "You're moving in with your brother?"

She nods.

"So you're not going to school with us anymore, and you won't be here to sand sculpt on Saturdays, and you'll be so busy with this restaurant I'll barely ever see you . . ." I ramble on, tears forming in my eyes against my will. It feels like my world is crumbling beneath my feet. "That's why you've been acting so weird. You knew you were doing this weeks ago, and you didn't tell me."

She purses her lips, on the verge of crying herself. "What else am I supposed to do, Mika? You're my best friend, but I can't stay here forever. I need my family, too. Being with Pavan and Rachelle makes me feel like I haven't lost everything."

I wipe at my eyes, knowing and hating that she's right. She has as many problems as I do, and it'd be selfish of me to be mad at her. "This sucks."

"I know." She sniffles. "I'm sorry I couldn't find the right words or time to tell you—I didn't want to hurt you on top of everything else. Because I know you need me, but . . . I have nothing to give unless I'm happy, too."

I force myself to nod. "So is Pavan coming to pick you up?"

"In about half an hour."

I suck in a deep breath, trying to be strong about this because Shreya needs me to be. She needs to think this won't break me, though it's tearing me apart inside. "Then I better help you pack."

Helping her fold clothes, I realize I've gotten good at pretending I'm fine. All the fake smiles at work have given me too much practice, because I can joke and laugh with Olivia and Shreya even though my mind keeps saying: *Everyone is leaving you, your life is over, and soon you'll have no one left, just like your grandma lost everyone.*

I really am cursed.

Pavan shows up right on time, and I give Shreya a big hug as he puts her things in the trunk. This is it. She's leaving. It might not be as far as San Jose, but it's still too far.

"You have to at least call me sometimes," I manage to say without even a squeak.

"Of course. Maybe we can still sculpt on Saturdays." Her tears wet my shoulder. "I'll miss you."

"Me too," I force out.

She lets me go and hugs Olivia, who is as strong as a rock like usual. We watch as they drive away, and I hold on to myself so Olivia can't see me shaking. She turns to me, looking sad. "Do you want me to stay?"

I shake my head. "I'm tired. I should sleep while Joel is here."

"Okay." She looks like she wants to say something else, but then lets out a long sigh. "Call me if you want to hang out later, okay?"

"Yup." I head back inside before she can see just how broken I am. Joel is right there to hug me as I cry. Though I'm glad, I also feel bad for making more work for him. Dylan should be here for me right now, and he's not.

"I don't have another appointment until this evening," Joel says. "I'll stay until your parents get home, okay?"

"Thank you," I whisper.

"You go rest."

I do. I sleep and sleep because being awake hurts. It's dark when my phone rings, and I fumble around for it as I pull myself out of the haze. When I see the number, I think I might still be dreaming. It can't be, but it is. Dylan.

I almost let it go to voicemail, but at the last second I hit "accept."

Chapter 45

"What?" I say, my voice every bit as cold as I hoped it'd be. Even if I've been dying to talk to him, I'm still pissed it took five whole days for that to happen.

"Okay, you're probably really mad at me," Dylan starts. "But I swear I didn't mean for it to be so long. I lost my phone. I think one of the maids saw it on the counter and didn't think it was—"

"So London's your maid now?"

"Whoa . . . what?"

"And you couldn't have emailed me or borrowed a phone?" It spills out, even though I don't want it to seem like I've been hurt. "I seriously doubt your giant mansion doesn't have internet access."

"Actually, the internet *was* down, but—"

"For *five* days? Really?"

There's silence for a second. "Yeah, really. But now that I think about it, that seems weird, doesn't it?"

"It doesn't seem weird. It seems like a lie. You're up there having a great time playing golf with your dad and soaking in all that money again. Why would you want to come back here?"

"Mika . . . what's going on?" He sounds concerned, but I'm too upset to worry about his feelings. "And why did you bring up London?"

"You mean your mom's tennis partner who's over at your house answering your phone and everything?"

"*What?!*"

"Why don't you ask her? Or didn't you know there's no place in your life for a girl like me?"

"What the hell are you talking about?" Finally he sounds frustrated with me, and that's just what I want. I need him to hurt like I am. "Did she talk to you?"

"You can figure that out on your own." I shouldn't, but before I can stop myself it comes out, "Or maybe I can leave a vague note with your uncle in the middle of the night with the explanation. And then I'll screw around for five days while you stew over why I disappeared and stopped talking to you."

"Mik—"

"Don't." I get up, slip my flats on. "I'm hungry, and I'd like to eat in peace. Bye." I hang up, which feels satisfying and also horrible. He immediately calls back, so I pull the battery out of my phone and chuck it on my bed.

I need to get out of here. No, I need to get out of my life. I can't stand it anymore, and there's no relief in sight. There's only one thing that might stop me from going completely insane.

My parents stand from the couch when they see me, looking worried as all get out. Joel must have told them what happened. They start to talk, but I hold up a hand. "I'm going out to eat. I'll be back. Don't worry, I'm not gonna kill myself."

And then I'm on my bike, pedaling like a mad woman. The air bites at my bare arms, but I don't care. A car honks when I recklessly cut across traffic. People curse at me as I barrel down a busy sidewalk. It feels good. Making other people angry somehow lessens my own pain. The more people I can piss off, the happier I feel.

By the time a guy in a truck throws a string of cuss words at me, I'm so determined to take out this injustice on someone that I storm into Shades of Bombay like a freaking bank robber. People stare at me as I stomp down the aisle, all the way back to the kitchen. I shove the swinging door open and stand there, probably looking wild.

Shreya's family stops working, all eyes on me.

"She's moving! Are you happy now?" I scream. "Because of your stupid prejudices my best friend is gone and I can't have curry and I want to hate you for hurting her. But I can't because I know she wouldn't want me to."

Her father's nostrils flare. "How dare—"

I point at him. "Don't even think about yelling at me! You've done enough yelling and hating and I'm sick of having to stand by and watch it destroy another family. This happened to my dad and his mother—and they both regret it like crazy. You're making it happen to your son and daughter when it doesn't have to. Families shouldn't be like this. There's enough out there to tear them apart without it coming from the inside, too!"

My breaths are heavy with pain, and I feel stupid for coming here and yelling at them. But I'm tired of keeping it in. I'm tired of taking the high road and being an example of tolerance. "Stop acting like idiots. Bring my best friend back."

No answer. Just angry glares. I figured as much, but speaking my mind has released the pressure building inside me. I put my hand on top of some take-out boxes. I don't know what's inside them, but I'm desperate enough to take any curry at this point. I grab them and say, "I guess this is the last time I'll be eating your curry. You owe me for all the crap you've put me through."

I run out with the boxes. Putting them in my basket, I speed off as fast as my bike will go. If I go home, my parents will want in on my food, so instead I head for Lovers Point. I commandeer a picnic bench and gorge myself on tikka masala and rice and *naan*. After not having Shades of Bombay curry for so long, it's like heaven in a Styrofoam box. I eat and eat and when it's all gone I wish there was more, even though my stomach might explode from so much food.

It's only after staring at my empty boxes that I realize just how crazy I am to do that. A wave of embarrassment washes over me, accompanied by the persistent fear that they might have called the cops. Arrested for curry theft—my parents would be so proud.

I thunk my head on the table, almost glad Shreya's not at my house. Then I'd have to tell her what I did, and she'd kill me.

"Stupid, stupid, stupid . . ." I mumble to myself.

What's wrong with me? I was never like this with my other boyfriends. I was calm and cool and prepared. But then again, I always felt in control. And as the end approached I could detach myself and move on. Dylan disappeared before I had a chance to see the end. Truth is, I never could see one.

My stomach flops like a beached whale with all the curry inside. Why did I yell at him when I still want him so much? I should have listened to him, told him I missed him like crazy, told him to come back and make it all better. I feel so petty, and here I am accusing Shreya's family of the same thing.

"Excuse me, miss?" a deep voice comes from behind.

I turn, and a flashlight blinds me for a moment. Once my eyes adjust, I realize there's an officer on the other side. Fear makes me freeze. They really did call the cops! "Yes, sir?"

"Don't you think it's a little late for a picnic?"

"Um . . ." I have no idea what time it is, but it's only now that I realize no one is around. "I guess so. Sorry."

"Are you a minor?"

I nod. Barely, but still.

"Probably not a good idea to be alone in a park so late at night. Make sure to throw your trash away as you leave."

I stand up quickly, trying to calm myself down as I gather the boxes. "Of course. I must have lost track of time."

"Get home safely." He walks off, shining his flashlight over other benches and bushes. I realize with a name like Lovers Point this place might attract a more romantic activity than gorging on curry alone.

And with that final blow to my pride, I head back to the house. My head spins. My stomach is so full I completely regret the crazed curry binge. I thought it would make me feel better. That lasted about as long as it took to eat it all. Now I have shame to add to my despair and anger.

It's not until I'm practically in front of my house that I notice there's someone sitting on the porch. I stop when I recognize the mussed hair and strong frame. My heart races when he looks up and sees me, and I'm hit by so many emotions I can't even begin to detangle them.

Dylan stands, his face unreadable. "We need to talk."

Chapter 46

I want to kiss him, hit him, scream at him, and let him hold me until all the bad things go away. But all I can think to say is, "Maybe I don't want to talk."

"Mika." Dylan doesn't move, and something in the way he says my name feels sad. "I didn't ask if you wanted to. Maybe I didn't handle this the right way, but can you at least listen to me?"

I put down the kickstand on my bike and take a few steps forward. "Fine. You have five minutes."

He clenches his jaw. "That should be enough."

"Good."

He sighs. "Yes, I left to apologize and it was impulsive and I should have thought more about how you'd feel. But I only did it because of you."

My brow furrows. "Excuse me?"

"It started when we talked about my family forgetting how to be happy. And then got even bigger when you explained how your grandma was family, and that you love her even though she's a horrible person." He looks away, embarrassed. "It had an impact on me, okay? I wanted to be the bigger person, to

301

tell my parents I was sorry and that I want them to be happy even though I'm *not* doing what they want me to."

A small pang of guilt hits, but it's not enough to stop me from asking, "Why couldn't you tell me that?"

"I don't know!" He throws his hands up. "Maybe because I was scared to face them. Or because if I thought about it too long I'd back out, and I thought you'd be disappointed in me if I did."

"Why would I be disappointed?"

He shakes his head, not in an angry way, but like he's upset that I don't get it. "Can you not see that I've been bending over backwards to impress you? You make me want to be a better person, and then when I try you get pissed off at me!"

"I didn't know what you were doing!" I say too loudly. "Your uncle said you ditched me. And then London answers your phone and tells me I'm just a summer fling. She basically called me trash."

"And you went along with it?" His voice is strained, like he's trying not to get angry but inside he's boiling.

"I didn't at first! But after five days what else could I do?"

He purses his lips, his eyes dark and sad. "Just so you know, I couldn't find my phone. I looked everywhere for it because I was dying to talk to you, but it was gone. London owned up to stealing it when she came over the morning I arrived. She planned the whole thing, and my parents didn't mind going along with it."

Another pang of guilt. "What did she plan?"

"She knew you'd call me eventually—you don't think she saw that as a great opening to hurt you? And my parents had

302

no problem lying about the damn internet being broken. I checked the router after I talked to you. It was turned off."

He balls his fists like he wants to punch something. "I should have known what was up after a few days, but I wanted to believe they were happy with me living my own life. Apparently they spent the whole week trying—and succeeding, it looks like—to sabotage my relationship and make me stay there."

My shoulders fall, and I feel about an inch tall because I can tell he's not lying. He's holding back a lot of pain over how they deceived him. "Dylan . . ."

His eyes meet mine, but they aren't soft. "It's fine. I should have known they'd do that. But you know what hurts?"

"What?" I ask.

"You believed it. Even after everything I've done to show you how much I care. Even after I've *told* you that you're the most important person in my life, you still see me as a guy who'd leave you like that." He pauses, gulping back what might be tears. "I know I'm not innocent in this, but you gave up on me after just five days. After I did everything to protect you, you couldn't have held on a little longer?"

"I . . ." No words will come. Why didn't I keep believing like I did at first?

"I'm new at all this relationship stuff—I'm bound to make a lot of mistakes—but I'm pretty sure I've fallen in love with you, Mika." Dylan doesn't say it sweetly, but as if the idea is agonizing. "You are stubborn and a little self-righteous and you have a temper that could stand a few anger management classes, and yet even those parts of you make me want to be with you every second."

I blush profusely, though I'm not sure if that was a compliment.

"But at the same time . . . this hurts. I spend every waking hour thinking about you and how to make you happy and how I can be the kind of guy you deserve. I feel like I keep failing at it, like I'll never be what you want me to be. And it kills me inside." He puts his hand to his mouth like he doesn't want to talk, but then continues, "I don't know if I can keep doing this. I want you so much, but I don't know if I'll ever be enough for you."

"Dylan, that's not . . ." I don't know what to say, because I feel horrible. I never thought he might be hurt. All I thought about was myself.

"I said my piece." He steps off my porch and walks up to me. "It's all raw right now, and it was a long drive home. Home, as in my uncle's house. Not that giant mansion you referred to. I don't have the energy to handle whatever you want to say. Good night, okay?"

I nod, completely shell-shocked.

He walks to his uncle's car. I watch him the whole way, wanting to run to him and yet positive he doesn't want to be anywhere near me. He gives me a single, mournful glance before he gets in and drives away.

Chapter 47

On Saturday, I go to the beach by myself and build a sandcastle like the ones Shreya and I made when we were ten. It's small and plain and no one comes to take pictures of it. The more I look at it, the more it reminds me of a grave memorial, a monument to losing my best friend. I lie in the sand and close my eyes, pretending life is still as simple as it was back then.

On Sunday, Olivia calls and we go school shopping. I keep mentioning how it would be more fun if Shreya was here until Olivia grabs me by the shoulders and shakes me. "Stop it!"

I stare at her, shocked.

"What am I? Sloppy seconds?" She pulls back, and her frown tells me I've hurt yet another person in my life. "You and Shreya spent all summer worrying about each other, and I had to sit and watch because I didn't have any problems. Unless you count my two best friends being too busy with their lives to even ask me how I've been doing with any of this."

Looking down, I have nothing to say but "Sorry."

"I know," she says. "Which is why I've been trying to swallow my pride and deal. But can you just be happy to be here with me? I know you wish they were here, too, but I'm not going anywhere, Mika. I need you as much as you need me."

That's when I break down right there in the mall. Because I'm so glad she's not leaving me, too. I end up telling her everything that happened after Shreya left—the call from Dylan, the shameful curry theft, and how he showed up only to leave all over again. She wraps her arms around me, and I feel small right next to her tall frame.

"Should I go to AnimalZone and kick him in the balls for you?" she asks.

"No. It's as much my fault as his." I squeeze her tightly. "Thanks, Olivia. I promise I'll stop moping. I am happy you're here—you're the one with the best fashion sense."

She laughs. "That's more like it."

I buy everything she tells me to, and when I get home I don't remember trying on half of it.

Monday morning, I sit in front of my laptop staring at my relationship status—as has become my new obsessive habit. Still together. Dylan obviously has internet access now, and yet he hasn't changed it. Is he waiting for me to thrown down the gauntlet?

I'm not touching it.

I can't. Not after how much I've already hurt him. The way he looked at me Friday night is burned into my memory forever—the aching pain in his eyes, the way his lips crammed together in attempts to hide just how much he felt. Since then, I've become completely convinced that it's not him who doesn't deserve me, but the other way around.

What have I done to be worthy of any of his attention? I've criticized him and judged him and never really told him how much he means to me. At least not in so many words. I've held myself back to stay safe, and yet expected him to bare his entire soul to me. I'm so selfish.

I lean back into my desk chair, soaking in the pain that squeezes my heart. I deserve to feel this way. And he has the right to throw the final punch. I'll wait for it, take it gracefully and pray he finds someone who won't hurt him so much. If I really care about him, that's the least I can do at this point. Let him fly away like the dragon he is.

There's a knock at my door, and I quickly shut my laptop. "Yeah?"

Mom peeks her head in. We haven't talked about what happened with Dylan, but I think she knows it's not exactly going well. "You'll be late for work if you don't get dressed soon."

"Oh yeah." I look down at my ratty tank top and shorts, wanting more than anything to stay like this all day.

Her eyes fill with concern. "Are you okay? You look sick."

"Not sick." But everything aches, and I still can't decide if I should dare show my face at work. Dylan will probably be there. But if I call in sick he'll know I'm avoiding him, and wouldn't that hurt him more? I don't know. "Well, not technically. But I'm not feeling awesome."

She nods. "I hope you can work things out. Dylan seems like a really sweet boy."

"He is," I manage to get out. Everyone kept telling me how great he was, how funny and attractive and kind. All I focused on was his flaws. I suck in a breath before I get worked up again. "Um, can you maybe call my boss and tell him I'm not coming? I'm . . . too scared to go. I can't do it today."

She doesn't seem pleased with my decision, but says, "Okay. How long?"

"Not sure. I have over a week of vacation time saved up. Just tell him I'll be back when I feel better. He'll understand. He knows." Clark even said I could quit. Surely he won't fault me on this.

"I'll call him right now." Mom shuts the door behind her, and I go back to my bed and crawl under the covers. I try to fall back asleep, but all I can think about is Dylan at work, what he might think of me not showing up. Will he be relieved? Sad? The selfish part of me hopes he's sad, because I still want him to want me.

Like I want him.

I spend the rest of the week in the pursuit of the perfect oatmeal. It feels silly, but it's also a good distraction, a goal, and maybe even a way to pay for what I did. Because Grandma stands over me every day, her scowl firmly in place as she watches.

"Too runny."

"Too thick."

"That tastes like sweetened cement."

"Not even a starving cat would eat that."

"Can't you figure this out? It's just oatmeal! What's so hard about making a decent bowl of oatmeal?"

On Wednesday, Grandma upgrades me from "edible" to "not bad." It is an oddly triumphant moment, since getting any compliment from her is a miracle. Which makes me think of how Dylan must have felt all summer. I guess I'm a lot more like my grandma than I ever thought. It is not a good feeling.

By Friday, I feel like I'm getting close to this mystical oatmeal concoction my great aunt Grace invented. It's less brown sugar than I thought. More cinnamon than seems necessary. It has to be cooked in milk, not water. And a pinch of salt brings out the flavors to Grandma's liking.

Still, she stands over me without so much as a hint of acceptance on her face. The one thing I'm changing today is saving the raisins for after it's done. In the hospital she said they came last, but I've put them in like that and she still complains. Yesterday she gave me a clue when she whined about them having "no bite." So instead of cooking them, I'm sprinkling them on top after I pour her serving so they stay chewy.

I fill a bowl, put the raisins on top, and hand it to her. She inspects it like the world's foremost expert in oatmeal. Maybe she is. Dipping her spoon in, she takes a small bite and sloshes it in her mouth for what seems like forever. Then she looks at me, not a smile in sight, "Now was that so hard?"

I raise an eyebrow. "Does that mean I did it right?"

She takes the bowl to the table. "Took you long enough."

I shake my head, trying to feel the victory of this moment no matter how hard she's making it. Clearly she likes it, because she's shoveling it in her mouth much faster than she ever has.

"Good job, Mika!" Joel smiles at me, and that makes up for Grandma's lack of excitement. "Your determination won the day."

I laugh. "As long as she's eating, right?"

He nods. "That will get more and more true as time passes."

"Yeah." I watch her, knowing there will come a time when her body forgets how to chew and swallow entirely. Today she is eating something she loves, and it was worth all the trouble.

As I make myself some toast, I can feel Joel watching me. He's been kind enough to keep coming though I've been home all week. Honestly, his company is more than welcome. He truly has a gift for turning any moment into a happier one.

"I've been really good not to ask," he finally says. "But you keep missing work and you don't seem very sick."

I sigh. "I don't?"

"It's about Dylan, right?" He nods when I pause mid-bite. "I knew it. You have heartbreak written all over you."

"Fine, you're right, but I don't want to talk about it. Not yet."

"Alright. I will provide chocolate and gossip and be patient."

"Thanks." It feels like I've become incapable of making any decision. Even after a whole week, Dylan hasn't changed our relationship status. It makes me hope, but at the same time I worry he's waiting for me to do it. One moment I want to apologize and beg him to take me back, and the next I'm too scared to hear him say it's really over. So instead I do nothing but stay at home and make oatmeal.

* * *

310

It's impossible for me to sleep in on Saturdays. Even without an alarm, my eyes pop open at five-thirty and I'm awake for good. So even though it's depressing, I find myself getting ready for yet another morning at the beach by myself. I don't take much, just a few tools to make my castle more elaborate than last week's tribute to Shreya's friendship.

It's probably too cold to be out today, but I brought a warm enough jacket and I can't be home anymore. It's starting to feel like a prison. I need to do something besides staring at my Facebook account and taking care of Grandma.

Lovers Point is fairly abandoned, with only a few die-hard runners facing the wind and threatening clouds. I lock my bike and head down the cliff to the empty beach, happy I have my pick of building spots. I choose a place behind a jagged rock, where the wind isn't so bad, and get to work.

Without Shreya around, I feel no need to plan anything exciting. I just want to make something pretty, something to help me escape for a day. Packing sand in an L shape, I go by instinct. Add towers haphazardly. Place doors and arches wherever I feel. As the morning goes on and the sun begins to beat back the cold, I imagine myself in this odd castle where nothing quite makes sense and it's wonderful. It doesn't have to make sense because it's just for me.

Though it's not a huge sculpture, I start to hear cameras clicking pictures. But I don't look up. I'm in my own sandy world, and I never want to leave.

I have no idea what time it is when I hear a familiar voice say, "Why don't you add a goldfish to the top? That'll put the final crazy stamp on it."

311

I pause, my eyes going wide. When I turn, there Shreya stands, smiling from ear to ear. And then I'm jumping up and hugging her and I think that squealing sound is me, too. "What are you doing here? I thought you were working on restaurant renovations."

I didn't think it was possible, but her smile gets even bigger. "I have been, but I needed to tell you something."

Chapter 48

My eyebrows pop up, though I don't dare to hope too much. "What?"

She laughs. "Well, Olivia told me about this crazy chick who stormed my parents' restaurant, cussed them out, and then stole someone's take-out order. Do you know anything about that?"

I cringe. "I'm never living that down, am I?"

"Nope." She grabs my arms. "But I wanted to thank you for being that crazy chick, who is still my best friend in the whole wide world."

"I am?" My heart hurts, thinking about how much I wasn't there for her this summer.

She nods. "Of course you are! Anyone who can yell at my parents like that for me is a keeper. Not that it helped in the slightest, but it reminded me that there's no way I can go months without seeing you."

"What does that mean?" The hope, it's threatening to kill me.

"It means . . ." Shreya looks back, and that's when I notice a blond woman waving at us. Then I realize it's Rachelle. She must have driven Shreya here. "I told Pavan I need to keep

313

sculpting on Saturdays, and Rachelle agreed to drive me here every week!"

I scrunch my face, determined not to cry. "I'm so happy right now I don't know what to do with myself."

"Me either!" She bounces around in a little circle. "I know it's not totally the same, but it's better than nothing, right?"

"Way better than nothing." Maybe we won't see each other at school anymore, and I'll still miss her like crazy during the week. But as long as I can have her on Saturdays, I'll never complain. "I can catch you up every week."

She smiles. "Then get to it, because Olivia mentioned you've been through some rough stuff, but she said it'd be better if you told me."

That Olivia. I need to buy her a present. "So, Dylan finally called, and—" I look away, the loss still a constant ache. "Can we sculpt something while I talk? I don't think I'll get through it any other way."

"Of course!"

We pack more sand a short distance from my crazy castle, and I spill it. Every little detail. It only makes me regret everything even more, because now it seems like I obviously overreacted to Dylan going. How I wish I'd just believed he would come back, like I told Clark when I first read his note.

Hindsight sucks.

"It doesn't have to be over," Shreya says, trying to sound positive but it doesn't quite ring true. "He said he's in love with you. That doesn't just go away."

"I know . . ." The words are so hard to say out loud, though I've thought them over and over for a whole week. "But maybe

314

it *should* go away. Maybe he should be with someone who deserves him."

"Mika." Her hand comes down on mine, and I look at her sincere eyes. "You *do* deserve him. He made a mistake—you made one, too. That doesn't mean you have to torture yourself and let him move on!"

That fear wells up again, the one that freezes me in place. "I don't know, Shrey. You didn't see how sad he was. Because of me. I can't do that to him anymore."

She shakes her head, almost laughing like she can't believe I'm so dumb. "Then don't! You know how to make him happy—if he can change, so can you."

"I'll think about it." I go back to the sculpture, which is an anime cat because that's what Shreya wanted to make. The more I think about asking him to give me another chance, the more my hands shake. If he said no, then it would really be over. There wouldn't be any hope left to hold on to. I'm not sure I can handle that kind of pain when limbo is already so horrible.

After we finish our little cat, Rachelle takes us out for ice cream and we kidnap Olivia for an afternoon movie at my house. Rachelle is nice enough to claim she needs to shop and will be back in a few hours.

Once I clean off the beach grunge, I join them in the living room. "You haven't picked a movie yet?"

"It's so much pressure!" Olivia says as she looks over our DVDs. "We only get one movie with Shrey a week."

"Oh gosh," Shreya says through a mouthful of popcorn. "I don't care."

315

I sit on the couch next to my grandma, who seems slightly perturbed by my friends taking over her TV. "Do you want to pick, Grandma?"

"The one with the giant," she says immediately.

I smirk. "*The Princess Bride*? I thought you didn't like that one."

She tips her chin up. "I changed my mind. Can't a person change their mind without getting the third degree?"

"Okay, okay." I hold my hands up, trying not to laugh. "We'll put it in, but you have to promise not to get mad when we repeat all the lines."

"I bet we could act this out from memory," Shreya says.

"For sure." Olivia puts in the movie, and we settle in to watch. Despite Grandma claiming to like it now, she gives the screen a big old crusty glare as we watch Westley and Buttercup do their "As You Wish" thing. "I hate this part. That girl is so stupid."

I snort. Here it comes. For a woman who has memory issues, she is shockingly predictable sometimes. "Don't knock Buttercup. She's a product of her time."

"That's not what I meant." She points at the screen, where Westley and Buttercup are saying their goodbyes. "There! She lets him leave. If she really loved him, she wouldn't let him leave. Stupid girl."

I knew that's what she'd say, and yet it hits me very differently today. "But what if she knows he needs to go?"

"Why does he need to? They're already happy together—why do they need money to marry? It's stupid." She folds her arms, upset. "Letting the people you love leave is stupid."

316

My heart pounds as I take in the words. "Do you regret that? Letting the people you love go away?"

Her eyes meet mine, full of surprise like she's been caught. Then she looks away, sadness weighing down her frame. "It's my greatest regret. I never tried to stop Martin or Stan or Greg . . . I figured if they didn't want to be around me, I shouldn't make them. But I should have tried. Maybe things would have been different if I did."

I tackle her into a hug, and she lets out a shocked screech. I don't care, because her words have given me courage, and I have to act on it before it fizzles out. "Thank you, Grandma. I needed that."

"Get off me!" she wails. "Don't touch me!"

"Guys, will you watch her?" Leaping off the couch, I run for the door. "I need to go right now."

"It's about time!" I hear one of them say before I slam the front door behind me. Grabbing my bike, I head for AnimalZone as fast as I can.

Chapter 49

I skid to a stop in front of the store and don't bother to lock my bike. When I burst through the door, Tanya the Gumsmacker gives me a what-the-hell look, but I don't care. I round the corner to Aquatics, my heart pounding like crazy in anticipation of seeing Dylan.

He's not there.

I frown, but maybe he's helping a customer or in the storage room or on break. I check every aisle, and when each one comes up blank I begin to panic. He needs to be here. I need to say this now before I freeze up and chicken out forever.

He's not in storage either.

The break room is empty, and it makes my soul sink. Why is he not here? I was sure he'd be working today, like destiny would make it turn out perfectly. But what if he gave up? What if he couldn't take working here anymore, either?

Clark pops his head out of his office, and his eyes go wide when he catches sight of me. "Mika! What are you doing here?"

"Please," I pant, only just realizing how fast I rode here. My legs are practically jelly. "Where is he? Tell me he didn't leave again. I messed everything up and I need to talk to him."

He frowns. "After his shift he disappears. Doesn't even tell me where he's going."

I give him a pained look. "No."

"But . . ." He raises a finger, a shadow of a smile on his face. "If you promise me you won't give him bad news, I might have a good lead for you."

I gulp. "I hope what I have to say isn't bad news to him, because then I might really have to quit working here."

A bright grin breaks under his mustache. "I hoped you'd say that. Come here."

I follow him to his office and watch him rifle through the papers on his desk for who knows what. "He doesn't tell me where he goes, but I found these in his jacket pocket yesterday when I was doing laundry. Figured I'd keep them in case he wanted them."

He holds up a handful of receipts, and I grab them from him. As I flip through them, I can hardly believe what I'm seeing—every single one is from the Monterey Bay Aquarium. I hold them to my chest, feeling like the most foolish girl in the world for not seeing just how much he loves me.

"Not sure what he does there for half the day," Supervisor Clark says. "But I have a good guess who he's thinking of."

"Thanks." I'm already half way out of the office when I say it, and then I'm back on my bike speeding in the direction of Cannery Row. The crowds get thicker and thicker the closer I get. Of course they do—it's the last weekend before school starts. Everyone is probably trying to soak in the final days of summer break.

There's a horrible line when I get to the Aquarium. I bounce and fret and almost consider calling Dylan, but I want to do this in person. I want to show him that he's not the only one willing to go to crazy lengths for this to work.

When I finally get in, I stare at the expansive lobby, suddenly very aware of just how large this place is. And the *people*. They are everywhere. I have no idea how I'll find him or if he'll leave while I'm looking, but there's nothing to do but start. I run for the Living Kelp Forest, scanning everything, hoping to see him. I even stand on benches to get a better look.

Not here.

I move on to the octopus exhibit and the touch pools, where there are way too many kids. I don't spend much time there—Dylan wouldn't hang out in such a loud place. I check the cafeteria and stores before heading for the other side of the museum. I'm frantic, worried to death that I won't be able to find him at this point.

Checking the deep ocean area is hard because the room is dim compared to the giant wall where turtles and fish swim right past me. After I'm satisfied he's not in there, I head for the jellyfish. It's another dark exhibit, and it's especially crowded today. I wish I was taller. It would make seeing through the masses much easier.

It's supposed to be dark so people can see the jellies, but I'm angry I can't see. Everyone is a black silhouette against the bright blue windows and ethereal floating creatures.

My breaths are shallow, and I can feel tears pricking at my eyes. This is crazy, to think I can find him here. I almost think about giving up, but then I catch something familiar in front of the Aquariou Jellyfish tank.

A slouching, sullen figure.

No one could look that depressed on vacation, so I push my way through the crowds to get a better look. The closer I get, the more my hope rises. It's definitely a guy, and his hair looks right—messy and a little too long.

The second I get his profile, I know it's Dylan.

That's when a new flood of fear wells up inside me, and I stop just short, watching him. I have no idea how to do this. Maybe I should have *planned* something. I'm about to look like an idiot walking up to him with absolutely nothing to say.

And yet I'm doing it anyway. Before I know it, I'm right next to him. He doesn't see me, just stares ahead like you do when you're surrounded by strangers. I wrack my brain for something clever, some kind of opener that says everything I want and feel in one little sentence.

"The Aquarium, huh," is what actually comes out. I'm super eloquent like that.

He looks down at me, and his eyes go wide as he jumps back a little. "How'd you know I was here?"

I bite my lip, the whole search for him suddenly seeming more like stalking. "Your uncle found a bunch of Aquarium receipts while he was doing laundry. So I followed the trail."

"I see." He relaxes just slightly, but there's still hesitation in his eyes. "And why'd you come looking for me?"

"Because . . ." I look down, as if the words I'm supposed to say are written on the floor. Sadly, they are not. "I needed to tell you something. Even if you never want to see me again, you need to at least know this."

"What?" His voice is quiet in such a bustling room, but I can still hear the hope in it. That's what pushes me on.

I meet his gaze. "You're enough. You're *more* than enough. You're so enough that it scares the hell out of me. I've sucked at making sure you know that, but if you let me try again I promise to tell you every day how much I love you."

He stares at me, and I have no idea what he's thinking. It's torture. Then one side of his mouth curls. "You love me?"

I nod slowly. "So much."

His grin gets bigger. "How much?"

"To the point that it hurts not to be with you. All I want is you. All the time. I don't know how to be without you anym—"

Dylan scoops me up, kissing me like no one else is there. I smile, laugh, and kiss him until some lady tells us we need to move. He doesn't seem happy about putting me down, but he does anyway. "C'mon, show me your favorite spots."

We talk about fish and steal kisses in dark corners and I never want this to end. I don't think he wants it to, either. And right now, that's enough.

Acknowledgements

I want to thank the people who believed in this book, and for that I have to start with my dear friends and crit partners who helped me get this book in shape: Kiersten White, Kasie West, Michelle Argyle, Sara Raasch, Sara Larson. You are amazing people and writers, and most of the time I wish I could be as cool as you guys. And to Jenn Johansson, Renee Collins, and Candice Kennington, thank you for always cheering me on through all the hard stuff as well. Thanks for sticking this out with me, guys, truly you are saints for dealing with my crazy.

I want to thank my Mom and Dad for being amazing parents who taught me how to be a good person through their own examples, even when they sometimes didn't have the best examples in their lives growing up. You two are amazing, and I miss you a lot now that you live so very far away. And to my siblings, Mark, Ariel, and Kenna, thanks for being excited for my little dreams and for being awesome people I can lean on even when you live half way across the planet. You all keep me going.

To Nick, I love you times infinity and am grateful you are so awesome. Thanks for being the best husband and for backing me up when I'm on deadline. To my kids, Ben, Kora, and Gilly, you are really the best ones I could ask for. You are all really awesome at playing video games thanks to my writing career, and I hope when you become pro gamers you will thank me for that.

I really have to thank the team at Hot Key Books for making this book a real thing that I can hold in my hands. It means the world to me, as this story is a very personal part of my heart. Thanks for taking care of it and treasuring it. To my editors Sara O'Connor and Jenny Jacoby, an extra special thanks for helping me make this book even stronger. I hope you're as proud of it as I am.

And to my agent, Ginger Clark, thank you for your endless support and confidence in my writing. It means the world, especially when I doubt myself. I know you're there rooting for me, and it makes a difference. Thank you for finding Mika a good home.

Finally, though she's not alive, I want to thank my grandma Carole for the good memories, and even for the not-so-good ones. Thank you for being a real person, flaws and all, and for teaching me in your own way. This book wouldn't have happened if it weren't for your influence on me, and I love you. I also know you loved me, no matter what words you might have said. You would probably kill me for this book, but writing it helped me keep a piece of you in my heart forever. For that, I'm the most grateful.

Natalie Whipple

Natalie Whipple accidentally killed three goldfish in the process of researching this novel (which Mika would be very ashamed of), but she hasn't killed any since. She grew up in California and spent many a family vacation in Monterey, but now she lives in Utah with her husband and three children and spends many days wishing she lived by a beach. Follow Natalie at betweenfactandfiction.blogspot.co.uk or on Twitter: @nataliewhipple

HOT
KEY
BOOKS

Thank you for choosing a Hot Key book.

If you want to know more about our authors
and what we publish, you can find us online.

You can start at our website

www.hotkeybooks.com

And you can also find us on:

We hope to see you soon!